THE SCUM OF ALL FEARS

SQUEAKY CLEAN MYSTERIES, BOOK 5

CHRISTY BARRITT

River Heights

COPYRIGHT

CHAPTER ONE

"YOU REALLY THINK your niece Clarice can handle cleaning crime scenes?" As I waited for my friend Sharon's answer, I leaned against the cool, granite counter of my favorite hang out, The Grounds coffeehouse, and took a sip of my iced latte. Warm drinks were my preference, but today was sweltering. Besides, the sugary, dairy delight was free, so who was I to complain?

Sharon averted her gaze from me and continued to clean amidst a mid-afternoon lull. "I think she'll be great, Gabby. She's desperate for a job."

Desperate for a job? Something didn't settle well in my gut about Sharon's statement—or her body language. Expertly averted gaze. Amazingly preoccupied at doing nothing. Suspiciously lacking in details.

I was about to ask Sharon exactly what her niece was like. Before I could, the bell over the door jangled, and Sharon nodded behind her. "Speak of the devil—I mean, the angel—here she comes now."

I turned, fully expecting to see someone who wasn't afraid to get dirty. Someone who could dress down. Who could pull their hair into a ponytail, slap on some rubber gloves, and scrub for hours on their hands and knees.

Instead, I saw a twenty-something girl wearing designer jeans, a ruffled shirt with glittery strands running through it, and high-heels. My mouth gaped open, and my hands went to my hips.

This could not be Sharon's niece. Not Sharon, the grungy woman with pink hair, uncountable piercings, and ripped jeans. Not Sharon, the woman who worked so hard at running her business that she almost never went home. Or the Sharon who did everything herself—fixed plumbing, changed light bulbs, gave herself tattoos—at least, that was Sharon's *I Am Legend* rumor about the town.

The woman who'd just walked in—more like a girl, if you asked me—extended her hand and flashed a wide smile that screamed "not-in-touch-with-reality." Not in touch with *my* reality, at least.

"I'm Clarice Wilkenson, and I'm so excited to be working for you." Her words came out high-pitched and fast, like she'd had too much sugar or caffeine—or maybe both.

"I'm Gabby." I *think* I extended my hand back to her.

She grinned, her teeth sparkling and white. I wondered if she could get my crime scenes that clean.

"So nice to finally meet you," she gushed, not letting go of my hand. She still pumped it up and down. "I love reading crime novels. This is going to be just like that. So cool. My friends won't believe me when I get back and tell them my stories. I'll be the talk of my sorority."

I pulled my hand away in an effort to stop my bones from vibrating. "You do know what I do, don't you?"

She nodded, her face the essence of happy-go-lucky, airhead utopia. "Auntie Sharon told me all about it. Crime scene clean up. Fascinating. I saw it once in *Pulp Fiction*. This is the perfect way to end my already epic summer."

I glanced back at Sharon and scowled. What had she been thinking? Sharon knew me better than this. I took my job seriously. And I seriously needed help thanks to a killing spree in my hometown of Norfolk, Virginia this past weekend. If this girl was with me, I'd practically be babysitting.

My so-called friend stole a sheepish glance at me and continued to wipe the counter. Suddenly, I got a better picture of how this whole deal had played out. Sharon's sister had probably pushed her to give Clarice a job here at The Grounds. Sharon had then probably insisted she had no openings, and that's when the coffee bartender—that's what I called her—had thought of me.

I'd been at the wrong place at the wrong time.

I was desperate for help. My business partner, Chad Davis, was on his honeymoon. I'd called all of my usual fill-ins, and they were all busy. My fiancé, Riley Thomas, was catching up at his law firm after a week of being away. My brother believed in living off the land—the trash of the land, at least. Long story. I'd even called my old assistant, Harold, but he was driving up to Pennsylvania to visit one of his kids.

I'd been on the verge of placing an online ad when Sharon had mentioned her niece.

She'd be great, Sharon had insisted. *She has a lot of energy. Enthusiasm. Drive.*

Liar.

My first clue should have been the fact that Sharon's eyes had lit, her shoulders had straightened, and her voice had lilted as she'd talked about the possibility. The thought of Clarice working for me had obviously lifted the burden off of Sharon. She'd seen a way out of her own dilemma. Brilliant on her part. Sadly naïve on mine.

Clarice smoothed her dark brown hair with her manicured fingers. "Is it okay if I run to the restroom before we leave? I just need to tinkle real quick."

"Absolutely. Tinkle away." Her temporary absence would give me a moment to not only fume but also to ponder the reality of working with someone who used the word "tinkle" without any shame.

As soon as Clarice disappeared from sight, I turned to Sharon and narrowed my eyes. I pressed my palms into the cool countertop. Nothing could make this better. Not even one of Sharon's homemade blueberry muffins . . . although, I wouldn't turn one down if she offered. It would be a start.

I put on my best game face. "Really?"

Sharon shrugged, suddenly busy making an espresso for . . . well, no one apparently since I was the only other person here. As the machine stopped screeching, Sharon took the hot coffee and downed it like a shot of alcohol.

Ouch. That had to hurt. Sharon hardly flinched.

"I don't know what to say," she muttered, squeezing the skin between her eyes. She lowered her voice and leaned toward me. "You don't understand, Gabby. Clarice drives me crazy. I couldn't work with her all summer. After I killed Clarice—and all it would take is one hour working with her and I'd want to strangle her—my sister would never speak to me again, and all the relationships in my family would suddenly be in shambles. I couldn't let that happen. My sister is all I've got left in this world."

"You've got a brother, multiple cousins, and both of your parents are still alive." I tapped my finger on the countertop.

Sharon frowned. "You've got a better memory than I thought. You've got to understand, Gabby. No one would hire her. She's—" Sharon stopped abruptly when the bathroom door opened.

Clarice emerged with freshly applied lipstick and powdered cheeks. She pulled her Coach bag up higher on her shoulder. I half expected to see glitter sparkling in the air around her as she glided back into the room.

Why hadn't Clarice been able to get a job anywhere else? She was attractive and perky and young. Certainly there were jobs out there for her. You know, restaurants that specialized in hot wings. Car shows with smiley women who drew attention to their vehicles. Reality dating shows where drama was king.

"I'm ready," she announced.

My hometown of Norfolk, Virginia was a nice mix of Southern quaintness and Mid-Atlantic briskness. Right now, I was tapping into my genteel, I-like-grits-and-sweet-tea side. "Sugar, where we're going, no one's going to see that lipstick."

She shrugged. "My mom says not to wear makeup for other people, but to wear it for yourself so you can feel good about how you look." She pointed to her lips. "Crimson Apple. Isn't is fabulous?"

I gave Sharon one more dirty look before forcing a smile. "Of course."

Clarice ran her hand down the length of her outfit. "Auntie Sharon said that you have a Hazmat suit I can wear over my clothes. Is that right?"

I pointed at her heels. "The shoes might be a problem. They could pierce the suit and render it ineffective."

She glanced down and frowned. She tapped her heels together like she was Dorothy from *The Wizard of Oz*. "But they're so cute."

"Blood born pathogens aren't so cute. They can really *tinkle* on your plans. But if you want to be exposed to them, then be my guest. Since you're part-time, I'm under no obligation to pay your medical bills, however. I don't care what the government says."

Clarice frowned. "Auntie Sharon, do you have something I could borrow?"

Sharon nodded toward the back of the store. She downed another shot of something. I had a feeling it wasn't coffee this time. "I have some tennis shoes in the office. Why don't you grab them?"

I almost hissed at Sharon, but I stopped myself. Clarice wouldn't last a day on the job. I wouldn't have to fire her. She'd quit before we finished the first crime scene. As soon as I got home, I'd place that classified ad.

I did not have time to train Miss Priss on cleaning basics—starting with how to dress when going to a crime scene. This job required a certain measure of common sense. Sense didn't seem all that common with Clarice, at least in the small amount of time since I'd met the girl.

Five minutes later, Clarice was wearing Sharon's fluorescent orange Converse sneakers, and we were bouncing down the road in my business van. I tried not to let a cranky mood settle over me, but I felt like I'd had the proverbial wool pulled over my eyes. I needed help. What I had instead was Clarice Wilkenson.

"Were you just humming 'You're So Vain'?" Clarice asked.

"Uh . . . I don't know. Was I?" Note to self: Must keep singing in check.

"I love that song." Clarice began her own off-key rendition of the piece. "You remember when Kate Hudson sings it on *How to Lose a Guy in 10 Days*? Totally loved that movie."

She continued rambling about all the other rom-coms she loved. Finally, she took a breath, so I decided to change the subject.

"So," I ventured, trying to sound chatty instead of irritated. "Is the job market pretty tough right now?"

The job market had been brutal for me, with budget cuts across the state. I'd lost my dream career with the Medical Examiner's Office and was now back to cleaning crime scenes. At least, for a while. I did have an interview coming up this week that might turn things back around.

But certainly there was a clothing store *somewhere* that was hiring bright young college students. Maybe a perfume counter?

"I have this bad habit of getting fired." Clarice shrugged and examined her manicured fingernails. At least the blood-red color would blend in at our crime scenes.

My muscles tightened as I turned my thoughts from her nails to what she'd just said. A bad habit of getting fired? "Oh really?"

She waved a hand in the air. "Oh, don't worry. I promise you I'm going to give one-hundred percent to Trauma Care."

"Why were you fired?"

She shrugged again, back to examining her nail polish. "Various reasons. Being late. Being bad with numbers. Being a space cadet. Destroying a display of expensive crystal."

I shouldn't have asked. I knew it.

"Speaking of which, only touch what I tell you to touch when we get to the crime scene." The last thing I needed Clarice to do was destroy something in a person's home. The people whose houses I cleaned had already been through enough. I didn't need to add a disaster named "Clarice" to their list of tragedies.

I needed to find something safe to talk about. "So, what's your major anyway? What do you want to do after graduation?"

"I'm studying business. But I really want to move to L.A.

and find some acting jobs. I don't know. I'd even be happy to work on one of those game shows or to start as an extra on a soap opera."

Someone who lived for fame. Perfect.

We pulled up at the crime scene. A woman had been shot here four days ago, and the crime scene had just been released. The police had already come and collected all of their forensic evidence. That's when the family called me and asked me to take care of cleaning up what they couldn't bear to think about.

The house was two stories, covered in baby blue vinyl siding, and had a well-kept lawn. This wasn't the typical neighborhood where you expected to find someone shot. Must have been a domestic case, I figured. A boyfriend? Ex-husband? I wasn't sure. Normally I looked into the background of my crime scenes before I arrived, but I'd been out of town last week and hadn't had the chance.

I parked my van. It was unmarked, white, and plain. Most people didn't want their neighbors knowing their business, so I tried to give people their privacy. It was the least I could do.

"I need your help grabbing the equipment from the back," I told Clarice.

Was it a coincidence that her name was the same as the young FBI agent from *The Silence of the Lambs*? It had to be.

"Sure thing." She bounced out and hurried toward the back of the van.

As soon as we had hauled everything in, a plan formed in my head.

I was going to freak this girl out so she never wanted to come to another crime scene with me again. I knew just the way to do it.

Was my plan devious? Slightly. But it was otherwise brilliant and necessary. That would override the devious part, right?

I glanced at the ceiling, as if to get approval from God. I had a feeling He might not be so keen on this plan.

The homeowner was waiting on the porch. Actually, it was the homeowner's mother-in-law. She seemed subdued and didn't have much to say. She let us in and then drove away, probably not wanting to see the disaster inside. I couldn't blame her.

I heard Clarice suck in a breath as we stepped into the foyer. Bullet holes littered a wall. A table was smashed. A TV turned over.

And this wasn't even the room where the real crime had occurred.

After we paused for a moment, I led Clarice to the bedroom. From what the mother-in-law had told me, the killer had tried to clean up all of the blood evidence, but the police had gotten here before he had a chance to finish. A neighbor had called 911 after he heard the gunshots. Still, there was enough blood to silence Clarice.

Her manicured fingers covered her mouth, and her eyes widened. "Wow. I've never seen anything like this."

"Count that as a blessing," I muttered. "Put on this suit—don't forget the mask or the gloves—and then we'll get started."

She nodded and wordlessly climbed into the Hazmat suit. I did the same. As soon as I was all protected—and Clarice was as well—I turned to my new, temporary employee. "I need you to start by scrubbing the blood off those baseboards over there." I checked out her outfit. "And don't forget your safety goggles."

"Can I wear these instead?" She pulled out some trendy

plastic framed glasses and slid them on her nose. "I'm near-sighted."

"Whatever," I muttered.

Suddenly, any hesitation Clarice had disappeared. She began chatting and chatting and chatting, scrubbing away without blinking an eye. She worked more slowly than I would have liked and she talked way more than I wanted to hear. But she was working.

How could this be possible? I thought she'd freeze up, shut down, freak out.

Instead, she was jumping in.

But I hadn't used my wild card yet.

I pulled out some powder I just happened to have in my van. I mixed it with a liquid containing hydrogen peroxide and poured it into a spray bottle.

"What are you doing?" Clarice rocked back on her heels.

"Spraying Luminol." I took my first squirt, thankful that my mask concealed my grin. I was proud of myself for thinking of a way to use up this product finally. I had no need for it. Not anymore.

"Luminol? Isn't that what those CSI guys always use?" She almost looked alarmed with her eyes wide and her lips slightly parted.

"Absolutely."

"It makes blood glow or something, right?"

"Actually, it detects iron in hemoglobin and creates a reaction, leaving the 3-aminophthalate in an energized state." I doused the mustard yellow wall. Normally, I'd turn the lights off before spraying the chemical. Any fluid detected wouldn't be as bright with the brief time lapse, but I'd still be able to get my point across.

She stared at me blankly.

I shrugged. "Yeah, so it makes the blood—or other bodily fluids—glow."

I continued to spray it on a wall of the bedroom where the crime had occurred, watching as the liquid appeared in patches. I hadn't actually used Luminol in my job with the Medical Examiner, but I'd learned to use it when I got my degree in forensics.

Just a couple of weeks ago, I'd ordered some of the solution because I'd been asked to do a little talk with the teens at church. I'd decided to use the Luminol to demonstrate how Christ's blood—shed on the cross—gave us even more reason to shine bright for Him. The talk had gone well, but I had some of the chemical left over. Now, I realized my over-order was like fate.

Clarice continued to stare at me. "Why are you doing that exactly?"

"I'm trying to find the blood so I'll know what to clean up."

"But if you can't see it, does it really matter?"

Normally, I'd just wipe all the surfaces down. But I wanted to make a point. Luminol would help me to do that. "When I do a job, I like to be thorough."

Guilt pressed in on me. That hadn't been totally honest. After I proved my point, I'd own up to what I'd done, I decided.

She shrugged and daintily began scrubbing another baseboard. We were going to be here all day if she kept cleaning at that pace. And she absolutely had to stop talking. I knew way more about the newest shows on MTV than I ever cared to.

I sprayed more furiously. Finally, I was satisfied that I'd soaked the wall. I closed the shades, pleased that they were room-darkening variety. They made my job easier.

Then I stepped back, feeling a little too giddy for my own good. "Check this out."

I flipped the lights, smugly thinking that I was about to shock her socks off.

Instead, what I saw made my blood go cold.

It wasn't just the amount of blood glowing on the wall. No, it was also the message written there.

One, Two

I'm Coming for You

Clarice screamed.

I almost joined her.

CHAPTER
TWO

"WHY IN THE world were you carrying Luminol?" Riley turned away from the stove for long enough to give me a questioning look.

I paused from making a salad in order to face him better. "Because . . . well, why not? That's why. But that's not the point." I crossed my arms and watched as he flipped chicken thighs on his stovetop griddle. "The point is that there was a message on the wall of the home."

He turned to face me, letting the chicken sizzle for a moment. "So the police missed something. Or maybe they didn't miss it. Maybe they just didn't tell the homeowner the message was there and the homeowner, then in turn, couldn't tell you."

"It wasn't there when the crime scene unit left," I insisted. The police had just questioned me for an hour or so. They'd made no mention of that. Not that they had to tell me everything—or anything. And they usually didn't offer any information. I was flying solo when it came to gathering information on crime scenes.

Still, the detectives with the Norfolk Police Department didn't look at me with the same disdain that they used to, back when I'd first started out. I'd solved a couple of cases and then been hired by the Medical Examiner for a whole month, so that had gained me some credibility.

Despite that, it had been a little hard to explain why I'd brought Luminol to a crime scene. It wasn't my usual M.O., but I'd just happened to have some on hand. And then there had been Clarice . . . one thing had led to another.

I tapped my finger against my cheek, the crime scene igniting something in me, a kind of primal need I had for answers to life's pressing questions. Thankfully, most of the time those questions went deeper than the "Which came first, the chicken or the egg?" variety.

I gave up on trying to make a salad in order to fully concentrate on this conversation. "Something doesn't feel right. Someone left that message in blood—or some other bodily fluid—then cleaned it up some, but not enough that it wouldn't show up under the right chemicals." If only I had access to a lab. I could have taken a sample and tested it to find out if it had been blood. Or some other fluid. But I was not officially a part of this case.

I was certain the criminal had left that message after the crime scene techs had come. That meant the bad guy had come back and risked getting caught just to leave that message. Why would someone take that chance?

Riley crossed his arms. The top two buttons of his white dress shirt were undone and his sleeves rolled up. He'd offered to cook dinner tonight at his apartment, and I was never one to turn down free dinner. In reality, I should be at another scene cleaning. But a girl had to eat. No one could fault me for that.

Riley looked all serious and lawyer-like as he stood there

discussing the scene with me. He'd finally shaved off his scruffy beard that he'd let grow out while he was on a once-every-decade vacation last week. His dark hair remained just a touch too long, but I liked that. It let people know that he wasn't all about the rules; he was just *mostly* about the rules.

Our wedding was coming up in four months, two days, and 56 minutes.

Not that I was counting.

He stepped closer, his blue eyes sparkling. "The message was for the police, not you."

"But it said, 'I'm coming for you,' and it was left after the fact. Isn't that strange?"

"I wouldn't worry about it. What I would worry about is that poor innocent girl who had to see it. She's probably traumatized."

I put my hand on his chest and nudged him playfully. "Poor innocent girl? She was driving me nuts! You have no idea."

Riley shook his head, a grin tugging at his lips. "You were trying to freak her out."

He knew me too well. Yet he still wanted to marry me. I still pinched myself sometimes.

I cocked a shoulder, trying to look innocent. "Okay, maybe I was trying to freak Clarice out. Just a little. Not *that* bad, though."

"Uh huh." Riley didn't sound convinced.

"You don't understand my dilemma. There's no way I could handle Clarice working for me every day until Chad gets back. I would go crazy. But if I fired her, Sharon would never speak to me again. In the very least, she wouldn't give me free coffee anymore. And you know how much I love my lattes."

Halfway through my diatribe, I realized Riley wasn't

listening. His gaze was fastened on the TV blaring from the living room behind me.

I turned around to see what could possibly be distracting him from my engaging story and latte confessions. I squinted as I saw the news banner stretched beneath a serious looking brunette news anchor. "Scum River Killer Escapes From Prison, Kills Two."

I glanced back up at my fiancé. "Riley?"

He still didn't hear me. He moved toward the TV, almost like he was in a trance.

I moved behind him, curious to listen in and maybe get a clue as to why Riley was so fascinated with this story. I'd heard about the Scum River Killer. He'd been all over the news when he first captured. But Riley seemed a little too interested.

Even Lucky, Riley's parrot, seemed to catch on to Riley's total and complete focus on the TV. He squawked across the room.

Riley turned up the TV volume, and a newscaster's voice blared into the room. "Milton Jones killed thirteen women before his murderous rampage ended nearly three years ago. He was put away for life without possibility for parole. While being transferred from the high security prison where he'd been for two years to a supermax prison, he obtained a gun from one of the guards and escaped."

"I can't believe it . . ." Riley muttered. He plopped on the couch and rubbed his cheek.

I put my hand on his back and massaged his taut muscles, trying for the life of me to figure out why he was reacting this way. Serial killers were bad. I got that. But Riley didn't generally have this reaction to them. It wasn't like either of us lived in a bubble. No, we dealt with scum every day; Riley, as a lawyer, and me as a crime scene cleaner.

When the news report was over, Riley fell back against the couch and stared at the ceiling. "I can't believe it," he repeated. He blinked as if absorbing life-altering news.

"I'm *so* not following a single thing that is happening right now. This Jones guy escaped from a prison in California. We're in Virginia—" I stopped myself. Riley had moved here from California. A year ago. There was no possible way that . . .

He closed his eyes. "I put him behind bars."

My hand dropped from Riley's back. "What?"

"He was the big case that made my career. I put him away and became a bit of a hero in the region when I nailed his conviction. The case consumed me. It was all I wanted to eat, drink, and breathe for months."

Some of this was coming back to me. I knew he'd been involved in some big cases, but his time as a prosecutor in California seemed like another lifetime ago. "I still don't understand why you look so shocked. I realize this is a big deal, but—"

He leaned toward me and grabbed my hand. "I don't think you realize just how huge this is, Gabby."

"Explain it to me then." I braced myself for whatever he might have to say. The only time Riley overreacted was when it came to my safety, and my safety wasn't in play right now. I had nothing to do with this case.

For once.

"As Jones was led out of the courtroom, he vowed that he would get out and that he'd get even. He said he'd pay me back for putting him behind bars and that he would make everyone in my life pay."

"Make them pay?" My throat felt dry.

"Make them pay just like he made those women he killed pay."

His words caused something ice cold to course through my blood. I barely even smelled the chicken burning in the next room over.

CHAPTER
THREE

"OKAY, well, he's in California. How's a fugitive going to get to Virginia? That would be crazy. No way he's sneaking on an airplane. If he steals a car or jumps on a train, he would still take a few days to travel across the country. By that time, the police are going to catch him." I nodded, totally convinced that my theory was correct.

Riley had turned the burner off and called for a pizza. With those all-important details taken care of, we could concentrate on more important things. Things like our lives.

"Milton Jones is sneaky. He's conniving. No one can still figure out how he got into those people's homes. He never told anyone and the police couldn't figure it out." He shook his head. "And what he did to those women . . ."

"What did he do to those women?" I was squeezing my own hand so hard that I nearly yelped.

Riley rubbed his cheek again before turning down the volume on the TV as a consumer report came on. "You don't want to know. It was horrific. The crime scene photos gave me nightmares for weeks."

They had to be serious if they gave Riley nightmares.

He leaned back on the couch, any sense of lightness and teasing that had been present earlier gone faster than my peace of mind. He stared into the distance, as if going back to a different time. "Everyone in the area was on edge. People wouldn't let their daughters go out at night. They bought extra locks for their doors. Tons of new neighbourhood watch groups started. People lived in fear over this guy."

As I pulled one of my knees to my chest, my stomach grumbled, and I really wished that chicken hadn't burned. "Let me guess, when they caught him, no one could believe he was guilty. They all said what a nice man he was. Isn't that what the neighbors always say?"

He went from rubbing his cheek to rubbing his temple. I don't think I'd ever seen Riley this distressed. "You're absolutely right. He was a deacon at his church. He coached his son's little league team. He worked as a sociologist by day, lived in a middle class neighborhood, took family vacations in between the murders."

I shivered. "That is creepy. And by creepy, I mean totally whacked out and sick. Tell me—how did he get the name Scum River Killer again?"

"He always dumped the bodies in this area that locals called the Scum River. It wasn't actually a river. It was this area of town, underneath an overpass, where there was a sewage leak. Filthy water flowed right down the middle of this street and walkway. People started calling it the Scum River."

Riley's cell phone rang, and he scrunched his eyebrows together when he looked at the screen. He stood as he answered, his body rigid and tight.

"What's going on? I see. Okay. Right. I just heard. Are you serious?"

That was the extent of what I could pick up on from this

side of the conversation. I sat on the edge of my seat, apprehension growing in me as I watched the strain pull tighter and tighter at Riley.

Really, this shouldn't affect Riley anymore. The police? Yes. The FBI? Probably. Riley had only prosecuted the case. His involvement was over.

And even though the man's threats toward Riley sounded horrific, what was the possibility the man could make it all the way across the country? I wasn't great at statistics, but the likelihood didn't seem high.

Riley came back into the room, and his face looked paler than I'd ever remembered it looking. Nausea roiled in my gut as I asked, "What's going on?"

He lowered himself beside me, his jaw flexing as he gathered his thoughts. "That was one of my former colleagues at the D.A.'s Office in California. He wanted to make sure I'd heard what happened. He told me that Jones actually escaped last night. Officials didn't release the news story until today in an effort not to send the public into a panic."

"Okay." I wiped my hands on my jeans, realizing my palms were sweaty.

"The FBI went through Jones' prison cell. He had some papers hidden in his mattress."

Waiting to hear what Riley had to tell me was worse than waiting for a shot at the doctor's office. "What are you getting at, Riley?"

He glanced up, his eyes intense. "They were news clippings about me, Gabby. About me since I moved to Virginia."

"Okay." The man had been carrying a grudge. I was sure a lot of convicts did.

"And about you."

I jabbed my finger into my chest, my anxiety torpedoing into shock. "About me? What do you mean?"

"You know that article that ran in the paper about you back in January?"

Of course I remembered it. I'd only framed four copies of it, and whenever I felt down in the dumps, I re-read it for an ego boost. I read it even when I didn't feel down in the dumps, for that matter. I might have even considered using it as wallpaper. "Yes, I remember."

"That article was there, too."

The blood drained from my face. "Why in the world would he have a copy of that? You weren't mentioned in the article, even."

"Somehow he's figured out that you're connected to me." He shook his head. "He must have had help from someone outside the prison. That's the only way he could have gotten those clippings."

I shivered. I didn't want to. I didn't want this to affect me at all. I wanted to be tough and reasonable. Unaffected. To wear my logic like armor. But the shivers kept coming.

Riley pulled me into his arms and whispered into my hair, "I don't like this, Gabby. I don't like it one bit."

I couldn't lie. I didn't like this one bit either.

CHAPTER
FOUR

I AWOKE the next morning with Milton Jones still on my mind. It hadn't helped that I'd done an Internet search on the man before I went to bed. In my defense, I'd hopped online to place an ad for a new temporary employee this week. I'd quickly gotten distracted.

Story of my life, it seemed sometimes.

As I read the details of his crimes, I'd shuddered. He'd tortured his victims before killing them. He was one big, bad dude, beyond the vile killers I'd encountered in the past.

He snatched women in the middle of the night. They were almost always in their early twenties, outgoing in nature, and thin in stature. No one could ever figure out how he got in and out of the homes. He always left a picture of his victims with their eyes Xed out after he abducted them. He kept the women for six days and then killed them, dumping their bodies in a public location afterward.

He was a psychopath. Yet he was meticulous. A planner. Devious.

I stared at my bedroom ceiling as the earliest of morning light trickled in from outside. Jones' threats to Riley had been idle, something he'd never be able to carry out. He'd probably threatened a lot of people for that matter. So why did he only have an unofficial shrine to Riley?

I didn't need to worry about it. For that matter, the FBI had probably already arrested the man. I was sure that when I turned on the news this morning I would see an update. I'd see video feeds of the man being led back to prison in handcuffs, taking the walk of shame.

Meanwhile, I'd forgotten to place my ad for a temporary worker, which meant I was flying solo today. I was already behind thanks to the debacle yesterday, so I had to get busy. I had a reputation for being reliable and thorough. I didn't want to mess that up, even if my days doing this job were potentially numbered.

I comforted myself with the fact that I'd still probably get my crime scenes cleaned faster *alone* today than I would have *with* Clarice yesterday.

Poor Clarice. I doubted she ever wanted to see me again. She'd looked pale and ready to throw up when she'd seen the message left in that house. Crime scenes could do that to a person. I'd dropped her off with Sharon, told her to take some Tylenol, and waved *adios*.

Now, it was time to start my day alone. I had four crime scenes on my docket to get cleaned between today and tomorrow. It was going to be a lot of work. I was going to have to hire some subcontractors to replace some dry wall and even a section of subfloor at one place.

I got out of bed, got dressed, grabbed a Pop Tart, and opened the front door, ready to get started. To my surprise, a woman was standing there, her hand poised to knock. She stepped back and smiled. "So sorry to scare you like that. I wanted to stop by and introduce myself."

"Introduce away then," I said, surprising even myself at the lameness of my words.

"I'm Rose Turvington. I'm your new landlord."

"New landlord? What happened to Mr. Sears?" Mr. Sears had been around since our country's forefathers signed the Constitution. I was pretty sure he'd used it as a guide when drawing up the papers to lease this place.

"He decided to go down to Florida. It was all very sudden, apparently." She pulled a lock of hair behind her ear. I noted her red, curly hair that bore a resemblance to mine. The difference was that she'd teased her bangs so they stood up in a gigantic curl.

The woman was probably in her mid-forties, so she had a good fifteen years on me. She wore skinny jeans with ankle boots and a black KISS T-shirt that emphasized her oversized apple figure. Her mascara was heavy, and she'd chosen an electric shade of blue to paint her eyelids. It was just a gut instinct, but I had a feeling she was thrilled that 80s clothing was back in style. In fact, maybe she'd never given up on it.

"I'm Gabby. Nice to meet you."

"Mr. Sears said you're one to watch out for." Her voice was low, kind of scratchy, maybe from smoking or possibly from yelling too loud at rock concerts.

"I suppose that's all in your definition of 'watch out for.'"

She laughed, deep and throaty. "You're funny. Anyway, I wanted to introduce myself. If you need anything, call me. I only live a few houses down, so I can be right over."

"Perfect." At least Mr. Sears had stayed out of my business. I wasn't sure I could say the same for this woman. People who had enthusiasm and energy to spare usually spent that enthusiasm and energy on other people. At least in my experience they did. Some people used it for good—by volunteering. Others used it for aggravating—by stirring up trouble.

I thought Rose was going to walk away, but she continued to talk. "I've already met Bill downstairs. No one else seems to be home."

I nodded. "Sierra downstairs is on her honeymoon, and Riley across the hall is probably at work. Mrs. Mystery—she lives in the attic apartment—sometimes doesn't come out or answer her door for days at a time."

"I see. It sounds like you're all a close knit little community here. I totally dig that."

I nodded. "Close knit. That's us." We were all as different as night and day, but we'd almost become like family. We watched each other's backs. Together, we could all make a really sappy music video to the song "Lean On Me." We'd been there and done that.

"I want to have a big cookout for all of you tomorrow. Please say you're available. Six o'clock outside on the lawn. I'm providing all of the food."

I wanted to object, to tell her I had too much work to do. But the woman put her hands together under the chin in an "oh please" motion and looked at me with wide eyes. Finally, I nodded. "I'll be there."

She raised her index finger and pinky in the air in a rocker's symbol. "Rock on! I'll see you then." She slipped a business card into my hand. "Here's my contact information in case you need me for anything. I aim to please!"

I watched as she practically skipped down the steps and out the front door, turning before she left to wave goodbye. The woman would certainly add some life around here. I'd give her that.

Maybe God was telling me that I needed more perky

people in my life. Between Clarice and Rose, that would certainly seem to be the case.

I trudged down the steps, holding my coffee with one hand, and my Pop Tart with the other. In vain, I tried to pull my Pop Tart wrapper off with my teeth. That's when I heard another door open. It had to be Bill McCormick, the radio talk show host who lived downstairs.

Sure enough, he stepped out, his bald head shiny and his stomach robust. His eyes, though . . . they looked different as he looked up the stairs at me. They looked brighter. "Did you meet her?"

I gave up on the Pop Tart and dropped it into my purse. "Did I meet who?"

"Our new landlady. She's a real looker, isn't she?" He wagged his eyebrows up and down.

"A real looker? I suppose." I noticed that Bill's face was almost glowing. And I'd never seen his face glowing. Usually, it was lit red with fury as he talked about either politics or his ex-wife.

"She told you about the cookout?"

"Sure did." I didn't really want to go into a long conversation about this. I had a lot of work to do, but I wanted to be a team player and the residents of this apartment were the closest things I had to a team. Well, the residents here and the members of my church. I'd known the residents here for longer, though.

He nodded and grinned. "I think my luck is changing."

"Have you been unlucky?"

"You didn't hear about my show?"

I stopped, my curiosity sufficiently pricked. "What about it?"

His lips suddenly pulled downward. "If my ratings aren't boosted, the station is dropping me."

My mouth gaped open. "They can't do that. You're their number one guy. You have been for years."

"That's what I thought! But ever since I had that little slip up a few weeks ago where I called that state senator," he paused and tugged his collar, "well, something I shouldn't have called him, sponsors have been dropping my show."

"Ouch." I couldn't begin to imagine what had come out of his mouth. Once Bill got going, there was no stopping him, and no thought was left unspoken.

There was a lot to be said for remaining quiet and appearing wise. What was that Bible verse? *Even a fool is thought wise if he keeps silent, and discerning if he holds his tongue.*

I'd been in Bill's position before, unfortunately. My impulsiveness and brashness did get the best of me sometimes.

Only once in a while, for that matter.

Okay, quite often.

"It's like I said. I think my luck is turning around." He nodded and grinned, a far off look in his eyes. "It's turning around." He waved at me and disappeared back inside his apartment.

Well, good for him. I hoped good things did come his way. He'd certainly been miserable for long enough. Of course, if he wasn't so angry all the time, ratings for his show might *really* drop.

I didn't have time to worry about it. I had to worry about cleaning this next crime scene and getting paid. This homeowner was using their insurance, which meant it would take forever for me to collect my compensation. It meant I'd have to haggle with the adjustor, who seemed to always have all the time in the world. But I'd take whatever jobs I could get. After all, I had student loans to pay.

I stopped cold when I saw my van.

Clarice leaned against it, a bright smile on her face. She waved enthusiastically, an energy drink in her hands and Converse on her feet. She was already wearing her trendy, oversized glasses, which seemed unexpected from someone as prissy as Clarice.

I wanted to run the other way or pretend like I didn't see her. I couldn't do either. Instead, I plastered on a smile and walked toward my van.

"Hello, Clarice."

"You almost sound like that guy from *The Silence of the Lambs.* Isn't that crazy? Hello, Clarice," she imitated before laughing. "That's so psycho."

Great, I was starting to sound like Hannibal Lector. This was what my life had come to. Next, I'd be talking about fava beans.

"So psycho," I repeated. I pulled my purse higher and sucked in a long, deep breath as I gathered my thoughts. "So, you're here. And you're wearing designer jeans again, I see."

"You didn't think one crime scene was going to scare me off, did you?" She tilted her head a moment before tugging at the leg of her jeans. "And these are last year's designer jeans, so I figured they'd be okay."

"How'd you know what time I was leaving? I didn't think we'd discussed that."

"I've been here since 7. Auntie Sharon said you like to start early. I didn't want to bother you in your apartment, though, so I just decided to wait outside. No one's going to say I'm a bad employee this time. Nope. That's not happening again. I'm getting all gold stars with this job-a-roo."

Perfect, I thought to myself. I wasn't getting rid of her, was I? I forced another smile and nodded toward my van. "Let's go, then."

Sharon. I wished I believed in voodoo. I might buy a doll with pink hair and a nose ring if I did. Of course, I was a Christian now, and as a Christian I was constantly reminded of both my need for forgiveness and my need to forgive. Sometimes it felt like I'd be struggling with those concepts for the rest of my life.

We started down the road. I tried to turn up the radio and listen to "Welcome to My Nightmare" by Alice Cooper. Instead, Clarice was talking about the crime scene yesterday and her sorority sisters. I tuned her out and tried to concentrate on driving.

"Oh my gosh! Did you see that?" Clarice screeched.

I nearly slammed on brakes. I looked for a lost dog about to wander aimlessly in front of my van. A woman being mugged. A nude man playing guitar on the street corner.

I saw nothing but a busy highway snaking through town, crammed with the gridlock of morning rush hour traffic.

"See what?" I was trying not to seethe. Really. I was.

"On that sign post back there? How could you have missed it? It was a flyer for Zombie Fest. Zombie Fest!" Her pitch rose with each word.

I bit back a sharp retort and tapped my fingers against the steering wheel. "Zombie Fest?"

"That sounds like the bomb. I can't wait to tell my friends." She held out her arms, limp at the wrists, and crossed her eyes. "Zombies. I'm a zombie. Brains!"

Oh my goodness. How was I going to survive a whole day of this? By the end of our first job, I'd be begging for a zombie to come and eat my brains.

She grabbed my arm and nearly had me jumping out of my skin. "You're totally going to go, aren't you, Gabby?"

Certainly she wasn't asking me if I was going to . . . "Zombie Fest?"

"It's this Friday. You've got to do it! Everyone who's anyone will be there."

I wasn't quite so sure her words were true. "Zombie Fest doesn't sound like much fun."

"It's zombies, for goodness sake! What's not fun about that? Except maybe monkey ninjas." She paused and turned her head sharply toward me. "You're not too old for it, are you?"

"Too old?" I wasn't even thirty yet. "Of course not."

"You're acting too old."

Too old? Some kind of survival instinct ignited within me. I was not some old stick in the mud. No way. I was young. Hip. With it. "I'd love to go to Zombie Fest. It would be the highlight of my week. Maybe my month. When I said it didn't sound like much fun, I meant it didn't sound like *much* fun—it sounded like the *bomb-diggity* of fun."

She grinned. "See! Auntie Sharon was right when she said I'd get along great with you. We're totally on the same wavelength."

Oh, please. Never. Ever. Shoot me.

I kept driving, wondering what I'd just gotten myself into. Clarice talked about it for the rest of the ride until we pulled up to our crime scene. The place was a small little bungalow located in an older but well kept area of Norfolk called Larchmont. Some larger homes here backed up to the water, but many were moderately sized. This house was painted olive green with white shutters and immaculate flowerbeds.

I cut the engine and prepped Clarice a moment. "There was a shooting inside. I'm fairly certain it was a drug deal gone badly. I'll spackle the wall where the bullets got lodged, scrub down everything, remove anything that would remind the family of the crime."

"Got it."

I met a man on the porch. He wasn't the same person who'd been here when I came out to give my estimate on Saturday. He had a curly gray beard, oversized glasses, and wore a trucker hat. His skin was pale and wrinkled, and he had an over abundance of ear hair.

"Thanks for coming," he mumbled, tugging at his hat.

"I'm sorry for your loss." I meant it. I never wanted to become immune to death's sting or the life-altering impact it had on the lives of the deceased's loved ones.

He nodded solemnly. "We all are. If you could make it look like this never happened, we'd sure be appreciative."

"I'll do my best," I told him.

He unlocked the door for me before walking to his car and making me promise to lock up after I left. I hauled out my equipment, including an industrial vacuum, an air scrub, and lots of cleaning products. We drug it all inside and paused for a moment.

I almost always paused first thing when I arrived at the scene. Maybe it was my subconscious way of paying respect to the dead. Every life, no matter whatever series of events that defined it, deserved a moment of honor. If God had created all of us, then it only seemed fitting to mourn the passing of one of His creations.

My cell phone rang. I glanced down and saw Riley's number. Hopefully he was calling to tell me that Milton Jones had been located and taken back into custody. At least I could breathe a little easier if that was the case, no matter how paranoid that might sound. I'd intended on watching the news this morning, but my pressing work schedule had won over the TV.

I hit TALK. "Hey, Riley. What's up?"

He got right to the point, not mincing any words. "A woman has been snatched here in Norfolk."

Okay, that wasn't the normal greeting I was expecting from Riley. "What?"

"It's on the news. A woman was snatched from her bedroom in Norfolk last night."

"That's horrible, but why did you call to tell me that?" Riley wasn't one to be random, so I knew he had a point. I had a feeling I knew what that point was, but I wanted to hear him say it, lest I sound paranoid.

"It's got Milton Jones' M.O. all over it, Gabby."

I leaned against the wall and lowered my voice so Clarice wouldn't hear. "It's ridiculous to think he's in this area, Riley. Are the police sure the woman didn't just disappear?"

"He left a photo there."

My blood got a little colder. "What kind of photo?"

"It was a snapshot of the woman taken at a Tides' baseball game." The Tides were our minor league here in Norfolk. "She had no idea it was taken. Her eyes had Xs over them."

I shivered. That was Milton Jones' signature calling card. I shoved aside my emotions for a moment. "How do you know the police in Norfolk found the photo? Are they actually saying it on the news?"

"No, Detective Adams called me a few minutes ago. He knew I was prosecutor on the Milton Jones case, and he wanted to talk to me about some details."

My throat burned as I swallowed. "I see. It has to just be a terrible coincidence or a copycat. Jones can't make it across the country without being caught, especially not in two days." I was going to keep telling myself that, at least. It made sense to me.

"You'd be surprised what that man can do. Promise me you'll be careful? Keep your eyes open?"

"Of course." I was always careful and kept my eyes open. Even then, I'd almost been killed several times.

"I love you, Gabby."

"I love you, too, Riley." My hands still trembled as I put my phone away and slipped into my Hazmat suit.

"Everything okay? You look like a ghost . . ." Clarice raised her arms and crossed her eyes again. "Or, should I say, a zombie?"

"Yeah, everything's fine." I didn't want to discuss this with Clarice, of all people. I nodded toward a room down the hall. "Let's get scrubbing."

"Aren't you going to spray the place with that chemical again?"

I scoffed. "Why would I do that?"

"Maybe someone left another message for you."

"They didn't leave a message for me. They left it for the police."

"Then why did that officer say the message had been left after the crime scene unit had already been through?" She crossed her arms and stared at me.

"Good question." I'd thought about that myself.

"Maybe someone wanted you to discover it."

"Nice theory, but it doesn't work. I don't usually spray Luminol," I admitted. "Yesterday was just kind of a . . . test. An initiation for the new girl, you could say."

"I get that. But was there any other way you might discover that message?"

"It was just a fluke. There's no way anyone could have known I was going to do that. I hadn't done it before. I won't do it again."

"Maybe someone knew you ordered the Lysol . . . inol."

"Luminol." I shook my head. "I really think that you're overthinking this. Let's suit up."

"So how'd you become a crime scene cleaner anyway?" Clarice asked as she pulled on her Hazmat suit.

"It's a long story. I went to school to study forensics, but I had to drop out. I was looking for something to keep me connected to the crime scenes and give me more experience. You know, something I could use later on. I heard about crime scene cleaning and decided to give it a shot."

"What is it that's kept you in this job instead of doing something else?"

I shrugged. "Various reasons, I guess. The job market isn't great right now."

"You, like, worked for the medical examiner for a while, right?"

I nodded. "Budget cuts happened, though, so I'm back to doing this. It's not that bad. I get to help people."

"And you've helped to solve some crimes, right? That's what Auntie Sharon said."

I nodded, snapping on my gloves. "I've got a few under my belt. It's been a mixture of following the evidence, following my gut, and not giving up."

Clarice smiled. "That's perfect."

I paused. "What do you mean?"

She shook her head. "I don't know. I just mean that you have a great story. Really. You do."

I pushed the door to the bedroom open and gasped. I backed out of the room, my heart drumming against my chest. Someone hadn't bothered to try and wash away his message this time.

"What is it?" Clarice asked, her eyes wide and frightened.

The image wouldn't escape from my mind. The blood. Dripping. Slashed across the walls. "It's another message."

"What does it say?"

I closed my eyes. "Three, Four. I'm hungry for more. Gabby St. Claire, are you ready for the gore?"

CHAPTER FIVE

DETECTIVE ADAMS STARED ME DOWN. We'd worked together several times before. Okay, well maybe "working together" was a slight stretch. In the past, we'd had encounters stemming from the fact that I'd been nosy. Like clockwork, Detective Adams had always shown up just in time to tell me to back off and let the police handle things.

Our professional relationship had progressed to the point where he'd helped me get the job at the Medical Examiner's Office. In many ways, he had grown to become one of my biggest supporters. He knew I was competent and that I lived to see justice served.

"No one knew I was coming here except the homeowner," I told him.

"Someone knew you were going to be here."

I shook my head, flabbergasted. "I came over on Saturday when I'd returned from my trip to the mountains to give the family an estimate. Maybe someone followed me then? I have no idea. Believe me. I've been turning this over and over in my mind. It makes no sense."

"Someone's trying to get your attention."

I crossed my arms. "It's working."

I glanced over at Clarice. She was breathing into a paper bag. If she kept that up much longer, someone was going to call for an ambulance. The poor girl. She really had gotten more than she'd bargained for. On the other hand, she would have some great stories to tell her sorority sisters when school started back up again in a couple of weeks.

"Be careful," Detective Adams urged.

"I wasn't even trying to stick my nose in this one, Detective."

He nodded, his gaze surveying the mayhem around us. The house had been flooded with law enforcement officials and Adams wasn't missing anything. He always kept one eye on his subject, but his other soaked in everything else going on around him. I'd found him to be competent, reasonable, and even-keeled.

"I know you weren't trying to get involved in this one," he said. "Unusual, but given the nature of the death here, understandable. Someone wants to draw you in. The question is: Why?"

"Your guess is as good as mine on this one." I started to walk away but stopped. "What am I going to tell the home-owners? Do you want me to contact them?"

"I'll call them and let them know new evidence has come to light. We should be able to clear the scene for you by tomorrow if you want to come back then and finish the job."

I nodded. "I know they're probably anxious to have all of these reminders erased."

"Anyone would be. If anything changes, I'll let you know. Otherwise, plan on being back here in the morning. The crime scene should be released by then."

"Got it."

I motioned toward the door, and Clarice followed me

THE SCUM OF ALL FEARS 39

outside. Humid air enveloped us, but the stifling heat still felt more comforting than the horror infusing the atmosphere inside of that home.

I paused and looked at Clarice a moment as we stood on the lush green lawn. The sparkle was gone from her eyes. Her skin was pale. Her shoulders sagged.

I figured this would be a bad time to make a zombie joke. Instead, I said, "You doing okay?"

She shook her head, silky brown hair swishing against her shoulders. This was soap opera angst at its finest. One day when she got her role as an extra on *The Young and the Restless* she could tap into these emotions for any especially dramatic scene. "I shouldn't have peeked into the room."

"I told you not to." But she just *had* to see.

Sounded like someone else I knew. *Me.*

She fanned her face. Some of that crimson apple lipstick would really serve to brighten her up at the moment. "What now, Gabby?"

I started walking back toward the van. "Now we head to the next job, which just happens to be the crime scene where we found the first message yesterday. It's been cleared, so we're okay to finish the job there."

Clarice stopped cold, her face seeming to freeze in place with eyes wide and lips slightly parted. "The next crime scene? What if . . . ?"

"Adams already sent someone over to check it out first. There shouldn't be any surprises."

She started walking again, a curious glint in her eyes. "Adams? You call the detective by his last name? You are the real deal, aren't you?"

I shrugged. "I'm not sure what you mean by the 'real deal.' I've earned his trust. It's been a long, hard road, though."

"What do you think of those messages being left? That one seemed specifically for you."

I guess my name had made that fact clear. I shrugged again, biting my lip before I said anything about being Captain Obvious. "I don't know. Eerie? Yes. Lacking in creativity? Absolutely."

"Lacking in creativity? What do you mean?"

"Hasn't the little numbers rhyme thing been done before?"

Her eyes widened. "Has it? I don't know. Not on *Criminal Minds*."

I cut my eyes at her but decided not to comment. "I've helped put some bad guys behind bars, so I've become an easy target, you could say. After that write up on me in a local newspaper, maybe I got too much attention. Attention from the wrong people, at least."

The curious glint turned into an all-out sparkle as she grabbed my arm. "You should have a TV show about you. Everyone would watch it. You're definitely pretty enough to be on TV. The camera would love you." Her voice went from flat to animated.

I shook my head as I climbed into my van. "Most people couldn't handle watching what I do. This is a reality they'd rather forget about." Crime scenes may look exciting on TV, and people thought they were desensitized. But when a real crime scene involved a loved one, they had a real wake up call. No amount of *CSI* reruns could prepare one to see that.

Clarice continued to talk as she climbed inside the van. At least the thought of my possible fame had distracted her from the eerie blood message inside that home. "It would sell. Totally. It would be like *Sunshine Cleaning*, Real World style. I wonder if I could be an extra . . ."

I shook my head, ready to be done with this conversation.

I had no illusions of fame and fortune. No, I was just happy to pay my bills and help out hurting families hungry for answers. Maybe if other people found justice in their lives, I could find justice in my own life as well.

I checked my directions and started down the road. The next scene wasn't too far away. I needed to knock it out and get on my way.

As I drove, I pondered whether or not crime scene cleaning was in my future permanently. I didn't know. I'd studied hard to have a career in forensics. It wasn't my fault the job market had gone south right around the time I'd finally gotten my degree. All the doors here in Virginia had effectively closed. Until someone died or retired, it looked like it was either crime scene cleaning here or taking a job in another state, which would require a move.

Which brought me back to the fact that I had a Skype interview on Wednesday with the Medical Examiner's office in Kansas. The opportunity seemed to be a good one. But Kansas . . . it was so far away from Riley and my friends. Did I really have to choose between my dream job and my dream man? That's what it was starting to feel like, and I resented the possibility of having to make that choice.

Besides, my dad was here. So was my brother, and we'd just begun to reconnect in the past couple of months. That much distance between me and my only sibling could seriously put a damper on my plans to make up for lost time.

I shoved those thoughts aside. I wouldn't stress out about it too much until I found out if the Kansas State Medical Examiner's Office was offering me a job. That's when I could have a little mini-crisis about what to do.

We pulled up to the next crime scene. A police cruiser waited in the driveway. I told Clarice to wait in the van, and I hopped out. An officer who looked so young he had to be a rookie stepped out.

"Even though you were just here yesterday, I'm going to walk through the house with you first. Those were my orders from above." He stood stiffly with his chin raised and a serious look in his eyes.

"Let's go then." Though I knew the scene had been cleared, I braced myself for any messages that would be a shock to my system.

Thankfully, everything appeared clear.

After the officer pulled away, I went through my normal routine of hauling things out of my van. Apprehension dug its claws between my shoulders, though. Even though the officer had said the scene was clear, I had a hard time believing it. I half expected to find another message waiting for me there.

One, Two. I'm Coming for You.

Three, Four. I'm Hungry for More.

Gabby St. Claire, are you ready for gore?

The messages were eerie, that was for sure.

Someone was taunting the police and me. Had the same person killed both of the people at the two crime scenes I'd cleaned? That's the only way they could have left those messages. Yet, the facts of the cases were so different. The homes were unalike, the motives were distinctive, and the means of death weren't the same.

I shook my head. I had no idea right now. Maybe things would come to light. Or, better yet, maybe this was some kind of sick joke. Maybe the sicko behind the messages would decide to let this drop.

I had the feeling that wouldn't be the case, though.

I got to cleaning, desperate to take my mind off my problems and concentrate on someone else's.

A grim reality but reality none-the-less.

Riley was working late, and I didn't feel like going back to my apartment after I dropped Clarice off at her car. Instead, I swung by to talk to Sharon. She was actually seated at a table reading the newspaper when I walked in. Her other employees were manning the register.

Before she even spotted me, I slid into the seat across from her. She nudged down the paper and frowned when she saw me. Immediately, she jerked the paper back up to conceal her face.

"Feeling guilty?" I asked.

She sighed and pushed the paper onto the table. "How's Clarice doing on the job?"

I shrugged. "I'm counting down the days until Chad gets back, if that tells you anything."

"She's a bit of a dingbat. She drives my sister crazy. She's the one who, once when she heard her car making a funny noise, turned up the radio so she wouldn't have to hear it. It turned out the engine was leaking oil and was totally ruined. It cost my sister thousands of dollars in repair bills."

"I kind of like that actually. Just turn up the radio. Ignore the noise, the worries of life."

"Or the warning signs," Sharon said. She straightened. "Not to change the subject, but how are you doing? How are the wedding preparations coming?"

"I need to make a checklist. I've got the church reserved, though. Still have to order invitations and all of that stuff." I remembered my dwindling checking account and frowned.

"What's going on with the job situation?"

"I have an interview with Kansas on Wednesday." In an

amazing turn of events, the barista set a latte in front of me. I *loved* this place. It was like they could read my mind. I muttered, "Thank you."

She straightened. "Kansas? Really? That's exciting."

"I doubt I'll take it."

"Why wouldn't you?"

I shrugged again. "My life is here. Riley is here. I don't know if I want to leave all of that behind."

"You shouldn't give up your career for a guy, Gabby. Respect yourself more than that."

Sharon's words felt like a slap in the face. *Of course* I respected myself. The issue here was a little more complicated. I took a long sip of my iced latte before speaking.

"I'm not giving up my career," I finally said. "I'm just trying to make some decisions about my future."

She raised a pierced eyebrow. "It sounds like you're not even seriously considering that job in Kansas, all because of Riley."

I straightened, trying not to let my voice go all high-pitched. No, I wasn't going to get flustered by this misunderstanding. "For starters, the job hasn't even been offered to me. My interview is coming up this week. And, for the second thing, it's not just because of Riley that I'm considering staying, but he is my fiancé, so of course he plays into this decision."

She leaned toward me. "Don't set it up so that he thinks his career is more important than yours. If you don't go to Kansas, that's what you're saying. You're going to have a lifetime of being less important than he is."

I sighed, frustration close to winning out over being sensible. "You know Riley. You know he's not like that."

She stared at me, dead serious. "All guys are like that."

Wow, I'd known Sharon how long now? I had no idea

she'd react like this when I told her I had a job interview in Kansas.

"We'll have to agree to disagree then." I desperately needed to change the subject before Sharon planted any negative thoughts in my head. I knew Riley. I knew he wasn't that guy. I stood and stretched. "You know what? I'm tired. I should be running."

"Think about what I said, Gabby."

I nodded, but I had no intentions of thinking about something that wasn't true.

———

By the time I got home that evening, I was bone tired. Not only had the scenes been physically grueling to clean, but the emotional toll the threats had taken on me was bigger than I wanted to admit. Then there was the conversation with Sharon that I'd rather forget. Yet it continued to echo in my mind.

I was ready for a long, hot bath and a re-run of *Psych*.

I dropped my purse by the couch and started toward my bedroom. I stopped mid-step by my desk, which was located against the wall in the Great Room, and stared down at the mess there. A mess I'd left, and an organized one at that.

Why did I feel like something had been moved?

I glanced over the papers, folders, and sticky notes cluttering the top. There was my new laptop. I'd bought it only a month or so ago. It was the first thing I'd purchased when I got my job with the medical examiner. Little did I know *then* what I knew *now*.

There was also an old Slim Jim canister that I'd covered in crime scene tape that held my pens and some spare change. My diploma hung on the wall above it, along with a framed copy of the newspaper article about me. Then there was a picture of Riley and me at my college graduation. My filing cabinet was overstuffed with business invoices, purchase order forms, and receipts.

Nothing appeared to be out of place. So why did I feel so unsettled?

I sat down for a moment and stared, trying to pinpoint the origin of my unease.

I picked up a couple of papers on top. Just some bills. Underneath that was . . . a list of my clients that I'd printed out.

Bringing the paper up closer to my eyes, I focused on the words. This week had ended up being so busy that I printed out the addresses of all my job sites, as well as my schedule for cleaning their homes, just so I could keep everything straight and organized.

Someone couldn't have . . .

I shook my head. No. No one saw this list. No one got an idea on how to leave me messages at crime scenes based on this paper.

Then Riley's words came back to me. *No one ever knew how Milton Jones got in and out of the homes. It was still a mystery to this day.*

What if he'd gotten into my apartment without leaving a trace?

I shook my head again, feeling like I'd taken a crazy pill. Milton Jones had not gotten into my house. He was in California. Hiding.

That woman who'd disappeared last night had been taken by someone else. It was a tragic coincidence, but a coincidence all the same.

A deranged serial killer was not after me.

He was not leaving messages for me at crime scenes in some kind of vast conspiracy to get revenge on Riley.

I refused to believe that.

But if I refused to believe it, then why was I having second thoughts about my bath? Why did I have the strange urge to call Riley and see if I could hang out at his place for a while . . . like until Jones was back behind bars? Even being with Clarice would be better than being in my apartment alone at the moment.

Just then, someone pounded at my door.

I grabbed my butcher knife and tried desperately to formulate a plan of action.

CHAPTER SIX

"GABBY? ARE YOU THERE?" someone called from the hallway.

My hand—the one without the knife—went over my heart. Riley. It was just Riley.

I put the knife down before calmly walking to the door, unlocking all four locks, and pulling the door open.

I had to stop myself from falling into Riley's arms like a damsel in distress. No, I was a damsel who'd charge my way into trouble and fight for myself. But even tough damsels sometimes wanted to be cared for and protected, even if we didn't want to admit it.

Riley wrapped his arms around me as soon as I opened the door. I didn't argue, but instead nestled my head into his chest. My heart still drummed a beat steady enough for a prisoner to walk to his death by.

"What's wrong?" Riley pulled back until he could see my eyes.

I rubbed my temple, wondering just how crazy I was about to sound. So, instead of sounding crazy, I went with a more watered down version of why I was jumpy. "My crime scenes are playing with my head."

"Maybe you should stay with someone tonight," he suggested. "Doesn't Sharon have an extra room?"

"I'll be fine." I walked to the couch, Riley following behind. I couldn't handle talking to Sharon any more tonight.

"Staying with someone would just be a safety precaution." He lowered himself beside me. "It wouldn't be a wimpy thing to do."

"You know me too well." I hated appearing weak.

"Sometimes you have to swallow your pride."

Pride did come before a fall. I sure didn't want my fall to be at the hands of Milton Jones. "I'll double check my windows."

Riley's tie had been loosened and, again, his sleeves were rolled up and the top two buttons of his shirt undone. Catching up on work after being away for a week had obviously exhausted him. Starting your own law practice could exhaust anyone, or so I'd heard.

I filled him in on my day, leaving out my suspicion that someone had riffled through the papers on my desk. I couldn't confirm it; all I had was a hunch. Science wasn't about instinct, though I was never one to dismiss gut feelings. If I told Riley my theory, he'd have the cops over here. I stuck with the eerie crime scene message instead.

Riley loosened his tie even more. "Those messages don't fit Jones' M.O. He was too meticulous, too careful."

"If it's not Jones—and I don't believe it is—that would mean we have two psychos on our hands. One is hard enough to handle."

"Jones is gone, Gabby. No one knows where he escaped. In this day and age where everything is on video, he's vanished. I wouldn't put anything past him."

"Have you considered that whoever snatched that woman in Norfolk was a copycat?"

"It seems too coincidental that a copycat would emerge now, just as Jones has escaped. I don't buy it." He shook his head, leaving no room for doubt.

"This has got you really worried, hasn't it?" I squeezed his forearm.

"What he did to those women . . ." His lips drew into a tight line.

He didn't have to finish. I knew what he'd done. I'd read about it online. It was the stuff nightmares were made out of. Methodical torture. Drawing out death for as long as possible. Things I couldn't bear to think about.

"On a happier note, we have a new landlord, and Bill McCormick wants to marry her." Yeah, I know. It was a rough subject change. But unless I turned the topic onto something else, I was going to start thinking about pain and people not being treated as humans. I didn't want to go there right now.

Riley shook his head like someone had just splashed him with cold water. "What?"

"It's true. She came by and introduced herself today. Her name is Rose. She's got this 80s rock vibe going on, and she wants to have a cookout for everyone here tomorrow."

"Mr. Sears never did that."

"Nope, he sure didn't." Mr. Sears barely showed up when there was a pipe leak or when an appliance broke. Most of us here had learned to take care of issues ourselves. There were advantages and disadvantages to his hands-off approach.

"You said the cookout is tomorrow? Isn't that when your interview is?"

So Riley did remember. He hadn't brought the job possibility up since I first mentioned it. He didn't talk a lot about what it could mean for us, but I wondered if he was worried that I might accept the job. Of course, he'd told me it was a great opportunity, but how great was it if it meant we'd live seventeen hours apart? And, if he wasn't worried about me moving, then how much did that mean he cared for me?

Was Sharon right? Did he think his career was more important than mine? I had a hard time believing it.

I was much better at deciphering science than I was figuring out my emotions. Or figuring out men, for that matter.

"My interview is actually on Wednesday. They called and asked if we could move it back a day. I'll squeeze it in between jobs."

He leaned back and propped his feet up on the coffee table. He looked tired. Really tired. Now wasn't the time I wanted to have a conversation with him about whose job was more important or who should sacrifice for the other.

"Did you eat dinner? Can I make you something?" I *thought* I had some Ramen noodles somewhere in my pantry.

"I'm good. Just a long day. I should probably get to bed."

Truth was that I wanted him to stay, but I knew he couldn't for more than one reason. Riley stood and headed down my hallway instead of toward the door.

I shoved my eyebrows together. "What are you doing?"

"Checking all of your windows." He moved from room to room, nudging and shoving and double-checking. Finally, I guess he was satisfied.

"Be careful. Promise me."

There was a time to be careful. And then there were times when careful would get you nowhere.

"I'll keep my eyes wide open," I told him.

And I would be careful, I decided, in a manner of speaking. I'd *carefully* figure out the mess around me until I got some answers.

I tossed to the other side of my bed as a night of restless sleep got the best of me. The sheets were knotted at my feet. My pillow had been punched more times than Mike Tyson's face. Sleep and my body were just not cooperating tonight.

My thoughts were going haywire.

They jumped from Milton Jones to the eerie messages at the crime scenes to my interview with the Kansas Medical Examiner. I thought about Riley, our future together, about everything I'd leave behind if I moved. I thought about my desk, the papers there, and the possibility that a serial killer could be taunting me.

Before I'd gone to bed, I'd opened my Bible and read from 1 Peter. *Your enemy the devil prowls around like a roaring lion looking for someone to devour. Resist him, standing firm in the faith, because you know that the family of believers throughout the world is undergoing the same kind of sufferings.*

I wasn't saying that there was a killer out there who was secretly the devil. But I did feel like there was someone out there looking for lives to destroy. I hoped I could stand strong in my faith throughout this storm.

Finally, I threw my legs out of bed and stood.

My alarm clock told me it was only 5:30 a.m. Way too early to be getting up. But I just couldn't lay down any longer.

I shuffled into the kitchen and flipped on my coffeemaker. I'd set it last night before I went to bed. Without any coffee, my mind was too groggy in the morning to make coffee. I know, I know . . . it was a tough life. I was hoping to add "I promise to make you coffee every morning" somewhere in Riley's wedding vows.

Five minutes later, I had a steaming cup in front of me,

topped off with some sugar and cream. I flipped on the TV and found a news station.

A story about Milton Jones was on. Of course.

I should have changed the station, but I couldn't bring myself to do it.

Instead, I listened as the reporter talked about the precautions people out in California were taking. That same, familiar fear had crept into their lives. Some had even planned vigils in honor of the man's past victims.

California seemed so far away. Yet, at the same time, it seemed so close.

How many miles? I pulled my cell phone from its charger on the end table and checked the distance. Two thousand, six hundred and some miles. To drive straight through would take one day, plus sixteen hours.

That didn't seem all that far.

Faces of Milton's victims flashed on the screen. I'd seen some of them before when I did my Internet search. They were all young. They were all pretty and ambitious and had a full life ahead of them.

Until Milton Jones had snatched it away.

I was pretty sure Lifetime had already made a movie about him. No joke. It had been called "The Milton Jones Story."

I reminded myself not to watch any Saturday night specials on the man. No, I didn't need a film to increase my wariness. Life was doing a fine enough job on its own.

Finally, I flipped the TV off and drank my last sip of coffee. Enough was enough.

I had to get to work. I walked over to my desk to check my schedule for the day.

What I saw there made my heart stutter a beat.

It was a picture of me. With Clarice. Leaving the crime scene yesterday.

CHAPTER
SEVEN

I FLEW across the hall to Riley's apartment and pounded on the door. He opened it, still looking sleepy and wearing his Redskins' PJs. I barged inside, my limbs shaking harder than a wet dog fresh out of the bathtub.

"What is it?" Riley raked a hand through his hair.

I held up the picture, which I'd been careful to only touch with a paper towel on the edges, just in case there were prints. My hand trembled so hard that Riley probably couldn't make out anything about the photo. "This. I found it on my desk this morning."

He ushered me inside before taking it from me. He knew the drill and watched out for any prints. His nostrils flared as he stared at the photo. "This was inside your apartment?"

I leaned against the door, my heart still pounding out of control. "It wasn't there last night. I looked through all of my papers on my desk before I went to bed. I would have seen it."

Riley started pacing. "How did someone get inside? All of your locks were latched, right?"

"Of course. Except, this morning, the chain to my door had been undone." I'd noticed in my mad dash to Riley's place.

He stopped. "What's that mean?"

I hardly wanted to say the words, but I'd only been able to draw one conclusion. "The only thing I can figure is that someone was inside my apartment the whole time." Shivers raced across my skin at the thought.

Riley stared at me for a moment before shaking his head and starting to pace again. "That's crazy."

"How else could this picture have gotten there? How else did that chain get unlatched?" I'd considered all the other possibilities as my mind raced on hyper-drive. I had no other ideas.

He ran a hand over his face and let out an exasperated moan. "Did you hear anything last night?"

I shook my head. "I was awake for most of the night, and I didn't hear anything. Not a squeak. Not a footstep. Nothing."

Riley stopped in front of me. Concern lined his blue eyes. "You've got to call the police, Gabby."

I nodded. "I know."

Riley grabbed his cell phone from a nearby bookshelf. "I'll call Detective Adams. You . . ." He shook his head, looking overwhelmed, an emotion I'd rarely seen on Riley before. "You just take some deep breaths."

I sucked in air, long and slow and hard. I closed my eyes as I did so and began fervently lifting up prayers.

Riley shoved the phone between his shoulder and ear. "Don't be surprised if he pulls Parker or one of his cronies into this."

Parker was my ex-boyfriend. Now he was a fed. Getting him involved would only add more fuel to the fire. The situa-

THE SCUM OF ALL FEARS 59

tion was stressful enough without adding an ex onto the scene.

"Adams is on his way. After you talk to him, you should get out of town," Riley told me when he hung up.

His words stopped me cold. "What are you talking about?"

"Maybe rent a cabin somewhere. Pay with cash. Give the person you rent from an alias. Stay there until all of this passes over." His pacing became more frantic, and he ran his hands through his hair. I'd never seen him like this.

"Riley, you're talking crazy. Besides, what if this doesn't pass over? I can't stay in hiding forever."

The far-off look in his eyes made it clear that he was running through scenarios in his head and really trying to think this out. "You need to be safe."

"Are we ever truly safe?"

My words seemed to get through to him. He pulled me toward him and held me. He was worried. Really worried.

I'd seen him worried about me before. Several times, for that matter. But this went beyond any of those times in the past.

"I can't lose you, Gabby," he finally muttered into my hair. He stroked my back, his voice tight and strained.

"Oh, Riley. I don't know what to say." I was good with the snarky and sarcastic. The serious and sentimental? That didn't come naturally.

He stepped back, a new light in his eyes. "Maybe we should get married."

I laughed, the sound airy and laden with surprise. "Married? Just because of a serial killer. I'm flattered."

There we go. There was that unfailing sarcasm.

He tilted his head so close to mine that we were practically nose-to-nose. "You know what I mean. We're getting married anyway. We could just move up the date. Then we could be together and . . ."

" . . . Milton Jones could sneak into our apartment and kill both of us?" The realist in me emerged at the worst times.

"I could stay up all night listening for him, if I had to. If he came, I could be there to protect you."

"And without sleep, your logic would be compromised. You need your rest in order to think clearly and help find this guy." I was being the reasonable one here. This was a switch.

He sighed and looked at the ceiling. "I'd just feel better if you weren't alone."

I wrapped my arms around his waist. "You know I want to marry you more than anything. But I don't want to rush the wedding just because of this Milton Jones guy. That would give him too much power in our lives."

Plus, there was always the issue of Kansas . . .

Riley let out a slow breath. "You're right. But we've got to figure out something until Jones is arrested again. Because having him sneak into your apartment again is not an option."

Twenty minutes later, Detective Adams sat across from us at the dining room table in Riley's apartment. Some kind of nervous tick had come over me, and I couldn't keep my hands still. I rubbed at a smudge on the tabletop. I cracked my knuckles. I twirled my hair.

"I don't have to tell you how serious this is," Detective Adams said. He leveled his gaze at me.

I glanced over at Riley, who sat next to me with his arms crossed as if he were guarding precious cargo. "Riley has already done a great job explaining that."

Adams tapped his pad of paper on the table and stared at his notes there. "Riley, I have a feeling we'll be in contact more, especially given your prior connection with this case. A task force has already been set up."

"I'll do whatever I can to help."

Adams nodded back toward my apartment. "We'll see if any of the prints the forensic unit collects in your apartment come back as a match to Jones."

Riley shook his head. "Milton Jones never left any prints."

"We have to keep our mind open to all the possibilities out there," Adams reminded him.

Riley straightened. "Who else knows about his threat toward me? Who else knows that Jones was collecting information on me from prison? Could this just be an opportunist trying to get to me, using Jones as a ruse?"

"We're trying to track down all of that information now. Details like those threats were kept under wraps. Only a limited number of people were aware of them, and most of them were people officially connected to the case."

Just then, someone rapped at the door. I expected to see one of the forensic techs. Instead, a man in a suit stood there. He was in his forties with brown hair that grayed at the temples. He had a lean build, a face scarred from acne, and he wore wire-framed glasses.

Riley took a step toward him, his face softening with some kind of male camaraderie. "If it isn't Dale Warren." He extended his hand in a chummy manner.

The man returned Riley's grin. "Riley Thomas. You're looking well. Your time away from the D.A.'s Office must be good for you."

"I can't complain. I wish I could ask why you're here, but I think I know."

Dale and Adams did a quick nod to each other before the

Norfolk detective put his notebook back into his jacket and rose. "I'm going to check on the scene next door. I'm sure we'll be in touch."

When Adams stepped out of the room, Riley turned toward me. "Gabby, this is Dale Warren. He's a detective out in L.A. We knew each other way back when."

"It wasn't actually that long ago," Dale said, extending his hand toward me.

I shook his hand. "Nice to meet you."

"Dale, this is Gabby St. Claire, my fiancée."

That still had a nice ring to it, even a month after Riley's proposal.

Dale grinned. "You always did have good taste in women, Riley. I see nothing's changed there."

I ignored the sexist undertones to his statement and forced a polite smile.

Riley pointed to a chair. "Have a seat."

Dale did just that, and Riley and I settled back in our seats. I wanted to offer him coffee, but I couldn't bring myself to leave the table and miss any news Dale might be sharing.

Dale's face lost any lightheartedness and turned serious. "The FBI has called together a joint task force that includes members of the U.S. Marshals, a prison representative, and some local police. Detective Adams is also a part of our team. We met yesterday. They want you to be a part of this search, Riley."

Riley nodded. "Of course. Whatever I can do to put Jones back behind bars. How did his escape happen? I'm still trying to wrap my mind around this."

He shook his head. "It was tragic. He'd almost escaped twice from the prison where he was housed. They decided to move him to the supermax prison out in Colorado."

"There's a supermax prison?" I asked. I really needed to

read up more on correctional facilities. I'd never had a need before, though. As long as criminals were put away, I was happy. Until now.

Riley nodded. "Only the worst of the worst go there. Terrorists. High-profile killers. It's a rough place."

"There's one other thing." Dale shifted and paused. "We think he might be headed this way. That's why I'm here and not in California."

Riley nodded solemnly. "Believe me. I've considered that possibility."

"I'm not sure why you're the one he's turned all of his rage on. But he's had you in his sights ever since his sentence was handed down. Up until now, his threats seemed idle and impossible to carry out."

Riley's jaw flexed. "We found a picture in Gabby's apartment this morning. It was taken of her yesterday."

Adams had taken the picture with him when he left so it could be examined at the lab.

He perked. "Eyes Xed out?"

Riley shook his head. "No. We think someone was hiding in her apartment, though, just waiting for her to go to sleep so he could leave the photo."

I shivered as he said the words.

Dale shook his head. "Why wouldn't he X out her eyes? Why would he just leave the photo without abducting Gabby?"

I felt invisible at the moment.

"That's exactly what I was wondering." Riley glanced at me. "Don't get me wrong. I'm exceedingly glad that he didn't abduct you. But something doesn't seem to fit here."

Dale played a little drumbeat with his fingers against the side of the table. "There's one other possibility we're considering. It's the idea that Jones is working with someone."

"Why would you think that?" Riley rubbed his jaw.

"Serial killers often have little fan clubs. Someone was sending Jones those clippings while he was in jail. He's had correspondence with somewhere around thirty people since he was put behind bars. We're looking into all of those people, but it's going to take some time. There's a chance someone is helping him."

Shivers ran up my spine. Usually, I stuck my nose where I shouldn't and that's when the bad guys came after me. I'd never had a case where someone threatened me just *because*. It made me feel powerless.

And I hated feeling powerless.

"We made up some sketches of what Jones might look like if he's using a wig or glasses." He pulled out some papers and handed them to Riley. "We thought you might want to take a look at them."

I looked over his shoulder. I still couldn't believe that Milton Jones would be able to make it across the country. He'd have to be one of the most clever criminals I'd ever encountered, if he did. The logistics of how he would work that out would have to be so precise. He couldn't have missed a step.

Riley rifled through the photos. I soaked in Jones' square jawline, the sagging skin beneath his eyes. He looked almost normal in most of the photos.

Other photos showed him with a tan. With bushy eyebrows and without them. With different hairstyles and glasses and clothes.

Riley shuffled the pictures. He paused at one. The face that stared back at me caused me to gasp. My finger jutted out, pointing at the photo. I shook my head as fear clutched my heart.

"What is it?" Riley asked, his forehead wrinkling with concern.

I stared at the picture of the man with a beard and glasses. I still couldn't believe it. It couldn't be.

But it was . . . "He's the man who let me into the house I cleaned yesterday."

CHAPTER
EIGHT

TWO HOURS LATER, Dale, Detective Adams, and the forensic unit had all cleared out of our apartment building. Riley was still as uptight as ever. I had to admit: At this point, I couldn't blame him. I was feeling pretty uptight, too.

I could no longer deny that Milton Jones was here and that he was bent on revenge.

"How'd he get here?" I rubbed my temples. "How in the world did Milton Jones make it across the country in that amount of time?"

Riley shook his head, looking just as perplexed as I was, as he leaned back on the couch. "I have no idea. The police are checking surveillance at airports and bus stations across the country. Maybe some kind of clue will turn up."

"Could he have planned his escape?"

"Prison officials didn't tell anyone when the transfer would be taking place. That's what would make it nearly impossible for someone else to have been working with Jones when he got away. The other fact is that it would have been extremely difficult for him to plan anything while in prison.

His phone calls were monitored and recorded." He shook his head again. "I just don't get it."

"Me neither." And the more I thought about it, the more my head pounded. Finally, I stood, stretched, and rubbed my hands together. "As much as I wish I could sit around and think about this all day, I guess it's time for me to get to work."

Riley had been sitting at the table, his jaw flexing and unflexing. Suddenly, I had his attention. He raised his head, his eyes wide with surprise and possibly agitation. "Get to work? Are you crazy?"

I shrugged, trying to look more casual than I actually felt. "What else am I going to do? Sit around here all day?"

"That sounds like a great idea, actually." From the intensity of his stare, I could tell he was serious.

I sighed and shook my head, hating to be the bearer of bad news. "I can't do that." I didn't want to be the idiot who went out and made myself easy prey for a killer who was bent on making my life miserable. But I didn't want to put my life on hold and hide out like a scared little rabbit either.

Riley shook his head . . . and kept shaking his head as he sliced his hand through the air. "I'm going to cancel all of my appointments and go with you today."

"That's ridiculous. I'll be just fine. Besides, you need to go to that task force meeting." I had to admit—I really wanted to be involved also. But I knew there was no way I'd be getting an invitation. "Crime scene cleaner" didn't quite fit with FBI, local police, and other authorities. "That will be the best way to help. Help find him and put him away again."

He leaned forward. "I don't want you to be alone."

"Riley, I'll be okay." I squeezed his hand. "Milton Jones only struck at night, correct? I don't think he snatched anyone in broad daylight. I'll be fine."

Riley stared at me, an unreadable emotion in his eyes. "You've done some research."

"Of course." That couldn't be a surprise to him.

His head dipped, as if his thoughts were too heavy to hold. "Jones was at one of your crime scenes. He's got you in his sights."

His words didn't comfort me, but I tried not to let it show. "Jones didn't try to abduct me. He was obviously just sending a message. To stay inside all the time would be showing my fear. It would be letting him win. I won't do that."

Riley's gaze, almost tortured, met mine again. "Will you check in with me throughout the day? I don't want to be overbearing, but . . ."

"Of course. And we have a cookout at six, so I'll be back for that. But I'm already way behind. People are going to start leaving bad online reviews for Trauma Care if I don't get busy."

Riley nodded slowly. "I get it."

I disappeared into Riley's bathroom to get ready. Earlier, Adams had given me permission to get a few things from my apartment. I'd grabbed some clothes, toiletries, and cereal.

After I was dressed, I grabbed the box of cereal to take with me, told Riley goodbye, and started down the stairs.

When I stepped outside, I stopped in my tracks . . . again. Clarice leaned against my van, a fruit cup in hand and trendy oversized glasses already on. I glanced down at my box of sugary cereal and guilt flashed through me. My metabolism wouldn't keep up with my bad eating habits much longer, I feared. Despite that, I popped another Fruit Loop into my mouth.

I raised my hands in the air in confusion as I walked toward her. "You're here . . . again."

She nodded and, for a moment, I felt like Reese Witherspoon had stepped off the screen of *Legally Blonde* and into my life. She wore a bubble gum pink fitted cotton top, white linen pants, and ballet flats. Malibu Barbie's brunette cousin, anyone?

"Of course. This is my job that I'm going to make stick, remember? I know some creepy things have happened, but nothing will persuade me to give up. I'm going to refine my reputation and become someone who has stick-to-itiveness." She leaned closer, like she wanted to share a secret. "That's my new word of the week. Isn't it great?"

Now of all times she decides this? Why couldn't she have decided this during her *last* job? I stopped in front of her, keeping my eyes on her face for a telltale sign that this was all an act.

"Aren't you at all worried after the messages we found?"

She shrugged. "I'm with you today. You won't let anything happen to me."

Perhaps she didn't know about all of the times I'd almost been killed. Instead of reminding her, I nodded slowly. "The police are going to meet us there."

"I hope the officer is cute." She paused and nodded behind me. "I hope *he's* the officer."

I glanced back as Riley stepped out of the apartment building. He wore khakis, a striped shirt, and his blue tie flapped behind him. My heart still skipped a beat when I saw him.

"Actually, he's not an officer. Clarice, this is my fiancé Riley Thomas. Riley, Clarice."

They shook hands.

Clarice's lips parted. "He would work well on your reality TV show."

"Reality TV show?" Riley asked. A wrinkle formed between his eyebrows.

I fluttered my hand through the air. "Long story."

Clarice turned to me, a new light in her eyes. "I talked to my friend. He wants to do a pilot on you. Maybe put it online first and see what the response is before approaching the networks about it. It could launch his career."

I couldn't care less about launching someone's career at the moment. "This is a really bad time to talk about anything like that."

"You're right. Of course." She nodded, but I had a feeling she was unconvinced.

"Besides, most of reality TV is fabricated."

Her eyes widened. "Really?"

I resisted a sigh and cocked my head to the side instead. "You do realize how serious this situation is, don't you?"

"Totally. It's like *Castle*."

"Not really."

"*Law and Order*?"

"Not so much."

"*Monk*?"

I shook my head. "I've got nothing."

Riley waved goodbye, sent me one last look of concern, and then climbed into his car. I nodded toward my van. "Let's get going. Time is money, right?"

"Of course!"

"You were just humming that song from *Wicked*. I think it's called 'Something Bad.' I love that musical," Clarice announced.

"I was?" Note to self: Must stop humming inappropriate songs around Clarice.

"You know what other musical I loved?"

No, but I was sure she'd tell me.

"*Little Shop of Horrors*," Clarice said. "It's such an odd little story, isn't it? Suspense, humor and romance. What a combination. But it works, I think."

"Sure."

"I love the dentist song from that movie. It makes me laugh every time." She started singing and even threw in jazz hands.

Was there any aspect of pop culture this woman was not in touch with? I doubted it. It actually made me like Clarice a little more.

"Speaking of dentists . . . I have a date with one tonight!" Her voice sounded sing-songy and way too perky for this hour.

"A dentist? Where did you meet him?"

"He was in the coffeehouse yesterday. Absolutely dreamy. He's a little old—almost thirty. But I've always liked older men."

I was feeling ancient right about now.

I focused on the road, trying to keep my thoughts from veering to social security and wearing Depends.

Silence stretched for a few minutes. That alone was suspicious. Clarice never stopped talking.

I glanced over at her. She was nibbling on a cotton candy colored nail and staring out the window.

"Everything okay?" I asked, hoping I didn't regret it.

She shrugged. "Do you ever feel like people pigeonhole you to be someone you're not?"

I thought about it before nodding. "Sure. People think I'm tough, but I'm not always that way. I guess we all put on fronts and wear masks at times."

She stared out the window again. Wordlessly.

I couldn't believe I was doing this, but I kept talking. "Why do you ask?"

"I was with a friend last night who referred to me as an

airhead. I know people say that behind my back, but hearing him say it to my face really knocked me off balance."

Guilt—my automatic go-to emotion—pounded at me again. Now would *not* be a good time to admit that I'd thought the same thing about her. Instead, I said, "Ouch."

She nodded. "I know people think that about me. So, sometimes, I play it up. It's who people expect me to be, so why disappoint them? The thing is, the more I think of myself as an airhead, the more I feel like I become one. Isn't that strange?"

"As the mind goes, so goes the rest of the body," I muttered. "What brought this up?"

"I'm thinking about my date. I know I sounded excited—and I am—but this dentist guy . . . well, he talks down to me, you know? Then I realized I was letting him. Why? Because sometimes I think guys like an airhead, you know? They don't want someone who's independent and strong."

"Not all guys are like that."

She glanced over at me. "I guess your fiancé isn't, huh? My Auntie Sharon always says I shouldn't care so much about guys. She says I'm obsessed and I find my identity in them."

Sharon had a tendency to lean toward the more feminist side of that argument. "You have to be happy with yourself, Clarice. You can't find your identity in other people. You can't live to make other people happy. At the end of the day—and at the end of your life—no one else will be accountable for your actions or how you lived except for you."

"You're right."

"You're still young. You still have time to figure things out. But never discount yourself. If you don't believe in yourself, no one else will either. You have a lot to offer, and don't let anyone tell you anything different."

She smiled. "Thanks, Gabby. That makes sense. I need to start making some changes. I need to prove to people that I'm better than they think."

"Don't prove it to other people; just prove it to yourself."

My little pep talk resonated in my head. How did what I say play into my decision about my career? Was Sharon right? Would I be crazy to give up a job I longed for to be with the man of my dreams? Was I discounting my own career so Riley could have his career?

I didn't have much time to ponder it. I pulled up to our crime scene and saw an officer waiting there. It was the same rookie I'd met yesterday. I hadn't given him a key to the place yet, so I took the one the homeowner gave me and put it in his outstretched hand.

We waited inside the van—with the AC blasting—while he checked out things inside. Just as I was searching for something to talk about, my phone rang. Saved by the cell. "Gabby St. Claire," I answered.

"Gabby, this is Ramona from *America Live*." *America Live* was Bill's talk show.

"Hi, Ramona."

"You're going to want to turn on your radio right now. Bill told me to call you. Said it was urgent. I think you'll agree."

I mumbled thanks and then turned on my radio. What I heard on the airwaves made my blood pressure rise.

"So, you're saying you are Milton Jones, the deranged serial killer who escaped from prison?" Bill's voice was full of disbelief.

"That's right. I've got a message I'd like for you to share." The man claiming to be Jones had a scratchy voice. Yet there was an underlying confidence there that made nausea roil in my stomach. This was a man with a plan.

"What's that? You want everyone to listen to my show?"

Bill obviously wasn't taking this call too seriously. His voice lilted. Was he amused? Entertained? Maybe he just didn't believe this was Jones.

"I want you to tell your friends that I'm coming. I'm coming," Jones repeated, his voice low and raspy. "You know who you are."

On second thought, maybe giving in to my fears and hiding away at some remote location *was* a good idea.

Too bad it wasn't an option, though.

CHAPTER
NINE

FIVE, *Six*

Getting my kicks

As if the phone call from Milton Jones hadn't been bad enough, the officer had found a message for me inside the crime scene. The police had come . . . again.

We'd stayed around for the usual questioning, and then Clarice and I had made it to another crime scene. This one had no messages waiting for us. Maybe one a day was this killer's quota.

We'd finished that job, I'd dropped off Clarice, and I'd made it back just in time for the cookout.

Right now, as I stood on the lawn, I couldn't help but put all the rhymes together in my head.

One, Two

I'm coming for you

Three, Four

I'm hungry for more

Gabby St. Claire

Are you ready for gore?

Five, Six

Getting my kicks

How sick was this guy? What I didn't understand was why he was leaving these messages. He'd never done something like this before. What had changed? Had he nothing better to do in prison than plot ways to torture Riley? Or was this truly a different crime? What were the odds that two killers were taunting me?

"You okay?"

Riley's voice pulled me out of my thoughts. I snapped back to the present. "I'm as okay as possible, I suppose."

I soaked in the cookout. A ratty picnic table that had seen better days had been covered with a mauve and blue flowered tablecloth. Rose had even bought some balloons that she'd tied to the branch of a live oak, to the handle of the grill (uh, yeah, that one had to come off), and a parking meter.

"The police been able to trace that phone call yet?"

Riley shook his head and flipped another burger on the grill. "Nope. It was too short. They have some equipment hooked up to Bill's phone in case he calls again."

"Milton Jones will probably know that and not call back."

"The man could be brazen at times. He just might."

I turned from Riley and looked at everyone around me.

Bill was here, of course. He was in radio talk show heaven. Suddenly, reporters from all over the country were calling him and wanting the inside scoop. This would definitely boost his show's ratings and maybe even make people forget about that bad thing he'd said about a state senator.

Adding to Bill's delight was the fact that Rose was here, and she giggled at his every word. Bill was eating it up. His chest seemed more puffed up than usual.

Mrs. Mystery had joined us, all 75 pounds of her. She sat at the wooden picnic table with her laptop, tip-tapping away at her new book. This was her idea of being social—writing with other people around her.

I wished Sierra was here, and I couldn't wait for her honeymoon to end so we could talk. She was a great sounding board for me. Besides, I had some questions for her about her spur-of-the-moment wedding.

Then there was Riley and I. Riley had agreed to man the grill. Waves of heat poured from it, and the 90 plus degree weather didn't help the miserable state of being outside. It was summer at its finest. Mosquitoes were out early in their quest to be annoying and flies had decided to dive bomb the potato salad and baked beans on the table.

Meanwhile, the rookie cop was nearby. Apparently, Adams had assigned him to remain stationed either outside of my apartment or at the crime scenes I was cleaning. The order was twofold: both for my safety and for the possibility that Jones might appear, allowing the police to catch him. Thank goodness he wouldn't have the officer following me everywhere. A girl needed some privacy, especially when she was snooping.

I'd found out the officer's name was Bobby Newell, he'd been on the force for a year, and he had a very anxious girl-friend who worried about him doing police work. He had closely cropped hair, a shiny complexion, and a Roman nose. We'd offered him a burger. He'd accepted, but he'd sat in his car with the AC on to eat. Smart man.

As everyone got lost in his or her conversations (or their computers), I turned to Riley, realizing we might have a moment alone to talk. "So, how did the task force meeting go?" I'd been dying to know.

Riley flipped another burger. "I'm not sure I learned anything new, per se. We're on a deadline. We have a ticking time bomb, if you will."

"What do you mean?"

"Jones always gave his victims six days to live. That was more than enough time to . . ." Riley shook his head, as if realizing he didn't need to spell it out. "Anyway, Nichole was taken yesterday. We have to find her before he kills her."

"You sound pretty confident it was Jones."

"We're operating on the assumption that it was, that somehow he got to Virginia. The details of how he got here aren't as important at this point as finding Nichole is."

"How was she abducted?"

He closed the grill. Sweat sprinkled across his forehead and wet the back of his T-shirt. "In her bedroom. He somehow unlocked the door, snuck into the house, and grabbed her."

"No one heard anything?"

"Not a sound."

I lifted up a prayer for the woman and her family. What an awful man to encounter. What an awful situation to live through . . . or die because of.

I shuddered.

I remembered talking to Jones on the porch of that house.

I remembered his voice on the radio.

I remembered the articles that had detailed what he'd done to his victims.

I wasn't one to get easily creeped out, but I was feeling a little freaked right now.

"Anyone know how Jones managed to make it across country?" I still couldn't wrap my mind around it. "I mean, I know you said those details aren't as important as finding Nichole, but could he have really done that without help?"

"They're trying to follow his trail now. Apparently, and I know this sounds cliché, but he somehow jumped on a train. From what authorities can tell, he got off in Colorado and stole a car. He drove all night. Stole someone's wallet and cell phone in Missouri. He kept driving until he got here."

"As soon as he escaped, he came right for you." Another shudder trickled down my spine. "It sounds like ya got trouble in Norfolk City."

"A *Music Man* reference? Now?" His eyes sparkled with amusement.

I shrugged. "I know. But musicals always trump reality."

Riley took the burgers and dogs off the grill, placed them in an aluminum tray, and dinner began. We all settled down at the picnic table, trying our best not to get splinters, and piled our plates high with food.

Rose seemed to take her role as host very seriously. She told us about how she'd moved here from Florida and that she'd lived in this area as a child. She rambled on about her collection of spoons. Then she talked about building her own snorkel so she could dive into Lake Drummond as a child. Apparently, her family spent time boating there and she'd been bored out of her mind.

I knew about two of her ex-husbands, how she hated anything with celery in it, and how she once followed the Grateful Dead for a summer. She also told us that she flipped houses for a living. I was actually grateful that she was carrying the conversation, because I didn't feel like doing it. Thankfully, no one brought up Jones.

But as we were cleaning up, Bill pulled me aside and slipped me something.

A gun.

"What's this for?" I asked. I glanced around, making sure no one else was looking, before sliding it into my purse.

"I've got several. I thought you could use one."

I wasn't sure how I felt about guns. I'd never owned one

before. I'd never even shot one. Normally, I might argue and say I didn't need it.

But, with Milton Jones on the loose, maybe I did need it, I realized.

I nodded "thank you" and continued to clean up.

After the cookout, I stopped by The Grounds again to get one of Sharon's chocolate chip cookies. Riley grabbed a butterscotch scone and retreated to a corner table to do some paperwork, so I leaned against the counter to talk to Sharon.

"Clarice is staying with me tonight," she muttered. "Apparently, she and her mother had a disagreement."

"Aren't you lucky?"

Sharon shook her head. "I know way more about designer clothes than I ever wanted to know."

"She's not all that bad, you know. We all put on fronts sometimes, wear our little masks that we think should fit us."

Sharon paused and cocked an eyebrow. "That's a change of heart."

I shrugged. "She's just trying to figure life out. Most of us did at her age."

Sharon nodded toward Riley and lowered her voice. "What's the word on your job?"

This was not a subject I wanted to talk about. I had to tread carefully. "The interview is tomorrow."

"You're going to take the position if they offer it to you. Right?"

I pulled up my shoulders, which felt stiff and tight. "I don't know yet."

"I'm telling you—you'll regret it if you don't."

I leaned closer. "Why are you so sure about that?"

She shrugged this time. "Experience."

Now that she mentioned it, I really didn't know that much about her past. Mostly, I just knew her as the pink haired lady who owned The Grounds, gave me free lattes, and offered a listening ear when I needed it. "Someone really hurt you, huh?"

She frowned, and I knew I'd guessed correctly. "I was married once. I gave up everything to be with him. In fact, that's how I got to this area. I grew up in Seattle, but my ex got some IT job out here that was supposed to secure a financial future for us."

"What happened?"

"He started working all the time. Then his new job didn't pan out. He was unemployed for more than a year."

"What were you doing?"

"I started working as a secretary."

"A secretary?" I blurted. Of all the things I could see Sharon doing, being a secretary wasn't one of them. She was too unconventional.

"It's true. I had been working as a graphic artist. I tried to get my old job back so we could move to Seattle again, but the position had already been filled. My husband and I ended up getting divorced, I worked that lousy office job for five more years. Finally, I decided to open this place."

"How'd your sister get out here?"

"Her husband left her too, so she moved out here to be closer to me a few years back."

I looked around The Grounds. "At least you had your happy ending, right? You have this place."

She locked gazes with me. "I remember feeling small. I remember feeling like I was a second-class citizen in our relationship. No one should ever feel like that. That's why I feel so strongly that you should make the decision that's best for you, not the one that's best for your relationship. I still resent my ex to this day for making me come out here."

I bit back another sigh. I did not want to end up resenting Riley. Were Sharon's words true?

I hoped not. I really hoped not.

I checked all of my locks several times before finally going to bed. I made a mental checklist as I laid in bed.

Locks latched? Check.

Windows secure? Check.

House phone under pillow? Check.

Gun in nightstand? Check.

Officer stationed outside of apartment? Check.

I had no reason not to sleep. Every base was covered.

Right?

Now my body was demanding rest.

Back when I first started cleaning crime scenes, I would have worked all day and all night if I had to. But I still needed a vacation from my vacation the week before. This whole psycho-killer-on-the-loose thing was wearing me down emotionally. Then there were the messages at the crime scenes and a potential second crazy person out there.

So, against all odds, when my head hit the pillow, I was out.

Until I awoke with a start.

Something had been tugging at me from my tumultuous dreams. Some kind of feeling that something wasn't right. Some fear that started in my gut and rose to my brain with the force of a puck flying upward toward the bell after a strongman smashed into the lever.

My eyes jolted open. Sickly fear invaded my every pore. Sweat covered my forehead.

Someone was on top of me. His hand covered my mouth. His other hand restrained my arms, pinning me down. His body straddled me.

Slowly, surely, a face came into focus.

Milton Jones.

CHAPTER
TEN

I WANTED TO SCREAM. My mouth was muffled.

I wanted to run. But I was trapped.

I wanted to fight. My limbs felt frozen.

Jones leaned down until I could feel his breath on my cheek. An odd, earthy smell spread like a vapor into my nostrils. He said nothing for a minute.

All I could hear was his breathing. There were no other sounds. Not the AC blowing. Not rowdy college kids out walking the streets. Not annoying dogs barking at nothing.

Just Milton Jones.

Just my heart beating erratically.

I soaked in Jones' features. His hair was short, shaved close to his head. He didn't wear glasses this time or a weird trucker's hat. No, Milton Jones looked like any good neighbor you could imagine having.

That thought made him even scarier.

"Hello, Gabby," he finally said.

Something about his voice ignited something in me. I began thrashing. I jerked myself back and forth, trying to get away. It was useless. The man probably weighed twice as much as me, and I had no leverage.

The gun.

I strained to reach my nightstand, tried to figure out a way to grab my weapon. Tried to conjure a way to grasp my phone. To scream. To do something!

He pressed down so hard that my teeth ached from the pressure. His hand smelled dirty. It felt calloused. It made it hard for me to get my breath.

"You mean the world to Riley, don't you?" he whispered. His eyes were wide, crazed, too excited.

A sickly feeling trickled down my spine.

"He's going to pay, you know."

I stared up at him. The man looked truly evil. His eyes appeared absent of a soul. He delighted in fear. That made him a monster.

But there was more. There was vengeance in the depth of his gaze. That made him even worse than a monster.

"Give him a message for me. Getting even will never be as fun. Understand?"

I continued to stare.

"Understand?" He pressed on my mouth so hard I thought my teeth would break off.

Finally, I nodded. The intensity left his eyes, and he smiled. "Good girl." His finger traced my jaw line. "You're a pretty one. It's too bad you're going to have to die."

Fear rushed through me, causing my body to ache.

I had to think, and I had to think quickly. He could kill me. I was powerless. Immobilized. Those were two things I hated being reduced to.

Despite that, I waited for him to pull out a knife, a gun, and to carry out his threat.

Instead, he slipped off me and slithered out the door.

I laid there for a moment, my heart pounding, the air barely reaching my lungs.

Then I came to my senses.

I lunged from my bed, grabbed the gun from my nightstand, and my phone from under my pillow. I darted through the hallway just in time to see Milton Jones disappear from my Great Room window.

He wasn't going to get away that easily. Oh no. Not when my nightmares could end right here and now.

I shoved the gun into my waistband and dialed 911, never easing from the chase. I climbed out the window and onto my fire escape. Below, I saw Jones reach the ground with a thump.

I explained to the operator who I was and what had happened. Hopefully she'd alert the officer outside of my apartment.

Just then, I stepped on a piece of glass and yelped. I'd had no time to grab my shoes. I ignored the pain and continued down the stairs. They squeaked and groaned with each step.

I reached the last landing and jumped down to the grass. I winced when my foot hit the ground. I hobbled forward, desperate to keep moving.

Jones headed toward the street.

I snatched the gun from my waist. I stared at Jones. There was no way I could catch him, not with the way my foot was screaming with pain. Not with the roots and gumballs and pinecones that stretched between the serial killer and me.

I aimed the gun. I didn't have time to think about legalities and being arrested or if I knew what I was doing. I pointed the barrel of the gun toward Jones.

The metal shook in my hand. My finger ached on the trigger.

Pull it, Gabby. Just pull it!

My finger wouldn't budge, though.

Jones threw me a glance, almost taunting me, like he knew I couldn't take another life. Then he jumped into a white sedan, and the car squealed down the street.

Someone else had been driving. Jones *was* working with someone. My suspicions were confirmed.

But was that person just a driver or was this person involved with his murderous scheme as well?

Officer Newell rounded the building. I pointed to the sedan zooming down the road. "Jones. Getting away. Go!"

He nodded and took off.

Riley appeared the next second. He grasped my arms, his gaze intense. "Are you okay? What happened?"

I pointed in the distance, not caring about my aching foot at the moment. "That was Milton Jones."

He took the gun from my hands, his eyes wide and his lips parted. "When did you get a gun?"

My hands trembled as reality hit fast. Milton Jones had been in my apartment. Should I have pulled the trigger and ended this whole nightmare? If someone died at his hands, would their blood be on me?

"Gabby?"

I shook my head, trying to get a handle on the large, overwhelming emotions that fought to overtake me. I suddenly knew what Nichole had felt like when she'd awoken in the middle of the night.

She'd been terrified.

More terrified than any scary movie could ever prepare you for.

More terrified than you could imagine in your worst

nightmares.

More terrified than any person ever should be.

Riley pulled me into his arms. He stroked my hair. Rocked me back and forth.

He mumbled things I couldn't understand, but I was pretty sure they were something like, "It's going to be okay," "I'm so sorry," and "You have cheesy toes."

Okay, maybe not the cheesy toes one. I hoped not.

My heart still raced as the reality of what had almost just happened settled in.

Jones could have killed me if he'd wanted to. But that hadn't been his plan. No, he wanted to send a message. He wanted to send fear.

People like that wanted to have a certain amount of control in people's lives. Simply killing me would have been too easy; it wouldn't have been as much fun as making me constantly look over my shoulder, wondering when he'd strike. Wondering what he would do.

He wasn't going to win, though. I was going to prove myself stronger than any of his threats, if it was the last thing I did.

That's right. "Girl on Fire" would be my theme song. When I got tired of that tune, I'd turn up "Eye of the Tiger" and start practicing some boxing moves Rocky Balboa style.

Because I wasn't going down without a fight.

A team of investigators had shown up and were now meeting in Riley's apartment. The small space seemed to be becoming an unofficial headquarters for this investigation. It was a good thing Riley always kept it nice and tidy.

Still, my chest felt tight and my thoughts were heavy.

Milton Jones had gotten away. I'd desperately hoped that the officer had gotten a license plate number, at least. But he hadn't.

We were no closer now than we were two days ago. I should have pulled that trigger.

Detective Adams and L.A. Detective Dale Warren wanted me to review what had happened with them again. Riley stayed beside me, holding my hand, squeezing it every so often. My foot, now bandaged with no serious injuries, was propped on the coffee table.

Halfway through my recounting of what had happened, Parker showed up. Of course.

I'd known there was a great possibility that the feds would be called in. Out of the agents who worked at the local FBI field office, why did it always have to be Parker who showed up when I was in trouble?

"I'm a local liaison for the task force," he told me. "Why is it that every big case I get to work, you're somehow involved with it?"

"That's an excellent question. I promise that this time, I was minding my own business when trouble found me."

He nodded. "I see."

He totally wasn't convinced. I could see it in his eyes.

Parker and I had an interesting relationship, much of it built on the infamous love/hate emotions. We either got along swimmingly or like cats and dogs. He looked like Brad Pitt, so when we'd first met I'd been willing to overlook his arrogance. But relationships built solely on physical attraction never went anywhere.

Riley extended his hand and offered a cordial greeting to Parker. I wasn't sure if it was simply my imagination—maybe I was seeing what I wanted to see—but I always thought there was tension between the men.

Parker pulled out his wallet and showed me a picture of a newborn. "Her name is George. We're kind of fond of masculine names for women."

I gasped. "You had your baby?"

He grinned like a proud papa. "Charlie would slap me if I said 'we.' She had our baby. C-section. Two days ago."

"Shouldn't you be at home with her?"

"She insisted I keep working. I think I was driving her crazy."

I looked at the picture again, my heart twisting with some kind of longing I didn't even know was present. It was funny. I'd never thought of myself as someone who'd wanted children, at least not at this stage of life. But staring at that baby made my insides feel like jelly. "She's beautiful. Congratulations. Where'd you get the name?"

He shrugged. "We came up with it together."

"You know there's a woman named George in the old Nancy Drew books, right?"

A hint of a smile tugged at his lips. "I think I heard that somewhere before."

Okay, so that was a little weird. I'm sure it was just a coincidence that his nickname for me used to be Nancy Drew and he named his daughter after a character in one of the books in that series.

Parker and his girlfriend Charlie weren't married yet, at least not that I knew about. Parker had a bit of commitment phobia after a bad first marriage.

Having a kid without the commitment wasn't the way I'd want to do things, that was for sure. As someone who grew up in an unstable home, I wanted to give my children a secure and steady future.

Parker lowered himself onto Riley's couch. "Okay, back to the case at hand. Tell me exactly what happened."

I filled him in on everything. My voice trembled as I recalled the events of this evening. However, this was easily my third time repeating the story. Each time, it got a little easier.

"You sure it was Jones?" Parker asked when I finished.

I nodded. "Positive. This isn't my first run in with him, you know."

"What I don't understand is how he got inside," Riley mumbled. He looked at Officer Newell. "You were outside of the house all evening, correct?"

He raised his chin. "I haven't left once. I heard the commotion and hurried to see what happened. But no one came or went all night. I would have seen them."

"The chain on your door was cut," Detective Adams said. "Somehow he got into the apartment building."

I closed my eyes, trying to think this out. One theory rose above the rest of the possibilities hovering in my mind. When I opened my eyes, I nodded, confident in my deduction. "He was hiding in Sierra's apartment."

"Why would you think that?" Detective Adams asked.

"She's out of town. The rest of us are here. Jones knew there was a good chance someone would be stationed outside of the building, and he must have known Sierra was out of town."

"How would he have known that?" Parker asked.

"Am I supposed to come up with all of the answers here? He does his research. He knew who I was. He knew that Bill McCormick lived in the apartment downstairs. That's why he called into the radio show today."

"So, what you're saying is that Milton Jones knew he couldn't hide out in your apartment again. So he broke into your neighbor's place and waited there until it was nighttime. Then he crept up the stairs and broke into your apartment." Parker stared at me like I was crazy.

I nodded. "That's the only thing that makes sense."

Detective Adams nodded. "I think Gabby's on to something. How else would Jones have gotten inside? The window leading to the fire escape was unlocked from the inside. There were no signs of tampering."

"I checked it before I went to bed," I agreed.

"Our forensic team is checking out her place now," Adams said. "In the meantime, you need to be careful, Gabby."

Why did people keep saying that?

Out of all of the snide comments in the world, I couldn't even begin to think of a way to make their pleas for caution funny, though.

After everyone left, I crashed at Riley's apartment for a few hours. I tried to sleep on his couch, but rest wouldn't find me. I had too much on my mind and ended up just tossing back and forth in the small space. Riley didn't even try to go back to sleep. He'd been at his computer, doing something there. Worrying about me, most likely.

Finally, I pushed myself up and raked my hand through my hair. I would look better if I'd been run over by a truck. My head throbbed. Whenever I remembered the events from last night, a tremble shivered through me. My stomach still felt tight with unease.

Milton Jones was toying with me, and I didn't like being toyed with.

"Morning." Riley turned in his computer chair and scooted toward me. "How are you feeling?"

"About as well as you can imagine." I nodded behind

him. "What are you doing?"

"Just catching up on some work. Trying to keep my mind occupied."

His words reminded me of how much I had to do. I stood. "Speaking of work . . ." Aside from the whole Milton Jones fiasco, I still had crime scenes waiting to be cleaned, and I didn't plan on taking any breaks from my work today. I didn't have the luxury of paid days off, so if I wanted to make ends meet, I had to work.

"Clarice will be with you today, right?"

"My luck wouldn't have it any other way," I said drily.

"And the officer will be with you."

"I'll be fine, Riley."

Riley had somehow gotten his hands on a box of donuts. I spotted them on the kitchen counter. I picked my favorite—chocolate glazed—and took a bite. "I've got to get dressed."

"Can you go into your apartment? Has it been cleared?"

I nodded. "Adams said it was fine."

"Do you want me to go with you?"

The truth was that I did. But I wasn't going to tell him that. "I'll be all right. I'll check in with you later, okay?"

He nodded, looking like he wanted to argue. But he didn't. He knew I liked my independence.

When I walked out to my van at 8 a.m., I fully expected to see Clarice there, waiting for me with an energy drink in hand.

Instead, all I saw was my van and Officer Newell's police cruiser. He waved at me from the front seat.

I was tempted to hop into my van and go to the job by myself. But I could use a hand today. Too bad that hand would include a very chatty mouth as well.

I hurried across the street, dodging morning traffic, and stepped inside The Grounds. I'd get a latte while I was here.

Better yet, maybe I should try an energy drink. They seemed to work for Clarice.

I recognized several of the regular patrons that frequented the place lingering at their normal tables. Some read newspapers. Others worked on laptops. All sipped away on their drinks.

"What are you doing here?" Sharon looked up from behind the counter as she twirled some whipped cream on top of someone's drink. "And what's with all of the cars over at your apartment? It's like Grand Central Station."

"I'll tell you about it some other time, some time when it's not quite as busy in here." I didn't need any listening ears. There was already enough panic in the area. I reached the counter and leaned against it for a moment. "Anyway, where's Clarice?"

Sharon paused and gave me a look that clearly said, "Are you losing your mind?" "You texted Clarice last night and told her to meet you at the crime scene."

That familiar sense of dread filled me. "I did not text Clarice."

"I saw the text, Gabby. You clearly did."

Adrenaline surged in me. "What was the address, Sharon? I've got to find Clarice."

"You don't mean . . ." Sharon's face went pale.

"We don't have any time to waste."

She ran back to her office and emerged only seconds later. "Here's the address. I only know because I was trying to give her directions. She hates using her GPS."

I took the paper from her and hurried toward the door. My mind raced a million miles a minute.

"Find her, Gabby. Please."

I glanced over my shoulder. "Call the police, Sharon. Get someone else out there. Now."

CHAPTER
ELEVEN

I RAN across the parking lot and rapped at the passenger window of Officer Newell's car. He sat up so quickly that he nearly spilled his coffee. Before he could even respond, I jumped into the passenger seat. "Officer Newbie—I mean, Newell—we've got to go. Now."

"What's going on?"

"I'll fill you in on the way there. We've got to get to 1592 Sycamore." I clicked my seatbelt on.

He continued to stare at me.

I sighed. "Milton Jones. Please. It's urgent."

He only stared another second before finally nodding. He turned on his lights and sped down the road. Sweat sprinkled across his forehead as he radioed in the situation.

My heart raced with each rotation of the tires. Couldn't the officer go any faster? Someone's life was on the line.

Grief clutched my heart, causing a physical ache. Not Clarice.

Milton Jones had used me to get to her. He was a professional when it came to toying with people, and I didn't like that one bit.

We finally pulled up to a rundown house in a less-than-desirable neighborhood. Just as we pulled in, two other cop cars stopped behind us, as well as an unmarked sedan.

I flew from the cruiser and sprinted to the front door, but Detective Adams appeared and pushed me back. "Not so fast. Me first."

I stepped back onto the lawn and lifted up prayers for Clarice, just as I had been doing since I found out someone had texted her from my phone.

Had Milton Jones grabbed my cell to text Clarice while I was sleeping? What else had he done in my apartment? Did I want to know?

It didn't matter right now. What mattered was finding Clarice. I prayed that we'd gotten here in time. I prayed that we'd beaten Milton at his own game.

I nibbled on my fingernails in the front yard. I couldn't remember the last time I'd chewed on my fingernails, but the intensity of this case was getting the best of me.

Detective Adams emerged a few minutes later with something in his hands.

It was another picture of Clarice. This time, her eyes were Xed out.

I was in a trance-like state as I drove to my first job of the day without Clarice. Officer Newell had driven me back to my van. I'd sat there, with the AC blasting on me, for several minutes as I'd tried to figure out my next plan of action.

Without access to the right information, there was nothing else I could do to help find my temporary assistant. I had to take a breather and remind myself that I was not some kind of crime fighting super hero. The police, and the FBI, and many of the most qualified people in the country were tracking this killer.

The forensic unit had searched for fingerprints at the house where Clarice had been taken. They talked to neighbors, checked surveillance footage from nearby traffic light cameras, studied the ground for footprints. At my place, they'd swept the floors for any trace evidence. They were searching for the white sedan.

I had to let them do their job.

And I had to do mine. Which, right now, meant that I had to clean another crime scene. I felt like I was letting Sharon down by working at a time like this. But sometimes working helped me to sort out my thoughts, and currently I had a lot of thoughts to sort out.

Before Jones had woken me, he must have gotten his hands on my cell phone. I'd left it plugged in on my end table, since the battery was nearly dead and it wouldn't have done me any good without charge. He'd been watching me, so he knew Clarice was working with me. In fact, he'd seen her that day he pretended to be the homeowner.

I'd guess also that the picture he left on my desk the night before was no accident. I'd thought that Clarice just happened to be in the picture. It was apparent that she was purposely a part of that photo now.

I stopped in front of another crime scene. This one was at a townhouse in an area where grass between the narrow driveways reached upward and toys cluttered porches. Multiple cars were in many of the driveways, evidence of not enough parking spaces.

Officer Newell pulled in behind me. We met at the front door. As I handed him the keys, I realized I was getting used to this new routine.

I remained on the porch, my body protesting the physical

labor that I knew was coming. I was tired—physically, emotionally, and maybe even spiritually. I really needed to hire some more employees. I could not carry this caseload alone, and I didn't want my business destructing before my eyes. Even more, I didn't want my life destructing before my eyes.

I had some reservations about hiring more employees. I'd had some problems with my assistants in the past. One person had a fascination with blood, and I think he secretly wanted to be a vampire.

One person had stolen things from crime scenes.

Harold had been my favorite assistant ever, but he'd decided to retire. He deserved a little R & R in his life, so I didn't try to convince him otherwise.

That's why Chad and I worked so well together. We'd started off with separate, competing businesses, but then we'd decided to join forces.

I was definitely going to have to consider expanding, though.

I shifted my weight on the porch, getting impatient. What was taking Officer Newell so long?

The door opened behind me, and a grim faced Officer Newell stepped out. I braced myself for another round of bad news.

"What now?"

"Seven, Eight, This is your fate," he told me.

I closed my eyes and began praying . . . again.

CHAPTER
TWELVE

I LEFT the crime scene and did something I rarely did.

I stopped by to see Riley at work.

I walked into the little one story building located in downtown Norfolk, on the outskirts where rent was cheaper and the traffic wasn't quite as heavy.

Mary Lou was his receptionist and secretary. She was in her sixties, plump, and had a halo of gray hair. She liked to talk about the price of eggs, the absurdity of rising taxes, and her grandchildren.

I really liked Mary Lou a lot. But I didn't want to chat with her right now.

"I really need to see Riley. Is he in?" I knew he was. I'd seen his car outside. Actually, it was a man's car from church that Riley was borrowing until he could buy a new one. Riley's had been totaled in an accident on our way to the mountains last week.

"Of course, dear. Go right on in. He's never too busy to see you."

That was nice of her to say and, to a certain extent, it was true. Riley always took time for me when I needed him. But I wasn't the only one who needed to hire more employees. Riley was slammed as well.

He twirled in his chair, and my heart did a little *thumpity-thumpity-thumpity-thump* for a moment. I loved this man, even if his office was so neat that it made him seem OCD.

He stood when he saw me, his body at once tight and straight. "Something else happened."

Of course he knew something was wrong if I was stopping by.

"Milton Jones snatched Clarice." I closed the door behind me so Mary Lou wouldn't hear too many details. I loved the woman, but she had a tendency to start prayer chains when no one asked her to. Sweet, I supposed, but there were some things better left out of the church grapevine.

I plopped in a chair across from him. "I don't know what to do. I don't say this very often, but I have no idea where to start to help."

"You could let the police handle it."

"I know. But I'm involved in this Riley, whether I want to be or not."

He came around to the other side of his desk and leaned against it, letting out a slow sigh. "Yeah, so am I."

"So what do we do? I've been racking my brain, trying to figure out something. Anything. I just keep drawing a blank." I rubbed my forehead.

"Let's talk this out. Maybe something will trigger something."

I nodded, loving how levelheaded Riley was. "Okay, first question. Where was Milton keeping his victims before he dropped them off near the Scum River?"

"He'd rented a house out in the middle of the country. It was more of a shack, really. He boarded up all the windows and kept the women shackled there. When they yelled for help, there was no one around for miles to hear them."

"How close was this house to the Scum River?"

He shrugged. "There was really no correlation to the two. The Scum River was in town, a good forty minute drive."

I tapped my finger on the arm of the stiff leather chair. "Do you think there was any reason he chose the Scum River?"

His jaw locked in place for a moment. "I think he wanted to show that he thought these women were scum."

"Why, though?" I shook my head, trying to think this through. "Why those women? I mean, I know some people call him a psychopath, but did he have any logic in choosing his victims?"

"He said his older sister used to abuse him. She was in her early twenties. He was in his early teens. Some forensic psychologists said that's why he picked pretty young women because he was comparing them to his sister."

"Where is his sister?"

"She died of an apparent heart attack. People theorized that Jones killed her, but there was never any proof."

"He never admitted to any of the murders, did he?" I tried to remember what I'd read.

Riley shook his head. "No, none of them. But Gabby, you should have seen the look in his eyes during the trial. I've never seen someone with that look before. It was like looking into pure evil. The man was soulless."

I remembered the look too well. "This is what still confuses me. His calling card was the photos he left. Why leave the messages at other crime scenes? It just doesn't fit."

"Even killers can deviate from their plans, I suppose. He's had a lot of time to think."

"And why is he targeting me so much? I mean, I know he

wants to get to you. But he's aiming a lot of fury my way, and that doesn't make sense."

"I wish I had some answers. But I don't."

I released a slow breath and leaned back. "How was he finally caught?"

"It was a fluke. A delivery driver got lost. He went to the house. Knocked at the door and got suspicious that something was wrong. He followed his gut instinct and called the police. When they showed up, they found evidence that the Scum River Killer had been using the location. They staked the place out. When Jones brought his next victim there, they arrested him."

"Let's assume then, that he's taken Clarice and this other woman to a location that's off the beaten path, but not too far away. How do we find it?"

"That's the question of the hour. This time, finding it can't be a fluke. One more life lost at this man's hands is one life too many."

His words were true. I glanced at the clock behind him and gasped. "I'm supposed to have my interview with Kansas in an hour. Maybe I should cancel."

"You shouldn't do that, Gabby. In fact, maybe you should fly out to Kansas for an in-person interview."

"You just want to get me out of Norfolk."

He raised his hands. "I can't deny it. I'm worried to death about you."

"Do not worry about tomorrow for tomorrow will worry about itself," I reminded him.

He nodded solemnly. "I know. This case just may be a test of my faith, though, because I can't shake this feeling of dread."

I stood. It seemed irreverent to look out for myself by

doing this interview since Clarice had been taken. But there was nothing else I could do at the moment.

<hr/>

I stepped into my apartment and immediately felt the thick heat in the place. I walked over to one of the AC vents and put my hand over it. Sure enough, nothing was blowing out.

Great. Now of all times.

This wasn't exactly a good time in life to crack my windows open. Not with Milton Jones on the loose.

I didn't have any time to report this to Rose.

Instead, I quickly fixed my hair and put on a blouse and jacket. I kept my jeans and flip-flops on, knowing that the camera would never see them.

Then I sat at my desk, pulled up the video chat, and waited for the Medical Examiner to call in.

Promptly at 3, my computer dinged and I accepted the request.

An older lady with bobbed blonde hair and plastic-framed glasses appeared on the screen. Sue Smith.

I went through the interview without any problems— except the fact that my mind was elsewhere. Not only was it on Clarice, but I was also reflecting on what a huge change moving to Kansas would be for me.

Was it a change I was ready for? And no matter how much I'd convinced myself that Riley and I could make it work long-distance, in truth, I had no idea how it would work out.

Sue Smith's questions were mostly expected. Why did I want to do this job? What kind of experience did I have? Why should they choose me over other applicants?

She'd also done some research. She knew I was a crime

scene cleaner and asked me how I thought that would help me.

She'd been polite and kind and had even sounded amused by some of my answers and my thoughts on crime scene cleaning.

We said goodbye, and I turned off my computer. Sue Smith was supposed to get back with me by the beginning of next week. I was going to try and not worry about a decision until I knew if I *had* a decision to make.

I wiped the sweat from my forehead, realizing my glistening face probably didn't make the impression I'd hoped for.

Rose had told me to tell her if I needed anything. I think this officially qualified. Though I sometimes tried to fix things myself, there was no way my budget could handle a repair like this.

I could call her, but a walk sounded like the perfect way to sort my thoughts. I grabbed my keys and, just as I started down the stairs, Bill McCormick stuck his head out of his door. I think he was missing Sierra because she was usually the one he stopped and peppered with stories.

"I had a date with Rose last night." He grinned a grin larger than any I'd ever seen on him.

"How'd it go?"

He rubbed his hands together. "I think things are looking up for me. It was a great date. She actually laughed at my jokes and listened to all of my many opinions on politics."

"Sounds like a match made in heaven."

"Ever since Milton Jones called into the station to talk to me, my ratings have been through the roof. No way the station is going to drop me now." He seemed to realize what he'd said and his smile dropped.

Or maybe it was my scowl that had halted his train of thought.

"I mean, I hate to profit from your misery. But," he shrugged. "You know. The state of today's media is terrible. Blood hungry. Sensational."

I forced a stiff nod. "I'm glad things are looking up for you." And I was. In a weird way. "Speaking of Rose, I'm walking to her house now. My AC is out. Yours?"

He shook his head. "Nope. Like I said, things are looking up for me. Tell Rose I said hi."

Oh my. He was worse than a teenager with a crush.

I waved goodbye and walked a few houses down until I reached a little bungalow that needed some upkeep. I checked Rose's card to make sure I was at the right place. Sure enough, I was.

For someone who flipped houses, Rose really needed to put some time and attention to her own. The yellow paint was faded, the flowerbeds overrun, and several shingles were missing.

When I rapped at the door, it creaked open. Someone hadn't latched it.

I waited for several minutes to see if anyone would answer.

No one did.

I pushed the door open farther and called inside, "Hello? Anyone home?"

There was still no response.

I should close the door so no one could break into the home.

But then I began picturing Rose lying on the kitchen floor, the victim of a heart attack. Or almost choking to death. Or fallen with a head injury.

What if someone had broken in and tied her up? What if

they'd made a quick getaway and that's why the door was unlatched?

That's when I decided to step inside and just check things out. I needed to be a good neighbor after all, didn't I? People needed to look out for each other.

I stepped inside and called for Rose one more time. There was still no answer.

Somewhere in the distance, a clock ticked. Something beeped—an answering machine, maybe? Otherwise, it was silent.

I walked through the living room. It was messy and smelled musty. The decorations were minimal. A cheap futon for a couch. Plastic tables meant for patios served as her end tables. An old, boxy TV sat on an upside down clothes basket in the corner. A collection of spoons was displayed on one wall.

I'd seen better. I'd seen worse.

I'd seen a lot of things as a crime scene cleaner, so very little surprised me anymore.

I'd just check everything out, I told myself. Just take a glance around, make sure everything was okay. Then I'd be on my way.

I continued through the living room and popped my head into the kitchen. I surveyed the place. Dishes piled in the sink. Mail on the counter. The stench of old coffee grounds.

But no one was there.

That was good. Right?

Then I wondered about the bedroom. Rose could have fallen. A quick check wouldn't hurt anything.

I veered from my exit plan and walked down a short hallway. I stopped in front of the first door I came to. Using my index finger, I nudged it until the door swung out on its hinges.

A bedroom came into view. The décor consisted of a mattress on the floor with a blanket on top. Clothes were stacked in tubs against the wall. An anthill of shoes formed in the corner.

There was one other door on this hallway. I tiptoed to the end of the hallway. My heart pounded in my ears.

Maybe Rose was just irresponsible and hadn't latched her door. Maybe she'd left in a hurry. Maybe the door was hard to close and a gust of wind had pushed it open.

If Rose caught me in her house and she wasn't injured or nearly dead, then my presence here was going to look bad. I could probably even be kicked out of my apartment for this.

Despite my reasoning, I pushed the last door open. It creaked before slowly swinging out on its hinges. I blinked at the dark room that waited for me. All the shades were drawn and the dark wood paneling, circa 1960, didn't do anything to help matters.

My eyes slowly adjusted to the light.

A bulletin board in the distance came into focus. I stepped into the otherwise empty room. The carpet beneath my feet felt matted and old.

I moved toward the bulletin board. There were all kinds of papers and envelopes tacked to the corkboard.

I looked more closely.

A sick feeling began gurgling inside me.

It was an autographed picture of Milton Jones.

CHAPTER
THIRTEEN

MY BLOOD FROZE.

What in the world? An autographed picture of a serial killer? I couldn't wrap my mind around it.

My gaze scoured the rest of the items there. A hair sample. A dirty sock. A postcard-sized painting of the sunrise.

I glanced at the initials at the bottom of the artwork. MJ.

Milton Jones? He'd painted this? I'd bet anything that the hair and sock was his as well.

This wasn't good. It wasn't good at all.

In the corner, I saw an article that highlighted Riley's accomplishments as a prosecutor.

My instinct to run became even greater.

I had to get out of here. I turned around, ready to flee.

Before I could take the first step, I heard the front door open.

Rose was back.

Or someone else.

Someone worse.

Someone like Milton Jones.

My eyes darted around the room. There was only one

place to hide in the barren space. The closet.

I quickly tiptoed to the door, opened it, and crammed myself into the space. I hadn't pulled the door fully closed when I heard someone step into the room.

I pushed myself back into the dark recesses of the closet.

There must be some clothes in the small, musty space. Maybe some boxes. The smell of mothballs and dust filled my nostrils.

The floorboards groaned in the room. My gaze refused to leave the sliver between the door and its frame. It offered me a glimpse into the room.

Rose appeared.

I could hardly breathe. What would I do if I was caught in here? How would I explain it?

For that matter, who cared about *explaining* things? How was I going to get out of this one *alive*?

Was Rose a serial killer's sadistic helper? She would have had the key to my apartment. Maybe she'd seen that Luminol delivery come and guessed that I might use it at a crime scene. Maybe those messages had been her idea.

Rose stopped at the bulletin board and stared at all the memorabilia there for a moment. She said something under her breath and giggled. Then she began pacing.

I tried to make out what she was saying, but I had no luck. It was all jumbled and low. As she walked closer to the closet, I pressed myself back.

The floor let out a telltale squeal.

Rose stopped pacing and stared at the closet.

Oh, no.

I had to hide. Now.

I pulled something from a hanger in front of me. A coat? It wasn't big enough.

I grabbed behind me again.

That's when I saw a hand.

A limp, lifeless hand.

Before I realized what I was doing, I screamed.

"Who's there?" Rose asked. Her eyes were wide and her gaze fastened on the closet.

I couldn't hide in the small, enclosed space with a dead body any longer. Besides, Rose knew I was there. The scream had made that much apparent. Staying here would only delay the inevitable.

Now I had to fight for my life.

And get this corpse off me.

I darted from my hideout, practically falling in front of Rose onto the sticky carpet. I pulled myself to my feet and backed against the wall. Rose stared at me like I was the bad guy.

"Miss St. Claire. What are you doing here?" Her voice sounded calm. Eerily calm. "Why are you in my house? In this room?"

"Dead. Body." I pointed behind me.

"Dead body? What are you talking about?"

"The bigger question is why do you have a dead person in your closet?"

"In my closet?" She let out a small laugh. "That's just Earl."

Just Earl? She really was sick and twisted. "Who's Earl?"

"He's my CPR dummy." One of her eyebrows rose toward the ceiling.

I turned around. A lifeless arm reached from the closet. A lifeless . . . plastic arm?

Sure enough, that hadn't been a real hand. My mind had

been playing tricks on me. My adrenaline had gotten the best of me.

Not my proudest moment.

But still, that didn't mean that Rose wasn't a sicko killer.

I pointed at her. "You're helping Milton Jones."

Her face went pale. "You don't understand. You're jumping to conclusions."

"What other conclusion could I possibly jump to? You have Milton Jones' stuff hanging on your wall." I nodded toward the bulletin board.

"I can explain."

We began pacing around each other in a circle, each hugging the edge of the walls and sizing each other up like boxers in a ring, waiting to see who would make the first move.

"Explain then."

"First you tell me why you're hiding in my closet." *She* was questioning *me*?

I sighed. "Because my AC isn't working. Your front door wasn't latched. I thought you might have had a heart attack or something, so I came inside to check on you. I found this little shrine instead."

"Likely story," she muttered.

"Your turn."

She shrugged. "I'm a collector."

"What does that mean?"

"It means that I collect souvenirs from serial killers, especially Milton Jones." She circled more.

"Why would you do that?" Seriously. I couldn't comprehend this. I'd seen some crazy things. I'd heard some crazy stuff. But never this.

"I find killers fascinating. Okay? It's my dirty little secret."

"Because you're one of them. You're a killer."

She blanched. "Of course not. I'm no killer. This is no different than watching those shows on TV. People dress like killers from the movies—Jason from Friday the 13th or Freddy Krueger—and no one bats an eyelash."

"You're helping killers profit off of their crimes. How do you think the victims' families feel about that?"

"It's a harsh reality. I can agree to that."

"So why do you do it?"

"It's just a hobby. Besides, you clean crime scenes. Don't tell me you have no fascination with crime and murder yourself."

I wanted to deny it, but could I? I wasn't sure. Rose was messing with my mind.

"Did you take Clarice?" I wished I had my gun. A knife. A lifeline from Regis. Something!

She stopped circling for a moment. "Who's Clarice?"

"Have you been helping Milton Jones?" I wasn't buying her story. Not yet.

"There's no way he's in Virginia yet. That's a long trip across the country." She sounded sincere, like she really didn't know. Maybe she was just a good actress.

"That's what I thought, too. But I've seen him."

Her eyes widened. Not with horror. With infatuation. "Really?"

"I'm still not convinced that you're not guilty here, Rose. Acting like a schoolgirl with a crush isn't helping your case."

The sparkle left her eyes. "I'm only guilty of being obsessive. I'm no killer."

"That's what they all say. Let's call the police. Let them sort this out."

She raised her hands in the air. "Sure thing." She slipped her phone out of her pocket. "In fact, that sounds like a great idea."

CHAPTER
FOURTEEN

"WHY WERE you in her house again?" Detective Adams asked me.

I stood on the lawn in front of Rose's place. The sun beat down on me, and I tried to ignore the trickle of sweat that started on my back. "When I found the door unlatched, I thought something was wrong. I just wanted to check and make sure she was okay."

"And when she came inside, why did you hide in the closet instead of letting her know you were there?"

I sighed, fighting exasperation. "Because she had mementos of Milton Jones hanging in her room. That kind of freaked me out, to say the least."

"She's threatening to press charges."

I could hear the woman inside the house, loudly and clearly expressing her side of the story. I knew this didn't look great for me, but couldn't they see the bigger picture here? There were more pressing issues at hand!

I threw my hands in the air. Why fight my frustration? "You should be pressing charges against *her*. She's obviously working with Jones. I don't care what she says."

"We're looking into it, Gabby." He sounded so even-keeled that I wanted to scream.

Instead, I crossed my arms. "Are you arresting me?"

"No, we're not arresting you, Gabby. We do need to finish up with Rose here."

"So I'm free to go?"

He nodded. "But please, no more breaking into people's homes."

———

An hour later, I sat across from Riley at a Mediterranean restaurant that had hummus and baba ghanoush so tasty it would knock your hijab off.

Despite that, I barely tasted it right now. All I knew was that I was glad not to be in my apartment. I had to clear my head.

I dipped my pita bread into the hummus and shook my head. "I don't get it. Why can't the police arrest Rose? Isn't it obvious she's guilty?"

He shrugged. "There's nothing illegal about buying souvenirs from serial killers."

"That's just sick. There's a whole business out there for this kind of macabre stuff? It's morbid and wrong."

"Some people call it Murderabilia. And yes, there's not only a whole business out there for these things, but there's a *big* business out there."

I tore pieces off my pita bread, wishing it was just as easy to pick apart this case. "Isn't this illegal? It seems like I read somewhere that murderers couldn't profit from their crimes by getting book deals and stuff."

"That was actually overturned back in the 1990s and declared unconstitutional. There are a lot of people fighting against stuff like this, though. It should be a crime, if you ask me."

I turned the thoughts over in my head. I reviewed each scene from today, slow enough to be play-by-play motion. Aside from the whole murder thing, there was one other thing bothering me.

I dropped my bread and sighed. I was doing way too much sighing lately. "Rose said I'm no different from her."

"Because you're a crime scene cleaner? Of course you're different. You're searching for justice. People like Rose are glorifying murder."

I nibbled on my lips in thought. "Do you think she's helping Jones?"

He shook his head. "It's hard to say. My first instinct was yes, but now I don't know."

Rose had insisted that the only reason she'd bought this apartment complex from Mr. Sears was because she knew Riley lived here now. She wanted one more reason to feel closer to Milton Jones. She'd definitely done her research.

The question was: Did that make her a killer?

I wasn't sure. Riley wasn't sure. The police probably weren't even sure right now.

But my mind was racing.

I sat up straighter, trying desperately to sort out my thoughts. "We can both agree that someone is helping Milton Jones, correct?"

"It makes sense to me. He can't be in two places at once. That's for sure. Plus, someone was driving that getaway car that night he was in your apartment."

I shook my head, hoping that would miraculously knock some pieces of this puzzle into place. "Clarice had a date last night with a dentist. I want to talk to him."

Could it have been an innocent date that just happened at

the wrong time? Maybe. But since I had no other leads, this one would have to do at the moment.

Riley stood. "I'm going with you."

I didn't argue. We paid our bill, I took one last bite of my pita and hummus, and then we were out the door. We walked three blocks and then played a not-so-virtual game of *Frogger* as we dodged cars and ran across the busy street between the restaurant and The Grounds.

We stepped inside. The place sounded and smelled as soothing as ever. But I knew there was something different here tonight. Grief had seeped in, the emotion nearly strong enough to be a vapor that mingled between scents of lattes and cinnamon cookies. It felt fluid, like it had invaded the otherwise peaceful conversations on how to solve the world's problems and what movies people wanted to watch this weekend.

I looked toward the office just as Sharon stepped inside the dining area. Her eyes were red, her nose pink enough to match her hair, and her shoulders hunched. I'd never seen Sharon upset before.

I rounded the counter, ignoring the dirty look from the barista. I reached Sharon before she'd even dropped her keys and pulled my friend into a hug. I felt responsible for Clarice's disappearance, even though I had nothing to do with it. Someone—Milton Jones—had pulled me into this when he used my phone to draw Clarice out.

"Any updates?" I asked.

Sharon shook her head. "You've got to find her, Gabby. She drove me crazy, but I don't want anything bad to happen to her. Especially not at the hands of the Scum River Killer."

"I'm working on it, Sharon." I shifted, took a deep breath, and tilted my head in a manner that I hoped conveyed compassion. "Listen, Clarice had a date last night with a dentist. Do you know anything about him?"

Sharon nodded. "He just started coming in here over the past week or so. His name is Stephen . . . Alexander, I think."

"Do you know anything else about him?"

She shrugged. "He seemed likable enough, I guess. He's in his late twenties. Works in Norfolk. I don't know."

"Anything else that stands out about him?" Anything would help, but putting pressure on Sharon might only make her freeze up.

She rested her hand on the counter and turned toward me. Her gaze was steady as she said, "You know, now that you mention it, our conversation the first time we actually spoke about something other than coffee was about Milton Jones. Of course, ever since that girl was kidnapped, that's all anyone is talking about."

I looked at Riley. We had to find this Stephen Alexander. Now.

CHAPTER
FIFTEEN

IT WAS eight o'clock at night, so of course Stephen Alexander's office was closed. Using my cell phone, I did an online search for his home address, but nothing came up.

Which left Riley and me back at square one.

Not the place I wanted to be.

Not when I pictured Clarice at the hands of Milton Jones.

Maybe Clarice would talk so much that Jones would just let her go in order to keep his sanity.

Of course, psycho serial killers weren't all that sane in my experience.

By the time Riley and I got back to our apartment, I noticed a crowd of people had gathered over in the parking lot of The Grounds. They each held candles.

A vigil.

Someone had planned a vigil for Clarice.

Riley and I walked over, took a candle from one of the girls handing them out, and found a place at the back of the crowd. I wanted to watch everyone, see if anyone acted suspiciously. Mostly, there seemed to be young college kids. I spotted a couple of regulars from The Grounds.

A girl—a sorority sister, perhaps—stood at the front of the crowd humming *Amazing Grace*. Some people wept. Some hummed. Others sang.

A camera crew stepped out from inside The Grounds. A reporter pulled out her microphone to do an on-the-scene update with the vigil in the background.

"What are you thinking?" Riley whispered.

"Besides how utterly sad this is?" I shrugged. "I guess I'm thinking that I hate feeling so helpless. I'm the girl who tracks down clues, who follows the evidence. And I don't feel like there's a single thing I can do right now."

"Milton Jones is good at staying hidden. He eluded the best of the best for three years."

I shook my head. "He has to be working with someone. I know that. I just have to figure out whom. If I can find out that information, maybe I can find Jones."

"Excuse me? Are you Gabby St. Claire?" someone said behind me.

I looked up and saw the reporter in front of me, a cameraman right beside her. Riley pulled me closer to him. I appreciated the fact that he wanted to shield me, but I could handle myself right now.

"I am."

The reporter looked beyond me just as the light on the front of the camera popped on. They were seeking a good story like a lion sought after its prey. "And you're Riley Thomas, the prosecutor who put Milton Jones behind bars."

He nodded stiffly. "I am."

"What do you think about the disappearance of Clarice Wilkenson?" She thrust her microphone in front of Riley.

I glanced at Riley, that unspoken couple's code passing between us. Riley's jaw was locked in place, and I could tell he wasn't comfortable with this. I wasn't either, truth be told. But how could we use this moment to help Clarice?

I glanced beyond the camera and noticed that the crowd had stopped humming. They all stared our way, waiting to see what would play out next.

"I think that the city and the country's finest are all doing everything they can right now to locate Clarice and to put Milton Jones behind bars again," Riley said.

"Are the two of you involved in the hunt for this madman?" the reporter asked.

"I'd rather not comment on that." Riley shook his head.

The reporter turned her sights on me. "Gabby, you've helped the police solve some other crimes in this area before. Rumor has it that you have a personal connection with Clarice."

I pushed a stray curl behind my ear. "I do know Clarice, and I'm working with the police and other law enforcement officials to insure that she's found safely."

"Do you think this is the work of the infamous serial killer Milton Jones?"

If I answered affirmatively, the whole city would be in an even bigger frenzy. I couldn't be responsible for that. "I can't speak to that issue at this time as I'm not an official part of this investigation."

"Is it true that Milton Jones has threatened you personally?" the reporter asked.

How in the world had she heard that? I knew the police hadn't leaked the information, and only a handful of people knew about it.

I shook my head. "No comment."

Riley tugged at me. I knew what that meant. This interview needed to be over. Like, five minutes ago.

The reporter continued to call questions out, and Riley

continued to lead me across the parking lot back to our apartment building. What a nightmare. To the media, this was the story of the year. To the people who were involved, this was the worst-case scenario of their lives.

One thing was for certain. Fear had a reign on the people in this area. I didn't see its grip loosening any time soon.

CHAPTER
SIXTEEN

JUST AS WE reached the front steps, I heard a footfall behind me. I braced myself for the reporter, for more questions. Instead, I saw a lanky, college aged boy. "I need to talk to you."

I soaked him in. He had acne on his cheeks, gages in his ears, and a pierced eyebrow. He was sweaty. Breathing fast. Cracking his knuckles.

This was one nervous man. But why?

"Who are you?" Riley asked, going into protective mode again as he nudged himself in front of me.

"My name is Colin Belkin. I have information that I think will be helpful to you."

"Helpful to us? Not the police?" Riley asked.

He nodded. "Yeah, I need to tell you both this first. If you'll give me a chance, you'll understand why. I promise you'll want to hear this."

There was no way I was asking this boy into my apartment. For all I knew, he could be the accomplice we'd been looking for. No, if we were talking, we were staying right here. "Go ahead. You have five minutes," I said.

I crossed my arms. I was cautious, and I didn't know whom I could trust at the moment. The last thing I wanted was to give details to an information hungry vigilante.

"I'm a friend of Clarice's," he started, looking back at the crowds behind him.

I glanced back, too. The reporter had wandered back to the vigil and stood there, talking to the cameraman now. People had raised their candles again, and I could hear them softly humming.

"You said you knew something," Riley prompted Colin.

The boy nodded, shifting uncomfortably. He rubbed his palms on his skinny, aqua blue jeans. "I don't know how to say this."

"Just say it," I encouraged.

He cracked his knuckles so hard that I cringed. "I know it's not right. Well, now I know that. At the time, we thought we could convince you. That you'd see things our way."

I shook my head. "What are you talking about?" I was clueless right now. Truly. "Who is 'we'?" I prepared myself for him to say Milton Jones.

Before he could answer, Officer Newell stepped from the shadows. "Do you need help?"

I shook my head. "I'm fine. I'll signal if things get hairy."

The officer nodded, looked Colin over again, and then went back to his car.

I turned back to Colin.

His eyes shifted. "I think Clarice may have mentioned me to you. I want to break in with Hollywood, you know? Maybe do some directing and producing and creating. I'm not sure which one yet."

I nodded. I did remember Clarice mentioning something about a friend of hers and reality TV. I still wasn't making the connections yet, though. What was he getting at here?

"I was with Clarice when Sharon told us you were looking for some help. Sharon told us a little about what you do. The whole crime scene cleaning and all."

"Okay." I wished he'd get to the point. However, I had a feeling I wouldn't like his point. That's what my gut instinct told me.

He cracked his knuckles more. "We thought you'd make great reality TV."

My hands went to my hips. "Clarice mentioned that. I told her I wasn't interested."

He looked down for a minute. "Yeah, we figured you'd change your mind."

Okay, all this hemming and hawing was getting to me. "What are you getting at, Colin?" I finally asked.

He sucked in a deep breath that filled out his bony chest. "What I'm getting at is the fact that Clarice wore some special glasses that had a camera in them. She was recording you on your jobs in hopes that we could convince you to let us go live with it."

My lips parted in shock. "Are you insane? Have you lost your mind? That's a serious breach of so many things, both legally and ethically. I could get in so much trouble for that. So could you, for that matter."

Indignation rushed through me. If Riley hadn't nudged me back, I might have lunged at the boy.

Colin raised his hands as if to surrender. "I know, I know. We didn't put anything online yet."

Riley stepped forward. "Nor will you, if you know what's best."

"There's more." Colin swallowed so hard over and over again that his Adam's Apple looked like it was involved in a Ping-Pong match.

"Go on." Why delay the inevitable?

"We had this crazy idea. You know most of reality TV is contrived anyway, right? Everything from the personalities they choose to showcase to the plotlines they develop to the editing of the tape. Producers prompt contestants with leading questions. They set up scenarios to bring out the worst in people."

"What are you saying, Colin?" Riley's hands were on his hips, and he looked none too happy about this turn of events.

"Sharon was telling us about the first scene you were going to clean. She didn't give any names or anything, but she gave us some details about the crime. I looked it up online, and we found the address. We had a brilliant idea. We decided to set up the crime scene. We snuck in and put that message on the wall using some blood I bought at a butcher shop."

"What?" I wanted to throttle the man.

He held his hand up. "We had second thoughts. We washed it off. At least, we thought we did. We realized we could get in big trouble. Then you used the Luminol. The reaction blew us away." He made a little blow up sound and fanned his fingers out like an explosion near his forehead. "It was some incredible footage. Totally made for TV."

"How'd you know where my next crime scenes would be?" I needed to stick with the facts or my emotions might knock me over.

"Clarice took a picture of your list of crime scenes with her camera. I guess it was in the van, and you'd run inside a house or something. The next time, we left the message instead of erasing it."

I sighed, trying to find the right words.

Colin shook his head. "We had no idea it was going to turn into this. We were just making up a storyline. We wanted to be . . . famous. We were going to call it *Little Job of Horrors*."

That's where all of Clarice's references had come from.

"You're going to be famous for something you don't want to be famous for," Riley said, shaking his head. "Messing with a crime scene? Breaking and entering? That's just the start. You could go to jail for this."

The boy's face went pale. "It was stupid. I know that now. But we really thought this would be our big break. I mean, come on. You're hot," he looked at me. "You're dating a former prosecutor. In some circles, you're already like a little mini celebrity. We could have propelled you to the top."

"You weren't concerned about propelling me to the top. You just wanted to propel yourselves." I had to push down my anger before I did something I regretted.

He glanced down and shuffled his feet. "You're right."

Riley's jaw looked locked in place, a sure sign that he wasn't any happier than I was. "Is Clarice's disappearance a part of this charade?"

Colin shook his head with enough strength that his brain was probably dizzy. "Absolutely not. That's the reason I came forward. I want to find her. Anything I can do."

Riley continued to stare him down. "You know we have to tell the police, right?"

"I figured." Colin's voice cracked. "I'm going to be in big trouble, aren't I?"

"Maybe since you came forward with the information willingly they'll cut you some slack." Riley didn't sound convinced. His eyes were still narrowed, and his body language screamed, "Agitated."

An idea had begun to swirl in my mind. "Wait one minute first. Colin, do you still have the video from those crime scenes?"

He nodded. "Yeah, the feed was sent to a server. Why?"

"Before we go to the police, I want to see the footage."

Maybe, just maybe, there was a clue there that would help me to find Clarice. We'd watch it until the police got here.

CHAPTER
SEVENTEEN

SINCE WE WERE short on time and Riley had left his computer at work, we all gathered around my laptop in my apartment. My home-sweet-home now gave me chills every time I stepped foot inside it. Watching this video of myself right now did nothing to make me feel better.

I suppose we could have gone to Riley's, but I was trying to push through this whole fear thing. Still, I wasn't ready to sleep here alone any time soon, not with Milton Jones acting like he could come and go as he pleased.

What really interested me, way more than watching myself clean and spray Luminol and call the police, was the video that Clarice had obtained after the police got there. We were standing out on the lawn, waiting to hear what our next step was.

I watched all of the people in the background, looking for a sign of someone out of place. Of course, there were neighbors. Neighbors always showed up when emergency vehicles appeared. Out of care and concern or nosiness? You could never be certain. Most likely, it was a mix of both.

Police tape cordoned off the first house. An officer stood

guard at the front door. I stood in front of Clarice, looking slightly ticked off with my hands on my hips. At that point, I'd stripped out of my Hazmat suit. It had been too hot outside to keep it on.

There was Officer Newell standing in the background. I pointed to the screen. "Go back some."

Colin scrolled backward. I leaned closer to the screen. "It almost looks like he has his cell phone out taking pictures, doesn't it?"

"It looks like he's taking pictures of you," Riley mumbled. His hands were in fists.

"That would have been the day that someone took a picture of me and Clarice and left it in the house," I realized.

Officer Newell as the accomplice? I'd never even considered it. Not until now.

He could have leaked the information about Milton Jones sneaking into my apartment, though. In fact, he could have let Jones into the building, all while under the guise of guarding me.

Fury began to burn in me. I knew there were nasty people in this world. I just really hated it when people who were supposed to be the good guys turned out to be dirty.

I had to talk to Detective Adams. Maybe even Parker.

And I had to do it now.

But before I could reach my phone, someone knocked at my door.

I looked up just as the door swung open. Someone was letting himself or herself into my apartment.

My stomach sank when I saw Officer Newell standing there, a strange glint in his eyes.

CHAPTER EIGHTEEN

"EVERYTHING OKAY IN HERE?" Officer Newell asked.

I nodded, all of my muscles suddenly tight. Casual, I reminded myself. Look casual. "Just fine, Officer Newbie—I mean, Newell. Why? Something strange going on outside?"

He scowled at my mess up. "No, everything appears fine. I just wanted to make sure you guys were okay up here." He stepped closer, his eyes narrowed suspiciously. "What are you watching?"

I stood, making sure I concealed the computer screen. "Nothing. Nothing at all. Just some silly YouTube videos."

"That didn't look like a YouTube video." His hands went to his hips, and he engaged fully in cop mode.

Riley stood. "Look, you were assigned to watch us, not to butt into our business."

Officer Newell took a step back, his lips pulling down in a frown. We'd ticked him off. Offended him maybe.

I just hoped he didn't break into a murderous rampage. I had to call Adams. I decided to use one of Clarice's tactics. "If you'll excuse me a moment. I need to tinkle."

Officer Newell's lips pulled back in disgust. "TMI."

I didn't take time to look back. Riley could handle himself here. I slipped inside the bathroom and pulled out my phone. I quickly dialed Adams' number and explained everything to him.

Before I hung up, I heard voices rising from the next room. "Hurry!" I pleaded.

I walked back into the living room in time to see Officer Newell draw his gun on Riley and Colin.

"I have a feeling you're both impeding a police investigation," he said. His hand shook.

I stepped forward cautiously. "This isn't a good idea, Newell."

Newell swung his arms toward me. Sweat poured down his forehead. "You don't know what you're doing."

"You should put the gun down. Don't do anything rash."

The front door flew open. Tim, my brother, barged into the house. "I saw the lights on and thought—" he started.

His entrance gave Riley the opportunity to tackle Newell.

A gun fired. A struggle ensued. Limbs blended with limbs. I couldn't tell who was who, or what was what.

Tim just stood at the doorway with a blank look on his face, an open target for any stray bullets.

"Get down!" I yelled.

He ducked to the floor. Colin jumped into the action, trying to wrestle the gun from the cop. Finally, the weapon slipped from Newell's fingers and onto the floor.

Riley kicked Newell's gun away. It skittered across the ground, and I grabbed it. I aimed it at Newell. I didn't trust him to handle this situation anymore than I'd trust a housewife to properly clean a crime scene.

Now we just had to wait until Detective Adams arrived.

"This is so far out," Tim muttered, grabbing an orange

from the breakfast bar. "I have the coolest big sister ever."

He wouldn't be thinking that if he ended up in jail because of me, I told myself. But at least we'd all be alive.

I wondered if they served oranges in prison.

Detective Adams and Parker had both shown up. They'd taken the gun, Officer Newell had muttered that they should arrest us, we'd muttered that they should arrest him, and Adams and Parker both looked equally as confused.

"What just happened?" Parker asked. He wore his ticked off look. He had many looks. Most of them weren't friendly.

I pointed to the rookie. "Newell is helping Milton Jones."

Newell's mouth gaped. "Helping Milton Jones? Why in the world would you think that?"

"You took the pictures that Jones left in my house."

"You're out of your mind." His voice rose.

"We've got the proof of it right here." I pointed to the computer.

Colin pulled up the scene. Parker and Adams both looked at Newell.

"Care to explain yourself?" Parker asked.

Newell's face reddened. "It's not what it looks like."

"That's what they always say." I stared at him.

Newell shook his head. "I was just trying to remember everything from the crime scene. I keep flubbing up, and I knew I'd be questioned about what had happened. I wanted to keep a clear picture of everything in my mind. So I pretended to talk in my phone, but I was taking pictures."

I crossed my arms. "Likely story."

Newell raised his hands. "It's the truth. I swear. You all know I'm a rookie. I can't afford to make more mistakes."

"Then why did you pull a gun on the people you're supposed to be protecting?" Parker asked.

That's when Newell turned on us. "I could tell they were up to no good. They wouldn't tell me what they were doing. They were impeding a police investigation! I knew I had to take them in, but they weren't listening."

Adams scoffed. "This is a mess. Would you guys like to tell me what you were doing?"

I filled him in. He grunted. Shook his head. Gave me "the look" that a father might give a daughter who'd made an unwise decision.

The police escorted Colin out of the house. They'd take him down to the station to be questioned more fully. I hated to admit it, but I felt sorry for the kid. His brain cells hadn't quite developed enough for his own good. He really hadn't thought things through in his quest for fame, and now he was going to have to learn that lesson the hard way.

In the meantime, Adams and Parker had reviewed the tape and sent the link back to police headquarters where their video experts would examine it. Before that, I'd copied the video to my hard drive.

I didn't have very many clues to go on in this case, so I wanted to hold on to everything I could.

As the police wrapped up their time in my oven-like apartment, the Bible verse from Psalm 91 echoed through my mind.

Surely he will save you from the fowler's snare and from the deadly pestilence . . . You will not fear the terror of night, nor the arrow that flies by day, nor the pestilence that stalks in the darkness, nor the plague that destroys at midday. A thousand may fall at your side, ten thousand at your right hand, but it will not come near you.

Lord, please protect us now, I prayed. Please protect us now.

CHAPTER
NINETEEN

I GLANCED AT TIM, who ever since he'd gotten here hadn't left my kitchen. He'd eaten my grapes, my crackers, and half a loaf of bread. He was what was called a "freegan." He only believed in eating free foods, often leftover from restaurants or even in dumpsters.

Right now, apparently my kitchen also constituted "free." I didn't care. I thought he was weird, but he was my brother and he'd been out of my life for a long time. I was just happy to have him back now.

"That was seriously whacked," he mumbled, eating another cracker.

Crumbs launched toward me with each word, and I wiped my face. "Tell me about it."

"Do I want to know?" He stuffed another carbohydrate-delight into his mouth and stared at me. He had a long, grotesque beard that was capturing all kinds of food. He wore plastic framed glasses that were too big and kept sliding to the end of his nose. He was tall, lanky, and had hair escaping from every possible route beneath his clothing.

I shook my head. "Not really."

"Oh, that's good. For a minute, I thought you were going to tell me you were somehow involved with that Scum River Killer guy." He chuckled and another spray of crumbs filled the air.

I offered a feeble smile. "That would be crazy, huh?"

I wiped my forehead. It was hot in here. Why we were all still in my apartment was beyond me. It was like a sauna, and we'd probably all lost a couple of pounds from the heat.

I glanced at Riley. He sat on the couch with his head back and his eyes closed. I knew that look. He was processing all of this. I knew he wanted to talk, but that was hard to do with Tim here.

I was the one who'd been watching my brother when he was kidnapped many years ago, and I still carried a guilt complex. I couldn't exactly ask him to leave, even though there were uncountable pressing issues at hand. "What are you doing here anyway?"

"I thought I'd see if I could crash here tonight."

He'd been living with my dad. Apparently, free housing was also a plus when you were a freegan. Of course, when I'd been in the hospital a few months ago after being assaulted, Tim had stayed with me. How could I say no? "I guess if you want to suffer through no AC you can. Why?"

"Dad snores. Did you know that? I need some serious sleep."

"Fine then."

Riley opened his eyes. "Why don't you go crash at my apartment? The AC is fine there, and I have an extra bedroom."

"You'd let me do that?" Tim asked.

Riley nodded. "Of course. You'll be my brother-in-law one day. We're practically family already."

Riley really tried to accept people. I knew he did. But Tim

was a stretch for him. Someone who didn't work, who didn't buy anything, and who didn't even care was everything that Riley was not. Riley believed in hard work, making a way for yourself, and being responsible.

Tim thought he was being responsible and being a freegan was his way of saving the world. Life was so tricky sometimes.

Riley walked Tim across the hall to his apartment, got him settled in, and then came back.

"That was nice of you." I brushed a kiss on his lips.

"It's the least I can do."

Riley leaned closer, exhaustion written into the lines of his face. "I never asked you how your interview went today."

I shrugged. "It was okay. Good, I guess. I won't know anything until Monday."

"I'm sure you nailed it." He grabbed an orange—it was a couple of weeks old, so I hoped it was still good—and turned toward the counter to peel it.

I crossed my arms, trying not to be too "girly" and read too much into things. "You seem awfully anxious for me to get a job in another state."

"It's not like that. I'm torn between wanting what's best for you and wanting what's best for me." He still faced away, peel curling toward the kitchen sink.

"What's best for you?" My throat felt tight.

He turned around, a half peeled orange in his hands and tenderness in his eyes. "Having you right here."

"And for me?" My words came out just above a whisper.

"I just want you to be happy." He squeezed my arms.

"Maybe I can't be happy if my dream job takes me away from you. What would we do when we got married?" Why was I almost tearing up over this? Where was all of my "I am woman, hear me roar" bravado?

Maybe Riley was my kryptonite. He made me weak. He opened up places of vulnerability in my life. I supposed those were the chances you had to take in a relationship, though. Or was Sharon right? Was I willing to give up too much for Riley? If I stayed here for Riley, would I be setting the precedent that Riley's career was more important than mine?

"I guess I'd have to move out to Kansas." Based on the grim lines on his face, I'd guess he wasn't thrilled with the idea. But at least he was open to it . . . kind of.

I stepped closer and gripped the front of his shirt. A fresh, orange scent rose between us. "You would do that for me?"

"If that's what I had to do."

"But your law practice is here." I still wasn't convinced that he was onboard. Nothing sounded affirmative. It was all "I guess," "maybe," "I suppose." Still, what did I expect from him?

"It's not where you are, but it's who you're with, right?"

I tucked my head into the nook between Riley's head and shoulder. I wished I didn't have to make these choices. I still had some time. But, if the job in Kansas fell through, then what? Would I apply for positions with the medical examiner's office in other states? If not medical examiners, then I could apply to be a forensic investigator somewhere.

No job openings were here in this area. Believe me, I'd exhausted every possibility. Everyone wanted to hold on to whatever job they had.

So I had to make a choice between using my degree in a respectable career and moving, or continuing to be a crime scene cleaner, something that wasn't nearly as glamorous, and staying here. Crime scene cleaning was hard work, but rewarding. It paid the bills, and I set my own hours. But it wasn't what I'd dreamed about for my entire life.

He still held me. "What are you thinking about?"

I didn't want to talk about my job situation now. I'd probably talked that to death. I'd *thought* it to death, at least.

Instead, I turned my mind onto more pressing matters.

On Milton Jones.

The Scum River Killer.

On finding Clarice.

"I'm thinking I need to talk to that dentist first thing in the morning."

CHAPTER
TWENTY

"YOU DO REALIZE this is your fifth cup of coffee," Riley muttered the next morning. I sat at his dining room table, my elbows propped on top, and exhaustion tugging at every cell of my body.

I shrugged and waited for him to fill up my mug anyway. I needed the caffeine. He obliged, and I pulled my cup back across the table and took a glorious sip. "It's either this or an energy drink. I'm beat."

He sat across from me with his own cup. "You didn't sleep well?"

Riley had offered to let me stay in his room last night, while he'd camped out on the couch. Tim had stayed in the spare bedroom, but even with Tim in one room and Riley in the other, I still didn't get much sleep. I couldn't blame it on lack of AC or even my adrenaline, which still coursed through me after that confrontation with Newell.

Mostly it was because I was thinking about Clarice.

I remembered the pictures of the other women at the crime scenes. I remembered reading what they'd been through before they died. My heart ached when I thought of anyone going through that, but especially Clarice.

I rubbed my eyes before taking another sip of coffee. "I don't think I will sleep well until Clarice is found and Milton Jones is back behind bars."

Even though I was both mortified and furious that Colin and Clarice had recorded me without my permission, I still didn't want to see Clarice—even Colin, for that matter —suffer.

Riley pointed to my Allendale Acres mug. The luxurious resort had gifted us both with one after I'd helped solve a missing person's case there. "Why don't you take that mug to go?"

"What do you mean?"

He stood. "We're going to go talk to Stephen Alexander."

"You're going too?"

"I have just as much at stake in this as you do. I want Milton behind bars. He's made this personal."

"What about your work?" I knew he was behind.

"I'll call Mary Lou and ask her to reschedule. I don't have any court dates for the rest of the week, so I should be okay."

"Sounds like a plan." I wasn't going to argue. Having Riley along offered an additional layer of security.

Tim emerged from the back bedroom, bedhead fully engaged. Of course, he always looked like he had bedhead. He looked halfway homeless for that matter, and it wasn't because he practically was. He had the means to look clean. He chose to forfeit them. "Where you guys going?"

"We've got to talk to someone about a case we're working on," I told him, standing up.

"Cool. Can I tag along?" He stared at me, no hint of jesting in his gaze.

I paused. "Really? It's nothing exciting."

He shrugged. "Yeah, I don't have anything going on. I was hoping to pal around with you." He stared back and forth between Riley and me.

I wanted to say no. I wanted to explain to him why it would be a bad idea. I wanted to keep this simple and stay on track. Instead, I nodded. "Sure, if that's what you want to do, you can come."

"Let's go." He started toward the door.

I squinted in thought, trying to find the right words. "Don't you want to brush your teeth or something?"

He waved his hand in the air, looking like someone who didn't have a care in the world. "Nah, I'm good."

Riley and I did our secret glance thing.

"All righty then," Riley said.

I'd never heard him do an Ace Ventura impression before.

From the way Riley flipped his keys in the air, I could tell he wanted to argue. But he didn't, and I appreciated that fact.

Fifteen minutes later, we pulled up to an office building with a sign that read "Alexander Dentistry."

"You're at the dentist?" Tim asked, peering between the two front seats.

I nodded. "Told you it wasn't exciting."

"How about if I just wait in the car?" He grabbed his foot and started examining his yellow toenails.

I wanted to barf. Instead, I nodded. "Sounds like a plan." A much better plan than Tim coming inside with us. He was a bit of a wild card, and I never knew what to expect. That wasn't always a good thing when you were talking to potential killers.

Even once we were alone, Riley didn't say anything about Tim. I thought he might express his real opinion or question my decision, but he didn't.

Besides, we had bigger fish to fry at the moment. Tougher steaks to sizzle. Rottener vegetables to vet.

I paused outside at the front door. The cars in the parking lot were reflected in the glass panels comprising the front walls of the building. I slowly turned.

"What is it?" Riley asked.

I pointed to a white sedan in the distance. "Milton Jones sped away in a white sedan."

"You remember the make and model?"

I shook my head. "I wish I did. It was dark. I could barely make out anything." I closed my eyes, picturing the scene again, but no details emerged in my memories. Mostly what I remembered was the fear I'd felt at the moment. Pure fear, unlike any I'd felt before, and I'd been in some sticky situations.

"So, someone else was driving, right?"

I nodded. "That's right. Maybe it was Stephen Alexander."

We stepped inside. I'd dressed conservatively today, despite the heat outside. I'd worn my best gray slacks and a silky purple button up top. I looked respectable and neat.

Riley wore his normal khakis and a soft blue golf shirt that brought out the colors in his eyes. If only I had time to simply stare into his gaze.

A receptionist greeted us. She was middle-aged with short brown hair and a heavy-set build that seemed to come on all too often past fifty. She wasn't overly friendly, nor was she rude. In a word, she was professional.

She nudged a clipboard toward us. "Go ahead and sign in."

"We don't have an appointment," Riley said.

"How can I help you then?"

I let Riley take the lead. I knew this case was burning

inside him. It was rare that we both had so big a stake in an investigation. This time, his investment might be bigger than mine. "We need to speak with Dr. Alexander."

"He's got a full docket today I'm afraid. You'll need to make an appointment. Are you having a dental issue?"

Riley was polite and cultured; he wouldn't want to cause a scene. I, on the other hand, didn't mind. "It's actually about that woman who went missing. Clarice Wilkenson." I said it loud enough that several conversations in the waiting room quieted.

She stared at me for a moment before snapping back into professional mode. "I'm sorry. Maybe you should speak to him about personal issues somewhere more neutral. This is his place of employment."

I leaned closer but didn't lower my voice. "Time is of the essence. We know he went out on a date with her on the night before she disappeared."

The receptionist gasped and glanced behind us, probably soaking in the shocked faces of the patients waiting to be served. "I don't know about that. But I'm going to have to ask you to lower your voice."

I spotted a man in a lab coat, like a dentist would wear, in the room across the hall, just beyond the receptionist. I didn't hear the squeal of a drill or the *whirl whirl* of a fancy toothbrush. I hoped Dr. Alexander could hear me. That was the whole point of my obnoxiousness at the moment.

"With every second we waste, Clarice could die," I said. "This really can't wait."

The receptionist gasped again. Okay, maybe I shouldn't be going for the shock factor, but desperate times called for desperate measures.

Apparently, I had a lot of desperate times in my life because I used that saying *way* too much.

That last statement did the trick. The man in the lab coat popped his head out of the room in the distance. "I'll talk," he muttered, simultaneous to scowling at me. He popped off his disposable gloves and stepped into the hallway. "Come back to my office. And please, keep your voice down."

We walked into a standard looking office. I quickly took in his decorations. Plain brown desk with a calendar spread across the top. Degree from Ohio State University on the wall. A picture of Dr. Alexander with a woman who looked nothing like a sister—not with the way their arms were wrapped around each other—on the bookshelf.

No wonder he wanted me to keep my voice down.

"To what do I owe this visit?" He laced his fingers together and set them on the desk, almost as if trying to appear older and more experienced than he actually was.

"I think you already know the answer to that question," Riley told him. "Clarice Wilkenson."

Splotches of red appeared all over the man's fair-skinned face. "I don't know what you're—"

"Don't bother to deny it, Doctor," I interrupted. "We have multiple witnesses. Let's not waste any time here."

He sighed and leaned back. A sprinkling of sweat scattered over his forehead and his breaths seemed to come more quickly. "Yes, we did go out on a date."

"How'd it go?" I asked.

He did a half-shrug, half-nod. "It was okay."

"Why were you talking about Milton Jones at the coffeehouse?" I continued.

The red on his face deepened. "It's what everyone all around town is talking about. That's why. People are talking about the Tides' winning season, about the weather, and about Milton Jones. There's no guilt in that."

I nodded behind him. "Who's the girl?"

He tugged at his collar. "My girlfriend, Stacey."

"Does Stacey know about Clarice?" Riley asked.

Dr. Alexander shook his head. "No, of course not. Stacey is still in Ohio, finishing up her last year of college. We only see each other once a month or so, if that."

"Tired of the long distance thing?" I asked.

"It's not my choice. It's a little lonely around here. I met Clarice and thought she'd be good company. I'm still trying to figure some things out since I moved to this area." He narrowed his eyes. "Not that it's any of your business."

"You from Ohio originally?" I asked. This was *not* a sign that long distance relationships couldn't work. Nope. I wouldn't believe it.

He tugged at his collar. "No, I'm not. I'm from California. I figure as persistent as you are you'll find out that information eventually anyway, so I might as well be forthcoming."

Riley leaned forward. "Why'd you move here, of all places? Why not stay in Ohio or move back to California?"

"There are more opportunities to make more money." He shrugged. "That's it."

"No other reason?" I just didn't buy it. He seemed like the type who'd *love* to be in the scene around California.

He sighed. "My father is from this area. I haven't been around him since I was four. I had the crazy whim that it would be nice to connect. I thought this was my chance. Are you satisfied now?"

I stared at him. I could actually understand where he was coming from. My father and I had a rocky relationship and only in the past few months had it started getting better. "Has it worked? Have you connected?"

He watched out the window for a moment before slowly nodding. "We've been cordial. It's hard to bridge a gap like that. I grew up with a single mom who struggled to make ends meet. I only got to go to college because of my grades and scholarships."

"What area of California are you from?" Riley asked.

Those red blotches appeared again. "Outside of L.A."

"Where outside of L.A.? I lived there myself for a while," Riley said.

The dentist swallowed, his throat looking awfully tight. "Boyle Heights."

"Near the Scum River?" Riley asked.

Dr. Alexander stared at us. He didn't have to say anything. The bulging muscles at his neck said enough.

CHAPTER
TWENTY-ONE

"HE'S GOT guilt written all over him," I mumbled to Riley as we stepped outside.

"The question is: Guilt about what?" Riley agreed.

"It can't be a coincidence that he's from the same area of California where Milton Jones left his victims. Maybe one of his family members was a victim?"

Riley shook his head. "I would remember that. There were no Alexanders. He could have been a friend of one of the victims. But I definitely didn't recognize that guy."

I climbed into the sedan and looked back at my brother, who'd apparently decided to clip his toenails in the car. Gross. I'd have to apologize to Riley later.

I craned my neck back toward him. "I need your help, Tim."

"With what?" He flicked another nail clipping onto the floor.

I ignored his bad hygiene for a moment, trying to focus on more important matters. "I need you to go dumpster diving."

"Awesome. Where? When? That's one task I'm always up for."

I pointed behind the building. "That's the where. The when is up to you."

"What am I looking for?" He shoved his clippers back into his jeans.

I shook my head. "I don't know. Not for sure. But there's something that dentist isn't telling us and I'm trying to figure out what. Maybe a paper. A picture. Cell phone records. I won't know until I see it."

"The best time is after the office closes. Otherwise, people get a little upset, especially in office buildings, when they see you going through their stuff. Grocery stores and fast food restaurants? They're awesome. And they've got so much food. How much we waste as Americans is unbelievable. Meanwhile, there are people starving in other parts of the world. It's a shame. A crying shame."

I didn't have time for his diatribe right now. I loved it that he cared about saving the world. He tried to do it his way; I tried to do it mine.

Right now, my crusade seemed more pressing and obtainable.

"I say we head back to the apartment and do a little more research," I said. "I also want to check in with Parker and Adams and see if they've come up with anything new."

Riley nodded. "Let's go, then."

My cell phone rang as we drove back. I didn't recognize the number, but I answered anyway. "This is Ramona, Bill McCormick's assistant. Turn the radio on. Now."

I didn't ask any questions. I hit the dial and found the station.

Chills raced over me at what I heard.

"I have a message for Gabby St. Claire." The voice was clearly Milton Jones'. He sounded as evil and sinister as ever.

"What's that message you'd like to get across?" Bill asked.

"Tell her that everyone around her is in jeopardy."

"Can you be any more specific?"

"Her questions aren't doing her any favors. Another will be taken, and it will be her fault. May her guilt be more painful than any physical pain. And may her pain only cause Riley Thomas more agony that he can imagine. Agony like the agony he caused me."

"You felt agony at being caught and sent to prison?" Bill asked.

"No, I felt agony at being unable to kill again."

I grabbed Riley's hand and squeezed. Riley was right. This man was pure evil.

The only way to protect people from Jones was to find him and have him arrested, back behind bars where he belonged. I should have shot him when I had the chance.

"Mr. Jones, are you there? Are you there still? Hello?" Bill said over the airways. "I guess we lost him folks. All I can tell the good people of Norfolk is to lock your doors. Keep an eye on those you love. And buy guns. Lots of guns. Good day, and good luck."

Nice *War of the Worlds* reference, Bill, I thought with the shake of my head.

"What did that mean?" I asked Riley. "Everyone around me? Who could be next?"

"He's playing games with us, Gabby."

"It's working. I'm feeling creeped out."

"You should be creeped out. Everyone should be creeped out. This guy is no joke. Are you sure you don't want to consider that cabin in the mountains, somewhere far away from everything and everybody?"

I shook my head. "Tempting. It really is. But the only way I'm going to have any peace is by finding this guy and putting him where he belongs."

Riley shook his head. "I don't know how to keep you safe."

"It's not your job to keep me safe."

"If not my job, then whose is it?"

Tim stuck his head between the seats. "I'll do it."

I frowned. I had a better chance on my own.

Before we reached our apartment building, I saw the police cars down the street from our place. My chest tightened, an all too familiar feeling.

We pulled up to the scene. Before Riley even put on brakes, my door was open and I stepped out.

Rose's house.

The police were at Rose's house.

Were they making an arrest? Was she the accomplice, just as I'd originally thought? Maybe they'd taken her into custody, and she was giving up important information.

I ran right up against the crime scene tape around the house, just in time to see Adams step out. "Detective!"

He looked over, a disgruntled look on his face as he nodded me across the line. I ducked under and met him on the front steps.

I nodded toward the house behind me. "What's going on here? Did you arrest Rose? Find evidence to convict her?"

Adams shook his head grimly. "Rose has been taken."

"Taken? What do you mean?" Riley joined me, shielding his eyes from the blaring sun.

"I mean that Milton Jones grabbed her last night."

CHAPTER
TWENTY-TWO

MY THROAT BURNED when I swallowed. Rose? A victim? This was not how I saw everything playing out.

"What happened?" I asked.

"The newspaper delivery guy noticed the door was open this morning. Everyone's up in arms about Jones, so he decided to call 911. The police found this inside." Adams held up a photo.

It was of Rose, taken at the cookout she'd hosted for all of us. Her eyes had Xs over them.

My heart sank. Rose had been telling the truth. She was innocent this whole time. And now she'd fallen prey to Milton Jones.

Riley squinted against the sunlight. "What about Officer Newell? Did he confess to anything?"

Adams shook his head. "No, but he's on desk duty right now. He acted in an unprofessional manner. A rookie will make rookie mistakes. Those mistakes will have serious consequences, though. Some people have to learn the hard way."

"How about Colin Belkin?" I knew he was probably innocent, but I'd take whatever information I could get.

"He's facing some charges for crime scene disturbance, among other things. But he's not guilty of conspiring with a killer. Just of being young and having poor judgment." Adams paused. "I heard about the message Jones left for you over the radio. You need to be careful."

"Was anyone able to trace the call?"

He shook his head. "He wasn't on the line long enough."

"That's no surprise," I muttered.

I filled him in on my meeting with Dr. Stephen Alexander. He took some notes and promised to look into it.

In the meantime, I had a few things to look into myself.

"Riley, look at this." I pointed to the computer screen. I'd brought my laptop over to his apartment, and we were crashing here until we could figure out our next step. Tim had disappeared to take a nap. Cutting his toenails must have really worn him out.

Riley wiped his hands on a dishtowel, fresh from making some sandwiches, and peered over my shoulder. "What am I looking at?"

"This is the website that sells what they call 'murderabilia.' It has stuff up for auction from some of the most notorious serial killers in this country. They even sell chips off of the tombstones from killers who are deceased."

Riley leaned over me and stared at the computer screen. He studied the information there for a minute before shaking his head slowly. "It's a sad reality that our world has come to this."

"Did you see the amount that some of these items are

getting at auction? It's insane. Someone's making a lot of cash on this stuff. I don't think it's always the serial killer, either."

"It makes me think of the verse from Ephesians. 'For we do not wrestle against flesh and blood, but against the rulers, against the authorities, against the cosmic powers over this present darkness, against the spiritual forces of evil in the heavenly places.'"

"Sometimes it feels like the world is such a wretched place," I muttered. "Man seems capable of so much destruction. Human lives have value. How do people so easily forget that?"

"It's nothing new to this era. Think back to Roman times when there were gladiators. Throughout the ages, there have been human sacrifices, and wars with brutal outcomes and horrific battles. Think of Hitler."

"I don't wear rose colored glasses, but sometimes I wish I did. I wish I could be like one of those beauty contestants who says she wishes for world peace. I don't have any illusions about world peace, not this side of heaven."

"Thank goodness our hope isn't in the world."

I nodded, my thoughts heavy with reminders of the capacity man had for evil. I'd never been reminded of it as much as I had the past few days.

I pulled my thoughts back to the matters at hand and pointed at the bottom of the screen. "I found out that the guy who runs this site is named Freddy Myers."

"Real name or a play on the names of well-known horror figures? Freddy Krueger and Michael Myers?"

I shook my head. "Play on words, I'm assuming. But his company is called 'Deadly Profit.' I did another Internet search on the company, and guess what?"

"Don't keep me in suspense. I have no idea."

"It's located here in Norfolk, Virginia."

Riley sat down beside me with a thud. "No."

"Yes. What do you think?"

"I think it's worth checking out. Strangely enough, I may have a lead for you. That is, assuming that Freddy Myers isn't this guy's real name."

"How's that?"

"I called Dale and asked him if he could tell me if Jones corresponded with anyone from this area while he was in jail. He told me, only because I'm on the task force. There was one person. His name was Freddy Mansfield."

This could be our first real lead. Adrenaline surged through me.

"I think we know where we need to look next."

___

We left Tim sleeping in the apartment, loaded Freddy Mansfield's address in Riley's GPS, and took off down the road. Maybe this was the break we'd been looking for.

We pulled up to a house that looked like something from a horror movie. It was old with all kinds of interesting angles and nooks and a steep roofline. Two large turrets rose on the sides. It was painted gray, perhaps to maintain a gloomy appearance whether rain or shine. The crepe myrtle trees in the front yard may have added some warmth to the place, but they'd been severed near the trunk so that no leaves or flowers would bloom.

Despite the massive size of the place and evidence of how beautiful it had been at one time, it looked neglected now. Something about the place made me wonder if it purposely looked like this, though. Maybe this Freddy guy wanted his house to maintain a mysterious aura about it, almost like a haunted mansion still burdened by the death of its inhabitants.

Or maybe I was reading too much into this guy's career.

After all, maybe people said the same thing about me. Maybe they heard "crime scene cleaner" and immediately thought of some sicko who got her kicks by seeing the places where people died.

It wasn't like that, though. I wanted to help people. I wanted to speak for the dead. I wanted the bad guys to go through the legal system, to pay for their crimes.

This man . . . he exploited the dead. He opened the wounds of the families who'd already suffered too much. He rewarded the evil acts of man.

I guess Rose's words were still messing with my mind. I knew that I was different than these people, no matter what she said.

Riley turned to me. "Shall we?"

I nodded. "There's no time to waste."

We climbed from the car and met on the lawn. His fingers intertwined with mine as we walked toward the front door. Dry blades of grass and weeds rose like skeletons all around the driveway and sidewalk.

We rang the front bell. Even from the porch, I could hear strains from *The Twilight Zone* playing as the doorbell sounded. Freddy Mansfield was creative, I'd give him that.

I don't know who I expected to answer the door. Maybe someone as pale as a vampire, as skinny as a skeleton, as sickly-looking as a zombie.

Instead, Freddy Mansfield was probably in his mid-twenties. He had a head full of dark brown hair, a medium build, and wore neat jeans and a plaid shirt.

No weird jewelry. No blood dripping from his mouth. No creepy tattoos—that I could see, at least.

No, he appeared like the boy next door. "I'll never convert and become a Jehovah's Witness. Sorry." He started to shut the door.

"We're not Jehovah's Witnesses," I called, stopping the door.

"Mormon?" he asked.

I shook my head.

"Christians?"

I pressed my lips together, determined not to feel flabbergasted. "Yes, but I'm not here to talk about religion. Do you have a minute?"

"Who are you?" He paused, his eyes shifting back and forth from Riley to me.

"I'm a crime scene cleaner. Gabby St. Claire."

His eyes lit. "You're the one Milton Jones has been talking about on the radio."

"That's me."

His eyes went to Riley. "And you're the prosecutor who put him behind bars." He shook his head, and then pointed to my "Don't Worry, Be Happy" shirt. "That shirt you're wearing. I could probably auction it and get a couple hundred off it."

"What?" My mouth dropped open.

He turned to Riley. "Do you still have that pen you obsessively clicked during Milton Jones' trial? That might bring in close to a thousand. I'll split the profit with you fifty-fifty."

"Sorry. I can't help you. But you might be able to help us." Riley shook his head, a look of disgust on his face.

"What's this about?"

"A woman named Rose," I started. "She utilized your site quite a bit."

"I don't keep track of all of my customers, and I don't have to. There's no law saying I need to background check my customers or invade their privacy in any way for that matter." He sounded like he'd recited that one a million times before. "Besides, the police have already been here. I've told them all of this stuff."

I licked my lips, charging forward. "Where do you get your merchandise?"

He shrugged. "It varies. Here, there and everywhere. People come to me with items they want to auction. I look for things from various sources."

Riley crossed his arms. "How do you verify the objects are the real deal?"

Freddy shrugged, having the naïve confidence that only someone who hadn't experienced that much in life could have. "I ask lots of questions. They sign an affidavit. Speaking of which, I'm sure you could get lots of good stuff from the crime scenes. We could go into business together. In fact, you wouldn't have to work anymore. You could just hire employees to do your work for you. You'd have the money for it."

"Tempting, but no. I'm not going to capitalize on murder."

He locked gazes with me. "You are already, aren't you? You wouldn't be in business without crime either."

"We're on different sides of this, no matter how you try to paint it." I wasn't going to back down from that conviction. I couldn't let doubt creep into my psyche.

"Whatever, lady. Listen, I don't know anything about this Rose. Anyone is free to bid on whatever items they want, and there's nothing illegal about it. As much as no one in our society may want to admit it, there's a market for this type of item. Society has made serial killers superstars, like it or not."

His words echoed in my head. This whole case was starting to bother me on so many different levels.

CHAPTER
TWENTY-THREE

I LET my head fall back into the seat as we drove down the road. My temples were pounding now as my conversation with Freddy replayed in my mind.

I rubbed my hands over my face, wishing I could get the encounter out of my mind. "He's right, you know."

"About what?" Riley asked.

"We've made superstars out of killers. That's how messed up society is."

"There are a lot of things messed up in this world today. Not many people can argue that. Certainly not me. But it does seem atrocious that people worship men who've gotten their fame from murder."

Heaviness pressed on me again. "Do you think Freddy is helping Milton?"

Riley sighed. "Gut instinct? No. I think he's greedy and without a conscience. But I don't think he's a killer."

"I've got to find Nichole, Clarice, and Rose. That's all there is to it."

"What are you thinking our next move should be?"

"First, let me say how much I love the 'we' in that statement. It feels good to work together." Riley and I had hit a rough patch last week when it came to my snooping. I was glad to see we were on the same page now. "Second, how about if we stop by to see Mr. Sears. Maybe he knows something about Rose that we don't."

"Didn't she say he was in Florida?"

"He goes back and forth. Maybe he's home." Riley must have talked to Mr. Sears more than I had. Riley was like that. Friendly, warm, and compassionate. I loved that he could also be tough, discerning, and solid like a rock.

"It's better than my plan, which was nonexistent. Let's go."

A few minutes later we pulled to a stop in front of a two-story house that bordered a bad area of town. A chain link fence surrounded the place, and a dog from the neighbor's yard barked furiously at the fence.

"Based on the upkeep of this place, it looks like he could still be in Florida and that he forgot to ask anyone to help him in the meantime," Riley muttered.

Mr. Sears had always been a cheapskate. He tried to do everything on his own, and it was never done well, which resulted in multiple calls to get him to come back again and reevaluate his previous work.

I'd had such high hopes that Rose would be different.

But then she had to be all crazy about a serial killer, and then snatched up by the very man she admired. Horrifying and sad, but ironic all the same.

I knew what it felt like to fear Milton Jones. I could still remember the panic that had rushed through me when I'd awoken to find him in my room and on top of me. None of this was a laughing matter. Yet, without a touch of humor, I might lose my mind with fear. Humor was my coping mechanism, right or wrong. Good or bad. Smart or stupid.

We climbed the rickety porch, and I pounded at the door. No one answered.

Finally, I turned to Riley. "It was worth a shot."

We started back to his car when someone called to us. It was the barking dog's owner. "You looking for Mr. Sears?"

I stepped closer so I could hear better, which prompted the dog to bark louder. The sun hit a window in the distance, and I squinted against it. Finally, a middle-aged woman with rollers in her dark hair appeared. She stood on her porch, holding her cat like a newborn.

I nodded. "That's right. I guess he's out of town. Florida, maybe?"

"I seen him two days ago."

Maybe this conversation was worth fighting for after all. "Oh really?"

"That's right. He was as grumpy as ever. Listen, if you see him, tell him to take out his trash. It's causing the worst stink I've ever smelt to pollute my backyard."

"His trash?" I questioned.

"You have no idea. Step back there. You'll see. It smells like something died."

As soon as she said that, all of my instincts went on alert. Riley and I exchanged a look.

The dog's barks and snarls became more vicious as we got closer to the fence. The owner never called him off. She stood still on her porch, watching everything.

When I rounded the back corner of the house, I stopped.

I'd know that smell anywhere.

It was the smell of death.

CHAPTER
TWENTY-FOUR

SURE ENOUGH, Mr. Sears was dead inside his home. I hadn't been able to go inside. No, I'd been a good girl and called the police. They'd come and checked out his house.

If anyone could recognize the smell of death, it was a crime scene cleaner and former medical examiner. There were some scents that were just undeniable. Rotting flesh was one of them.

Thankfully, your sense of smell became immune after about five minutes around a scent. That was good at crime scenes, but not so good if you had B.O.

The most Detective Adams could give me on the case was that Mr. Sears had been murdered. He wouldn't give me a hint as to what the cause had been.

But the neighbor had said she'd seen him two days ago. He must have been killed that very day she'd seen him for his body to smell this bad already.

But that meant Mr. Sears had been killed *before* Rose had been abducted. I still wasn't sure how this all tied in, but I was confident it did somehow.

I also found it interesting that the neighbor told us a police officer had been looking for Mr. Sears either one or two days ago. The bad news was that she couldn't remember what he looked like, if he was young or old, or what he drove. She only remembered his badge. I had a feeling the woman was on some kind of drug that had deadened most of her brain cells.

Had Officer Newell stopped by? Why would he?

After we left the scene, Riley and I went to a little Mexican restaurant down the street, deciding that food might be a good way to revive our minds and spirits. A TV played in the corner. It was the five o'clock news, and all they were talking about was the Scum River Killer, whom they'd dubbed simply as "Scum." People all around us had stopped eating in order to listen. The restaurant staff even killed the overhead music for a moment.

The information the police gave to the media was simpler than what I knew. But the facts were that three women had been abducted, and the police had hardly any leads. Time was ticking away. Nichole only had two more days to live, if Jones stuck with his previous time schedule.

The station then launched into a recap of his terror spree in California.

I turned to Riley and shook my head. "I don't often say that I'm scared, but this guy scares me."

He reached across the table and squeezed my hand. "I know. But he'll mess up and the police will catch him."

"But how many women will be snatched before then? How many will die?"

Riley shook his head, and I could see the melancholy that washed over him. He didn't have the answer to that question. I didn't expect him to.

I'd been involved in some nasty cases before, but I was pretty sure this was the nastiest. Most of the people I'd tracked down had killed to cover up something or to hide the truth or out of fear they'd get in trouble for something else.

Milton Jones murdered for the fun of it. I wasn't sure how to come to terms with that.

"I need to change the subject for a minute," Riley started. "When are you and Teddi going dress shopping?"

Teddi was my dad's new girlfriend. She'd offered to help me pick out a wedding gown, and, for some reason, I'd agreed.

"Tomorrow, now that you mention it. I'm going to have to reschedule, though. I'm behind on my work. Clarice is missing. Rose is missing. There are other things more important."

"Just how behind are you on your jobs?"

"I'm *behind* behind. I just can't work with everything else going on. One lady said she was staying with relatives out of town for a while, so it wasn't a big deal. Another location is where the homeowner actually died. He lived alone. Relatives want to get the house cleaned up so they can put it on the market, but they're not in a big hurry. They're still planning the funeral for that matter."

"The good news is that Chad will be back . . . on Sunday, right?"

I nodded. "Last I heard."

As the waitress set our food in front of us, my stomach grumbled. I felt guilty even feeling hungry. Three beef and cheese enchiladas waited for me to devour them, along with some rice and refried beans.

Riley and I prayed for our food, for Nichole and Clarice and Rose and Mr. Sears' family. We prayed for sound minds for all of those involved in finding Milton Jones. I felt better after saying "amen."

I took my first bite and savored the spicy, warm food. What had Riley said before we prayed? That's right. He'd mentioned Chad and Sierra. I couldn't wait for them to get back, for more than one reason. First, I needed Chad's help. Second, Sierra was my best friend and I always bounced ideas off of her. Third, I had to get the inside scoop as to why they'd decided to elope while I was away on vacation last week.

I thought about my own wedding. We'd picked out a church in Norfolk. The place had stained glasses windows and white, wooden siding. Riley and I would get married in the evening and soft candlelight would create a warm atmosphere in the sanctuary.

I had so many other details I needed to attend to. I had to find a caterer. Pick out dresses. Send invitations. Choose my flowers.

Maybe eloping was a better idea. I knew I wanted to marry Riley, so why wait? Besides, I still hadn't figured out how we would afford the wedding. Money was already tight, and Riley and I wanted to pay for the wedding ourselves. Now he had to buy a new car. Sometimes my business was busy and lucrative. Other times, it dragged. That meant I saved money when times were good, so I could pay my bills when times were bad. Such was the life of the self-employed.

I couldn't even think about all of that right now.

"Let me talk this out for a minute," I started. "We know Milton Jones is behind this. He's the mastermind."

"Correct, although he has veered from his usual M.O."

"We know someone is helping him. Maybe that's why he's veered from his previous routine. Maybe his little apprentice isn't sticking with the plan completely."

"I can accept that."

He sounded so lawyerish when he said stuff like that. Ordinarily I might give him a hard time. Not today, though.

"Okay, so Rose was my first suspect. Now she's missing, so we can rule her out."

"Agreed."

"Then there was the rookie cop who took pictures at the crime scenes."

"He could have just had bad judgment as he claims," Riley pointed out.

"It's true. The police have their eye on him. He would have to be pretty brazen to continue to help Milton Jones, if he's our guy. Certainly he has to know he's under the microscope right now."

"I haven't completely ruled him out as a suspect."

"Then there's Freddy, who runs the online auction. Freak or killer's right-hand man?"

Riley shrugged. "That's debatable, I suppose."

"There's Colin, Clarice's friend who wants to find his big break into show business. He did come forward with his video. Again, I think he's a case of someone with bad judgment. I don't think he's a killer."

"From what I understand, he's been under police surveillance. There's no way he could have snatched Rose."

"Then there's Stephen Alexander. Last person, other than Sharon, to be seen with Clarice."

"Maybe we'll get some answers when we look through his trash tonight."

"A person's trash can say a lot about a person. That's what Tim would say." I'd scoffed at his Yogi Berra-like phrases, but he had a point.

We both leaned back, lost in thought.

Riley pointed to a sign hanging in the window beside us. "Zombie Fest?"

I nodded. "Clarice was really excited about that."

My heart sank when I remembered it. Even if the woman

had set me up and secretly recorded me, I didn't want her to suffer. I wished more than anything she could be here to enjoy Zombie Fest. I wished she was around to tell me how much she'd enjoyed it, even if it meant I'd want to throw something at her.

Riley and I finished eating, each of our thoughts obviously heavy. Any attempts at conversations about anything other than Milton Jones seemed to fall flat.

Finally, I looked at Riley. "You think the dentist office is closed yet?"

He glanced at his watch. "It's past six. I'd imagine they're either closed or will be closing any time."

"Let's go get Tim, then."

CHAPTER
TWENTY-FIVE

I STOOD outside the dumpster while Tim rummaged around inside the smelly metal container. Riley had to take a call from a client, so he paced in front of the building, promising to alert us if anyone came our way. The sun was beginning to set and sink lower into the sky as we began our mission.

Luckily, most of the shops in this area were professional, so they'd closed up rather early. That made our job easier.

It wasn't that I was opposed to jumping into a dumpster myself—I mean, I did clean up blood and other bodily fluids for a living. It was just that Tim was so good at digging through trash. And someone needed to go through the items that he tossed onto the ground. That seemed like a good job for me.

Even though this dumpster catered to an office building, the stench that crept from it was nauseating, like it had seen one too many rotting bags of food scraps. From what Tim had told me, some locals must take to dropping bags of dog doo into this dumpster after they took their evening walks as well.

Tim stood up. "I found something."

I hurried to the side of the dumpster and tried to peer in. I was a little too short to see inside.

He raised his hand in the air. "A free toothbrush. The wrapper is still on it and everything, so it's clean. Can you believe people would throw away a perfectly good toothbrush? I bet it was someone who got one of these for free after getting their teeth cleaned. They probably have some fancy one at home, so they just tossed this on their way out. Can you believe the nerve of some people?"

"A toothbrush, Tim? I thought you'd found something good." I wanted to scream at my brother sometimes. But then I remembered what it was like to have him gone from my life, and I was filled with gratitude, despite his quirks.

He shrugged. "This is good . . . to me, at least. I just stopped a perfectly useable product from entering the landfill."

"I need clues, Tim. Not clean teeth." Too bad he hadn't been all that concerned about using a toothbrush since he'd been staying at Riley's. We'd been the ones who had to endure his morning breath, and it hadn't been pretty.

"All right, all right. If I find any more, I'm donating them to the homeless shelter down the street, just for the record." He glanced down at the trash around him. "It would help if I knew what I was looking for."

What was he looking for? Even I didn't know for sure. I just knew that I'd know when I saw it. "Pictures. Cell phone records. Written admissions of guilt."

Tim popped his head up. "Really? You think it's that easy?"

"Of course not." I sighed. "I'm grasping at straws here, aren't I?"

Riley slid his cellphone back into his pocket and approached us, just to hear the last part of our conversation.

"Dr. Alexander was the last person, other than Sharon, who had contact with Clarice," Riley said. "He's worth looking into. He may not be guilty of anything other than being unfaithful to his girlfriend, though."

Was there anyone I was missing? Of course there was. For all I knew, I'd never even seen this accomplice.

We knew that someone had mailed Jones items to his jail cell. That's how he'd ended up with the article about me. It would seem logical that he had someone helping him.

But all that mattered was that we found either Milton Jones or someone else who could lead us to him.

Suddenly, a bag landed beside me.

"Look through that," Tim yelled.

I ignored some kind of greenish-yellow gel that covered the outside of the plastic bag. "Sure thing." I snapped on some gloves and pulled the plastic apart. Riley squatted beside me to help.

Inside, there were papers. Some were shredded. Others were flyers and junk mail. It looked like someone had cleaned out their desk.

I riffled through a lot of it but found nothing useful. Just as I finished that bag, Tim threw another bag out.

"Try this one, too," he yelled. "It's too hard to look through bags like that while I'm in the dumpster."

The truth was, he'd probably rather be looking for things he could either use or things he could sell to make a few extra bucks. My family was so interesting. A crime scene cleaner. A freegan. A washed up surfing champion turned alcoholic.

Did Riley really know what he was getting himself into when he married me?

I wasn't about to tell him. Not that I thought he'd change his mind. Sometimes, it was better to keep these thoughts quiet, though.

I dug through a lot of the same information that I'd found in the other bag, which wasn't very much.

I stopped when I saw one stray piece of paper. The words there made me pause.

You can use the family hunting cabin whenever you need it. State Road 172, Surry, Virginia. Love, Dad.

A hunting cabin? Could this be where Milton Jones was keeping his victims?

There was only one way to find out.

───────────

"Should we call Adams?" I asked as we bumped down the road.

Riley shook his head, his neck looking tight and stiff. "We're just following a hunch. I say we call him if we discover anything. This could be nothing."

"Or it could be everything."

Riley nodded, his hands tight on the steering wheel and his knuckles white. "If Milton Jones is there . . ."

I reached into my purse. "I have this." I pulled out my gun.

Riley's eyes widened. "Put that down before another driver sees you and calls the police! You're carrying it with you? You don't have a permit."

"There are some things that are bigger than a permit. Like my life."

Riley shook his head. "I agree, but . . ."

I held up my free hand. "Don't worry. I'll be careful." I put the gun back in my purse. Truth was, I felt a little weird about carrying it.

But then I remembered those crime scene photos and I

thought about what Milton Jones had done to his victims, and I forgot any of my hesitations.

The stench in the car after Tim had been in the dumpster was nearly unbearable. Even though the heat was stifling outside, I still cracked my window. Tim, in the meantime, was sleeping in the backseat.

Apparently, he *and* my father snored.

The drive to Surry County would take at least an hour. The sky was now gray, and by the time we arrived at the cabin, it would be dark.

I knew that going out there alone had all the warning signs of being a bad idea. But I also knew that sending the police out there based on a scrap of paper would be foolish. They had better things to do right now. Still, a shudder raced up my spine.

The car made a weird sound and thumped a couple of times as we sped down the interstate. It was an old Ford Taurus, probably nice in its day. But right now the blue car was on the verge of not passing inspection.

Someone at church had been thinking about selling it, and when they found out Riley was carless after the accident last week, they volunteered to let him use it. The paint was faded. The plastic covering the steering wheel peeled. The seats were stained—being a crime scene cleaner, my mind went to the worst places concerning *what* exactly those stains had come from. No, I'd seen too much to simply think "spilled soda."

And those were just the physical aesthetics that were unappealing.

The car also made a strange noise when you turned left, the engine sometimes groaned, and the windshield wipers mysteriously turned on and off without anyone ever touching a button.

Right now, as we rattled down the road, I wished we'd stopped back by my apartment to get my van. I wasn't sure this vehicle would make it.

We traveled off of the interstate, on some smaller highways, through a couple of small towns, and finally headed down a rural road surrounded by trees. Outside, the light became dimmer and dimmer. Darkness was close.

The thought chilled me as I realized its double meaning. We truly could be approaching one of the darkest people and crimes I'd ever been involved in. The thought was unsettling.

I lifted up a quick prayer that God would keep us safe.

Though I walk through the valley of the shadow of death, I will fear no evil.

The Scripture ran through my mind. I repeated it over and over.

For the Lord my God is with me.

He could do much more than any gun could. He'd proven that time and time again in my life. And I felt like the most undeserving person ever when it came to God's protection. I was thankful He didn't give me what I deserved, but that He showered His love on me.

I looked at the GPS on my phone. "Turn right here."

We veered off one narrow road and onto another. The trees closed in closer to the car. The sun sank deeper into the horizon.

Out here, there was mostly woods, so it was the perfect place for a hunting cabin.

"This is like the area where he kept the girls in California," Riley said quietly. His jaw looked locked in place and his neck muscles tight. This case had obviously affected him in a big way.

"What do you mean?"

"It was in the middle of nowhere, well off the beaten path.

Woods had surrounded it. If one of the girls had been able to break free, there was only a slim chance that she would have survived running through the woods to get help. There was too much space between the cabin and the rest of the world."

I could sense this was hard for him to talk about. "Did you go to the cabin?"

"Once. I wanted to get a feel for what had happened there."

"What was it like?"

He shook his head. "It was horrible. What happened between those walls, although it was over and done with, still seemed to fill the air in the room, if you know what I mean."

I nodded. It wasn't like Riley to talk about things in the abstract. He liked relying on facts.

That being said, the realization that he was talking about something other than the facts spoke volumes.

"I don't believe that places can be haunted," he continued. "But I definitely felt like something malevolent had happened there."

His words left a sick feeling in my gut. We should have definitely called Detective Adams. Maybe this whole case was beyond my scope.

I pointed to another road. "We have two more turns before we get there. This one is next."

"I'm going to cut my headlights. Just in case this is the right place, I don't want to alert anyone that we're here. Do you still have a phone signal out here?"

I checked my screen. "I sure do."

"Good. We have to be careful."

We rolled down the gravel road labeled "Private." With each inch closer, my muscles tightened. Whenever we did find Milton Jones, I feared we were going to need the protection of an angel army, as the song we sang at church said.

I remembered what Riley had said. *When I looked into his eyes, it was like looking into pure evil. The man was soulless.*

"I see some lights over there." I pointed through the trees, down toward the end of the lane.

Sure enough, the faintest trickle of light could be seen through the trees. Riley pulled to the side of the road and cut the engine. "We should walk from here," Riley said.

I couldn't agree more.

"Do you want me to look through his trash can for you? You can tell a lot by—" Tim appeared in the backseat, like Lazarus raised from the dead. How long had he been awake?

"—what a person throws away," I finished. I shook my head. "No rummaging through garbage now, but I will give you my phone. Come with us, but stay back on the outskirts of the property. If anything happens, you have to call the police. If this is Milton Jones, he won't suspect that you're here with us."

"There are advantages to being a third wheel."

I sent him a small smile. "You're always welcome, Tim. Always."

I actually got a grin back from him. "Thanks, big sis. That means a lot."

Our relationship was slowly developing. I'd take slowly developing to nothing, though.

I tucked the gun into the waistband of my jeans and stepped out of the car. Riley and Tim joined me.

Darkness was on us at full force. Out here in the country, the darkness was different than in the city. It was blacker, heavier.

The woods were alive with crickets and owls and other creatures that made leaves crackle and branches shake.

I was thankful that Riley reached for my hand. "You're trembling," he whispered.

I was hoping he wouldn't notice.

I didn't say anything. What was there to say? Yes, I'm terrified. This man gives me nightmares.

I couldn't think like that. I had to keep focused on finding Clarice and Rose.

We reached the edge of the woods. A log cabin stood in the distance, a white car parked beside it. A white sedan.

Stephen Alexander's sedan.

Possibly the one I'd seen Milton Jones pull away in.

My heart pounded against my rib cage. This was it. The moment of truth.

Part of me desperately wanted this to be Milton Jones' lair. I wanted to find Nichole and Clarice and Rose and save them.

The other part of me wanted to be safe.

Of course, I rarely choose the safe courses in my life.

"What now?" Tim asked.

I pulled out my phone and slapped it in his hand. "Here you go. You could be our lifeline here." I still had some doubts about my brother's level of responsibility. Certainly he wouldn't let us down in a life or death circumstance, though . . . would he?

Just then, a scream cut through the silence.

A woman's scream.

Coming from the cabin.

CHAPTER
TWENTY-SIX

"DO you want me to call now?" Tim held up the phone.

"Yes, find Detective Adam's number in my phone book and tell him where we are," I told him.

"You should wait here with Tim," Riley told me.

I pulled my gun out. "Not on your life." I really hoped I didn't have to use this thing. But if I had to, I would.

Riley and I stayed low as we hurried toward the cabin. All the windows were lit, and I could see movement inside. Adrenaline honed my senses, making me feel alert and sharp.

We reached the wall of the cabin. Riley ducked low so he was on one side of the window, and I was on the other. He motioned to me before slowly creeping upward and peering into the house.

"Stephen Alexander is here. That's definite," he whispered.

I slid up the wall so I could get a better look. I spotted a woman cowering in the corner of the room.

I blinked. It wasn't Nichole or Clarice or Rose, however. This wasn't even the girlfriend I'd seen in the pictures at the office.

No, this was a woman with long, blonde hair. She was young, and she looked terrified.

"What did I tell you about this, Angela?" Stephen Alexander screamed from inside. "You're only making this worse for yourself."

"Please, I just want to go home," she whimpered.

Riley nodded toward the front door. I ducked low again and made my way there. We couldn't wait for Adams to arrive. This woman might be dead before that happened.

"You women are all alike," Stephen mumbled.

The woman screamed again.

Riley and I crept onto the porch. His steps were steady but soft as he went to the front door. Slowly, he reached for the knob and turned.

It was unlocked.

I raised my gun, ignoring my fear as I pictured Nichole, Clarice and Rose in the recesses of this place, hurting and in desperate need of help.

On the count of three, Riley threw open the door. We both rushed inside.

"What in the—" Stephen Alexander turned toward us, fire blazing in his eyes. "What are you doing here?"

"Let the girl go," Riley mumbled.

Stephen pointed to the woman in the corner, an incredulous look on his face. "Her? It's not a crime to cheat on your girlfriend."

I aimed my gun at him. "Don't make him repeat himself."

He held up his hands, as if pleading with me. "I think you're misunderstanding."

The woman screamed again. "There it is. Get it. Get it!"

What?

"The police are on their way," I explained.

The woman, Angela I assumed, looked at me with startled eyes from the corner of the room. "The police?"

"We know you're helping the Scum River Killer," I told Stephen.

"The Scum River Killer?" He started to lower his hands when I nudged my gun his way again. He raised his arms higher. "I have no idea what you're talking about."

"I knew it was a bad idea to come here. You're helping the Scum River Killer? You pig," Angela muttered.

I shook my head. "You came here willingly?"

"Yeah, some romantic getaway, huh? There are mice here, and animal heads on the wall, and a carving of a nude woman in the dining room. Not my idea of romantic."

I blinked, trying to process all of this. "You were screaming. We heard you."

"I saw a mouse. I'm terrified of mice."

"What?" Riley's voice held disbelief.

"Maybe we should all just calm down," Stephen said. "I can explain all of this. I'm a jerk. I can agree with that. But I'm not a killer, and I'm not helping a killer."

"So, you'd be okay with Riley checking the rest of the house?" I asked.

"Be my guest, but you won't find anything," Stephen said.

I kept my gun raised to him. Angela had moved from the corner, and she now stood behind Stephen, hunkering there.

"Why don't you put the gun down?" he asked.

"Not until I know for sure that you're innocent." I shook my head.

"Of course I'm innocent." His voice rose with emotion.

"You were the last person to be seen with Clarice. That makes you a suspect. How many times do I have to remind you of that?"

"How'd you know I was here?"

"I have my ways." Like a dumpster diving brother and an insatiable curiosity.

"You dated that woman who was abducted by the Scum River Killer?" Angela took a step back from him.

"It was a coincidence."

"You were one of the last people to be seen with her. But she just disappeared . . . a few days ago, if that. That means . . ." Angela slapped him. "You are scum."

"Now, Angela, it's not what it looks like."

"Let me get this straight. He never threatened you," I clarified.

"No, he didn't threaten me. But he did turn on his charm and make me feel like I was the only woman for him."

Yeah, what he'd done was no crime, but it should be illegal. He'd led a woman on, made her believe she was the only one, and soon enough he would have probably dumped her.

Riley came back into the room. "It's clear. There's no one else here."

I lowered the gun.

Stephen's face reddened. "Now let me call the police. You're guilty of breaking and entering, pulling a gun on me—I'm sure there's a charge for that, too."

"I saw your girlfriend's modeling photo," I started. I hated to play my hand like this. But I had no choice. Not if I wanted to preserve this investigation.

"What about it?" He stared at me, sweat trickling down his forehead.

"I have her email address and phone number. I'd hate for her to get an anonymous call informing her of your indiscretions."

His eyes narrowed. "You wouldn't do that."

"Oh, I would. Stacey Bennett. 614-555-3789." I'd seen a stack of her modeling pictures in the trash. Not very nice of him to throw away pictures of his girlfriend. I imagined she'd given them to her oh-so-faithful boyfriend in hopes one of his patients might be a talent agent or advertising manager.

Stephen's mouth gaped open. "Fine. I won't report this. But I don't want to ever see you again."

"As long as your name isn't associated with a crime scene, I think I can handle that."

As we trudged back to the car, I found myself humming the song from *Little Shop of Horrors*. Yes, being a dentist and inflicting pain on people just might be the perfect career for Dr. Alexander.

But that didn't necessarily make him a killer.

CHAPTER
TWENTY-SEVEN

WITH MY AC still out and Rose not available to fix it, I decided to camp out at Riley's again that evening. Though Riley was totally into "avoiding the appearance of sin," there were times when safety trumped people's judgments.

Riley and I had set a lot of boundaries. Truth be told, neither of us had always abided by the standards we had now, and, in some ways, that made the boundaries we had harder to stick with, but even more necessary.

At least with Tim staying with us, that would clear up some of the misconceptions people might have. Besides, everyone else in the apartment building thought there was nothing wrong with us just moving in with each other. To save on rent, if nothing else, they'd argued.

But when I'd become a Christian, I'd changed. I had new standards, and I had to turn my back on the way I used to do things. I was like someone who used to smoke. I couldn't even allow myself one puff or I knew I'd be back to where I started.

I paused at the second floor landing and stared at my door. I'd been in my apartment since Jones had broken in. It was just that, it had been daylight then. In the dark, the place seemed more ominous. "I just need to grab a few things."

"I'll go with you," Riley said.

"You don't have—" I started to argue.

"I'm going with you."

As I unlocked my front door, I realized I'd never called a locksmith about getting a new chain to go across my door since Milton Jones had cut through my old one.

Images of his invasion into my home flashed into my mind. I closed my eyes, trying not to let the thoughts explode into hyper-charged fear. I had to take rein of these emotions before they carried me away.

The inside of my apartment was hot and muggy. I would have cracked a window, but circumstances being what they were, I'd decided that was a bad idea. Even the nighttime air hadn't cooled down the inside of this place. In fact, I think my apartment had trapped the heat, and now every room felt like the inside of an oven.

"I'll be back." I started toward my room. I twisted the knob and pushed my door open. What I saw there made my heart skip a beat.

Blood. There was blood all over my walls.

And pictures of me with my eyes Xed out.

The whole crew was in my apartment again. And, by the whole crew, I meant Detective Adams, Special Agent Parker, and L.A. Detective Warren. A forensic team was there collecting all the evidence they could.

In a twist of luck—if you wanted to call it that—Tim had accidentally called my old science partner Drew Adams instead of Detective Adams. On one hand, the police hadn't come out to the cabin, nor had my reputation been tarnished after a false lead. On the other hand, my brother was so unreliable.

At my apartment, I had to physically stop myself from following behind the CSI crew and discussing any possible clues and my theories behind them. Let them do their jobs, I told myself. But part of me missed being in on the official action.

Another part of me resented Milton Jones for making the apartment of a crime scene cleaner a crime scene. That had happened once before when a man had died here, and I still had nightmares about it.

"It sounds like you've been busy," Detective Adams said. "You are being careful, aren't you? You should leave the detective work to this task force. We've got every available cop in Norfolk, as well as every neighboring city, working this case.

"I'm involved here, Detective, whether I want to be or not." I trembled again as I thought about my bedroom. Why had Jones turned so much rage on me? This seemed to go beyond just making Riley pay for putting him behind bars. But why?

"Maybe you should get out of town for a while." Parker joined our conversation. "This guy obviously has you in his sights. Maybe you should make this a little harder for the killer and a little safer for yourself."

"I tried to talk her into that," Riley said.

Great, I had all the bossy men in my life surrounding me now, and they were all in agreement. I was like a contestant on *American Idol*, standing before the judges' panel, and listening as they all tried to decide my fate.

And for tonight's selection, I'll be singing "Safe and Sound" by Taylor Swift . . .

I shook my head, coming back down to reality. "There's nowhere I can go where he won't find me."

"Maybe we could help you out" Parker said. "The FBI has some resources at hand. I'm sure I could pull a few strings."

I shook my head. "I can't do it. What if this guy isn't caught for months? How long was his rampage before? Three years? I can't stay in hiding for three years. For more than one reason, starting with the fact that I have bills to pay."

"Maybe you guys should move up the wedding date and take an early honeymoon," Adams offered, raising his eyebrows. "In Europe."

"I'd be okay with that." Riley nodded. "We could take in the Eiffel Tower and Big Ben. Or maybe explore some castles in Scotland. Take a siesta in Spain."

"It's not a bad idea, Gabby," Parker agreed. "There's nothing like some good old haggis to distract a person from their problems."

Really? When had all three of these men ever agreed? But now that it came to my wedding they were on the same wavelength?

"My wedding day is supposed to be special, not influenced by the likes of Milton Jones." I crossed my arms.

"Do a big wedding later," Parker suggested.

"Says the man who's not married."

He shrugged. "Marriage isn't for me. You know that."

I shook my head and sliced my hands through the air. "Milton Jones will not have any control over my life."

"If he takes your life, I'd call that the ultimate control." Detective Adams said the words so quietly that I almost wondered if I'd imagined them.

I didn't imagine the familiar way my blood seemed to freeze, though. I could deny it all I wanted, but the truth was that Milton Jones was getting in my head. He was playing with me, playing with my emotions and fears.

I was letting him win.

That's what he wanted to do. Just murdering someone? What fun was that for a psychotic serial killer? No, he wanted control of his victims. He wanted me to live in terror until D-Day—the moment when he actually tried to grab me.

Tried being the key word here.

I wasn't going to let my guard down.

"We've got a new officer assigned to keep watch over this place," Adams started. "You'll have someone stationed outside of your apartment at all times."

I nodded, wishing his words comforted me.

"What about Officer Newell?" I asked. I mean, who could you really trust?

"He's on desk duty for now, but he appears to be all clear. We searched his phone records and his emails. He gave us full access. We found no hints that he was associated with Milton Jones."

"I think he may have stopped by Mr. Sears' house this week. That's what the neighbor hinted."

"I'll see what he says."

"Do you have any other leads?" I asked.

"You know we can't tell you that. But we're on top of this. We have someone on this 24-7. I've only gotten probably two hours of sleep in the past three days, if that tells you how seriously we're taking this." Adams stared at me.

"What about Mr. Sears? How did he die? Can you at least tell me that?"

"You know I can't tell you that either." Adams ran a finger across his throat as he said the words.

I got the message.

Mr. Sears' throat had been slit. But I didn't hear that from Adams.

That didn't fit Milton Jones' M.O., but I couldn't buy that the man's death just coincidentally happened in the middle of all of this.

Nope, I sure didn't. My gut had told me those messages at the crime scenes didn't fit and I'd been correct. But how did all of this tie in?

"Can you give me something else? Anything?" I asked.

Adams leaned closer. "You didn't hear this from me. Got it?"

I nodded.

"That Freddy Mansfield guy you told me about? He has a prior record."

"For what?"

"Breaking and entering. Funny thing, at all the places he struck, he never left any clues as to how he got inside."

"Just like Milton Jones?"

Adams nodded. "Just like Milton Jones."

I awoke with a start.

Panic raced through me. Where was I?

Then everything came back to me. I must have fallen asleep at Riley's.

I rubbed my cheek, still feeling the impression from Riley's shirt.

The TV screen was blue in the distance. Riley and I had sat down to watch a movie, ready to do something to take our minds off the madness at hand. He'd let me pick. I'd almost gone with *Little Shop of Horrors*, but instead I chose *The Sound of Music*. I needed something light and happy and hopeful.

Something that involved no murder or gore or blood covered walls.

Maria and her adventures never failed to cheer me up.

I smiled when I looked over and saw Riley snoozing on the couch, his head propped up against the back. He was wearing khaki shorts and a Georgetown T-shirt. His dark hair was tousled, and a couple stray pieces of popcorn dotted his clothes.

I hadn't intended on falling asleep out here. No, Riley had offered up his room again since Tim was using his spare. Riley was going to take the couch. But I guess we were both exhausted from everything that had happened.

I stared at his face, at the soft blue light from the TV as it illuminated him. Riley Thomas was more than my fiancé. He was my best friend. When I wasn't with him, I wanted to be with him. I couldn't wait to tell him about my day. I couldn't imagine my life without him, for that matter.

Maybe I should listen to everyone's advice. Maybe we should just get married and take an extended honeymoon. We could furiously pray the whole time that Milton Jones would be caught in the meantime and that we could resume our lives.

My life rarely worked out that way, though. I vowed that would only make me stronger; that it would make me a fighter. But it definitely seemed like just when one trouble rolled out of my life another one was waiting to roll in.

A sound caught my ears, and I stiffened. What was that? It wasn't Tim. It had come from the other side of the apartment, the side opposite the bedrooms.

I surveyed everything around me. The bookcases looked the same. Lucky's cage was motionless. The curtains hung without movement.

But I'd heard something. I knew I had.

Adrenaline pumped through me. I felt like a cat ready to pounce. Like a giant Venus flytrap sensing an incoming fly and poising for action.

Why had Clarice filled my head with songs from *Little Shop of Horrors*? Why? Why? Why?

I didn't have time to ponder it now.

Something was waiting in the distance. Something wasn't normal. Something caused danger to crackle through the air.

The questions were: What? Who?

I hoped my guesses weren't correct. I hoped there was some wild misunderstanding going on in my mind. Chad and Sierra were back early and wanted to stop by for a visit? Bill McCormick remembered something about his conversation with Rose during their date? Mrs. Mystery wanted to discuss a plot idea with me from her latest book?

My spine straightened. The sound. I'd heard it again.

I continued to scan my surroundings, looking for some kind of sign. My eyes stopped at the front door. My gaze became hyper-focused on the doorknob.

I held my breath, wondering if my eyes were deceiving me.

They weren't.

The doorknob turned.

Someone was trying to get inside the apartment.

CHAPTER
TWENTY-EIGHT

I STIFLED A SCREAM.

"Riley, you've got to wake up!" I whispered, nudging his shoulder.

His eyes popped open, confusion washing over his features as he pushed himself up. "What . . . ?"

I shook my head, put a finger over my lips to motion "quiet," and pointed at the front door. The grogginess disappeared from his eyes when he saw the knob turning. He jumped to his feet.

"Lock yourself in my room and call the police," he whispered.

"I'm not leaving you out here. Are you crazy?"

"Gabby, I can't stand the thought of anything happening to you. Don't you understand that?"

"Well, I can't stand the thought of anything happening to you, so, yes, I can understand that. We're in this together. I'm not leaving you."

He stared at me a moment before nodding. "Fine. Get your gun."

My purse was right beside the couch. I pulled out the

weapon, which was starting to feel an awful lot like an appendage lately. I really didn't want to shoot someone, but I would if I had to.

I couldn't shoot to kill, for more than one reason. Morally, I couldn't stand the thought of taking someone else's life. But the fact also remained that, if I killed Milton Jones, we might never find Nichole, Clarice or Rose. He was the only one who had knowledge of their whereabouts. Well . . . him and his accomplice. I just wasn't certain how deep the accomplice's involvement went.

Riley motioned toward the door. He took his place on one side of the threshold, while I stood on the other side—behind the door. My skin was alive with dread and if my pulse pounded any harder I feared I might either throw up from anxiety or go into cardiac arrest.

I froze as the doorknob twisted again. Someone was determined to get inside Riley's apartment. How had they gotten past the police officer parked out front?

Riley nodded at me and reached for the door.

"Do you think I could get some milk?"

I jerked my head back. Tim stood there, scratching his stomach and looking at us like we were crazy.

I frantically motioned for him to be quiet.

"What?" He held up his hands. "It's just milk. If it's yours, that still means I didn't buy it. Free is free. I'm a man of principle."

I growled.

The doorknob stopped jiggling, and footsteps hurried away outside the door.

Riley threw the lock off and opened the door.

"Call the police!" I yelled to Tim.

Riley and I stepped outside just as a figure disappeared out the front door.

He had too much of a head start on us. We flew down the stairs. I practically fell out the front door before skidding to a halt on the small slab some might call a porch. Riley stood on the front step. He pointed toward the street. "There he is!"

Riley darted down the sidewalk. I followed behind, wishing I had shoes on. Rocks stabbed at my already tender feet as I hurried down the front steps. I spotted the police cruiser in the lot.

The police! Why hadn't the officer seen what was happening and taken action? Did everything have to be spelled out?

I pounded at the window of the cruiser. The officer inside stared straight ahead, unmoving, unblinking.

I gasped and pulled myself back. My heart stuttered a beat when I realized the officer was . . . dead?

Tim had called 911. Backup should be on the way. Satisfied with that reasoning, I sprinted across the street, headed toward the residential area behind my apartment complex and away from the busy retail and restaurant area.

I could no longer see Riley or Milton Jones. I wasn't even sure which direction to look. I paused and heard some dogs barking. That seemed like a good indicator of where to look.

I pushed myself to move quickly—quickly enough that my lungs screamed for air and that my legs pulled tight with strain. This was our chance. I didn't want to blow it.

I rounded the corner, following the canine tattletales that alerted me something was going on. As my lungs burned, I reminded myself that I needed to work out more, for this very reason. *What if I need to chase a serial killer one day?* I'd given this as an excuse before and people had laughed at me.

I stopped running at the next street corner and bent over, trying to catch my breath. I prayed that Riley was okay. As the image of the downed police officer filled my thoughts, I prayed even harder.

Movement in the distance caught my eye. Riley appeared between two houses. His hands were on his hips, and he shook his head. I could tell by his expression that he wasn't happy. I jogged to meet him halfway. Though I hoped for good news, I knew I wouldn't be receiving any.

"I lost him." Riley shook his head, his jaw hard and his chest quickly rising and falling. "He had too much of a head start. He was weaving between houses, throwing over trashcans. Then I heard a car squeal away."

I closed my eyes as disappointment filled me. I'd been expecting the news, but still. We'd been close. So close.

Milton Jones was always a step ahead of us.

Riley sucked in another long breath as we began walking back to the apartment to see if the police had arrived. "There was something strange, Gabby."

"What's that?"

"Milton Jones is in his early fifties. The way that man ran . . . he was so agile, like he was someone much younger."

"You think it was his accomplice?"

Riley nodded. "Yeah, I do."

"Any tell tale signs as to who he could have been?"

Riley shook his head grimly. "No, not a clue. It could have been Dr. Alexander, Freddy Myers, or even Officer Newell, for all I know."

I kicked a rock, watching as it rushed across the pavement and hit the curb. When would we ever catch a break? Lately, it felt like never.

CHAPTER
TWENTY-NINE

THE POLICE HAD COME, the police had searched, and the police had gone. Now the sun was rising, I was going on my—how many? I'd lost count—night without sleep. I was tired. Riley was agitated. Tim was confused.

The good news was that the cop in the car wasn't dead. He'd been knocked out. I'd assumed the worst in my haste to catch Jones.

The bad news was that the police hadn't caught Jones or his accomplice, despite the manhunt that had ensued.

At 7 a.m., Riley and I went across the street to The Grounds to get some coffee. I think that for once in his life Riley understood my "I'm too tired to make coffee without any coffee" mantra. Besides, I wanted to see Sharon and find out how she was doing.

Before I even reached Sharon, Bill McCormick appeared from a corner table, an extra large cup of coffee in hand. Gone was his earlier glibness. Instead, his eyes looked sad. "I know it sounds crazy. It was one date. But I really thought Rose and I had something."

"I'm sorry, Bill."

He continued to talk. He'd thought they had a real connection, a great date, and now all of that was gone. The earlier celebration over his boost in ratings had disappeared faster than his hairline.

Riley and I had done our best to comfort him, but Bill finally shuffled back to his apartment to get ready for work. I didn't like people who hurt other people. I really didn't. And that meant Milton Jones was at the top of my list of Most Despised People.

Sharon was at her normal place behind the counter. But instead of her normal smile, her eyes looked puffy and dull. She frowned and her chin trembled when she looked up and spotted me. Riley gave me a nod and went to sit at a table, so I could talk to Sharon privately for a moment.

I went around the counter and pulled her into a hug. We shared a moment of grief.

When we stepped back, I rubbed her arm. "How are you holding up?"

"Not well. I haven't slept in days. I keep having night-mares. I keep thinking about what might be happening to her . . ."

"Have the police given you any leads? Any updates?"

"Only that they're working around the clock."

I nodded. "And they are. The lead detective doesn't look like he's gotten a moment of rest. I know this is top priority, not only for local authorities, but the FBI is in on this, too."

"You're the only one who can find her."

I shook my head, honored that she thought so highly of me, but skeptical at the same time. "All my leads have led nowhere."

"You're not giving up, are you?"

"Of course not. It's been all I've been breathing and eating since it happened."

She squeezed the skin between her eyes. "This is all my fault."

"Why in the world would you think this was your fault?"

She sagged against the counter. "I should have just given her a job here, but did I want to work with her? No. I pawned her off on you. That led her right into the killer's hands."

I pulled her into another hug. "This is in no way your fault, Sharon. You can't blame yourself for the actions of a psychopath."

Her cry told me that she hadn't heard a word I said, though.

And I had no idea how to convince her otherwise . . . except by saving Clarice.

Riley and I walked back to the apartment building, one that I was starting to think of as *Calamityville Horror*. No one would want to buy this place in the future, not with everything that had happened here.

Then I thought about Rose and about Freddy and changed my mind.

Some people would buy it *because* of the things that had happened here.

As soon as we stepped inside, I saw Teddi standing at the top of the steps. She was the only girlfriend my dad had since mom died who'd stuck around long enough for me to remember her name. She was the epitome of a Texas beauty queen, only with about twenty years of tarnish on her crown.

I almost hated to admit it, but I liked her. She wasn't my mom. No one would ever be my mom. But my dad liked her. He'd straightened up a lot since they started dating, so I couldn't complain.

"Are you ready to go dress shopping?" She stood at the top of the stairs, a wide smile on her face.

Dress shopping? That's right! How had I forgotten? I wanted to do a face palm at my stupidity. In my defense, a lot had happened this week.

"Teddi, I'm so sorry, but I forgot. I can't make it today."

"You've got to make some time for yourself. That's what I always say. No one else is going to take care of you like you can." She glided down the stairs in high heels with more ease than I did walking on flat surfaces wearing flip flops. Amazing.

"I know, Teddi. I really do. And I want to go shopping with you, but some things have come up. Some really important things that I can't put off."

"But your wedding . . ."

"Can we reschedule? Maybe for next week instead?" Provided a serial killer wasn't still chasing me.

"I was so looking forward to some girl time today." She frowned, pouted almost.

I smiled sincerely. "Some girl time does sound nice, and I do want your opinion."

Apparently, Teddi didn't have a TV in her house. Otherwise, she would probably realize that the Scum River Killer was in town, and that Riley and I had been affiliated with the case. Everyone in the area seemed to know that after the killer had called Bill McCormick's show.

I hated to do it, but I was going to leave her in the dark about this one. The facts of the case were enough to raise anyone's blood pressure. Worry about loved ones was worse than worrying about yourself.

She squeezed my arm. "Listen, I wanted to let you know that your dad and I have talked, and we want to help pay for part of the wedding. We wish we could pay for the whole thing, but that's really not an option right now."

I stopped cold and blinked. Certainly I hadn't heard correctly. My dad had bummed off of me for years, refusing to work himself. It was a long story, but I'd enabled him to do so. Each request for cash had prompted my guilt complex to kick in.

"We couldn't do that," Riley said. He put his hand on my back.

I shook my head. "Besides, my dad doesn't have the money."

"He's been working some extra jobs lately, just so he can help you out."

"My dad?" Certainly she was talking about someone else. Someone responsible. Someone not related to me.

"Yes, your dad." Teddi laughed softly. "Of course. Who else?"

"The two of you . . . you're not even married yet. You don't have to help. You have no obligation." I was still in shock. I wasn't sure if I was making sense or not, or even if I was being rude. But this was almost as confusing and mind-blowing as the search for Milton Jones.

She squeezed my arm again. "I told you. You're like a daughter to me. I want to help."

"That's really kind," I finally said. "But Riley's right. We can do this on our own."

"I won't take no for an answer. We're buying your dress, at least. You do know that I won Best Gown in the Miss Texas pageant, right? It was back in '76, but I still know what a good dress looks like."

I smiled. My dad had a thing for the beauty pageant types. My mom had won a few titles herself. At times, I wondered if Mom and Teddi had ever met. I wouldn't be asking.

Teddi took a step toward the door. "Monday. We're going shopping. No ifs, ands, or buts about it."

She winked and stepped closer. Before she strode outside, she leaned closer to me and whispered, "Let your dad pay some for your wedding. It will help him with his guilt."

Before I could say anything else, she left. Riley and I stood there speechless. The wedding was important. I mean, of course it was important! But how could I even begin to think of myself right now when people were in danger?

"That's really sweet," Riley finally said.

I replayed Teddi's words over and over in my mind. "I can't believe my dad wants to pay for something."

Riley shrugged and pushed one of my curls behind my ear. "I know we agreed to pay for the wedding on our own, but maybe you should think about it. Maybe your dad is finally trying to make things right."

My dad? Making things right? It was enough to make my brain nearly freeze up from overload. When I saw that Riley was waiting for my response, I nodded. "I'll think about it. No promises, though."

———

Before making my way upstairs, I decided to step outside and grab my mail. I knew my box was overflowing, because I'd neglected to check it all week.

You never knew what kind of nasty messages or threatening letters might be waiting for you there. Been there, done that. I'd also been on the receiving end of my father's bills before. Maybe that subconscious thought was what had prodded me to check now.

We stepped outside, and I waved at the new officer who'd been assigned to sit outside of my apartment. He waved back from his patrol car. We trotted across the parking lot toward the cluster of mailboxes at the street.

"This is where we first met, you know," I reminded Riley as we walked. Probably a bad time to reminisce, but I did it anyway.

He grinned. "Yeah, I know. All because of that parrot up in a Bradford pear tree."

"I'd just come from a crime scene and I had soot on my face, and my hair had frizzed out because the house I was cleaning was set on fire." I grinned. "Memories."

"A year later, and look at us now."

The trip down memory lane had been a nice distraction, but only for a moment. I leaned toward the mailboxes. Something looked different. Finally, I pointed at Riley's. "The name from the front of your mailbox is missing."

Riley peered over my shoulder. "What do you mean?"

I pointed to the empty space below his box number. "I mean, your name is missing. Usually, it's right there beside mine. Mine is missing too, for that matter."

"That's strange."

I shook my head. Something was bugging me. But what? I needed to figure it out soon. Because the more questions that swirled in my mind, the less peace I had in my life.

Before I had time to figure it out, Dale pulled up.

There were retail stores that got less traffic than this apartment building did lately. The difference was that retail stores made a profit. Me? All my money was disappearing with every job I put off. Truth be told: I didn't even care at the moment.

A few minutes later, I'd put the thoughts of my mailbox aside and went back upstairs. Dale plopped down at Riley's dining room table, and Riley went to make a cup of coffee. The detective looked tired, as did everyone who was involved in this investigation. No one was getting any sleep; this case haunted everyone's nightmares, whether they were investigating it or hearing about it on the news.

I looked down at a note Tim had left on the table. He'd gone to hang out with some friends. That meant we might not hear from him for anywhere from a few hours to a few days. Maybe it was better that he kept himself occupied.

"I don't suppose you're interested in going back to your old position out in California? I know they'd take you back in a heartbeat." Dale stiffly leaned back in his chair. I had a feeling he'd be more comfortable at a bar than at someone's dining room table.

Riley shook his head and poured his former colleague a cup of coffee. "No, my life is here."

Dale looked over at me. "He was the best prosecutor the office had ever seen." He took the coffee from Riley and raised his mug in thanks.

"I don't know if I'd say that," Riley argued. He crossed his arms and leaned against the wall casually. I could see the strain of this investigation on Riley, also. His eyes had lost their usual brightness, and he'd almost seemed to age before my eyes.

Dale shook his head. "He's too humble. You should have seen him in action. Nothing could ruffle him. He was thorough, ethical, and determined."

"I'm sure everyone's doing just fine out there without me."

"Jane Willows just left, you know. They're looking for someone to fill her position."

Riley straightened. "Jane left? I thought she'd be a lifer."

"We all did. Of course, none of us thought you'd turn

from pursuing criminal justice to taking social justice cases, either. Just proves you should never assume anything." Dale took another sip of coffee.

"Assumptions never get you anywhere. Isn't that the truth?" Riley took another sip of coffee. "So, did you just stop by for a chat or did you have some questions?"

"I wish I was just here for a chat." Dale leaned forward and abandoned his coffee mug for a moment. "I thought you should know that we got some results back. It turns out the perp used propofol to knock out the officer last night. Someone injected it right into his neck."

Dale had my attention now. "Propofol? Wasn't that the drug that killed Michael Jackson?" Leave it to me to come up with a pop culture reference.

Dale nodded. "It was. It's used as an anesthesia by doctors all over the country."

I sat up straighter. "What about dentists? Do they use it?"

Dale shrugged, leaning back in his chair again. "I suppose they could use it also, especially oral surgeons."

Riley and I exchanged "the look."

Dale raised his eyebrows. "What was that about? Does someone want to tell me what's going on?"

We filled him in on the dentist.

He nodded slowly when we finished. "We'll look into it." He paused and stared at me a moment until I squirmed.

"What?" I asked.

"We could use you as a decoy to draw Jones out."

Before I could respond, Riley beat me to it. "That's the worst idea I've heard in a long time. No way."

Dale held up his hands in surrender. "I know, I know. It would be risky."

"Too risky," Riley insisted, his eyes narrowed and his jaw rigid.

"You're right. It was just a crazy idea." Dale stood and extended his hand to Riley. "No hard feelings. I'd feel the same way in your shoes. I'll be in touch."

Riley nodded as the two shook hands. "When this case is over, before you leave town, let me know. Maybe we can catch up."

Something about the way Riley said the words made me wonder if he was considering applying for his old position with the D.A.'s office. I shook my head. That thought was ridiculous. Riley had started his own law firm and was doing what he loved now.

"Will do."

I stood, paced over to the window, and shoved the curtain aside. From where I stood, I saw Dale climb into his car and pull away.

Something about his sedan caught my eye. What was it?

It wasn't white, so I knew it wasn't Jones' getaway car.

No, it was a black hybrid. A suit jacket hung in the back window.

"What is it?" Riley asked.

I shook my head. "I don't know. There's something about his car . . ."

"A lot of people drive cars like that."

"I know. I can't put my finger on it."

"You don't think Dale is involved in this in some way, do you? He's a stand up cop."

I shrugged. "I'm not drawing any conclusions. I'm just trying to find the truth." I dropped the curtain and plopped back down on the dining room chair. Riley brought me a cup of coffee, and I took a sip. It was black, but I didn't care.

I didn't argue when Riley set two bowls of cereal on the table, either. They weren't the sugarcoated, fruity kind that I liked. No, this was healthy with lots of fiber and whole grains.

It would do.

"Tell me about Jones' family," I said. "Please."

"What about them?" He took a bite of his cereal.

"How did they react when he was arrested?"

"They stood by him at first. They denied that Jones was guilty, said he couldn't hurt a fly. According to his wife Julie, he couldn't even spank his kids. But as the evidence came out in the trial, Julie changed her mind. She actually came to me and offered up more evidence."

"She didn't have to do that."

Riley shook his head. "No, she didn't. But she felt an obligation to the families of the victims."

"Have you heard anything about Julie since the trial?"

He ran a hand through his hair. "I know they divorced. Last I heard Julie was dating someone else and they'd moved away from California, somewhere they could start fresh."

"I wonder if the children ever talk to their dad?"

"I doubt it. They were upset, as you can imagine."

"Maybe Milton Jones blames you for taking away his family. Maybe that's why he's targeting both of us right now and not just you."

"Sounds like a good theory to me."

I leaned back and nibbled on my nail in thought. It had about as much flavor as Riley's cereal. "What about his victims? Do you remember how he chose them? What was his method?"

"They were all similar to his older sister. I think I mentioned that to you before. Young, thin, bossy."

"But how did he pick them? Did he meet them some-where? Did he stake out college campuses? Were they all waitresses? Was it all simply random?"

"No, he was purposeful, which is part of what made him more scary. He was a sociologist. All of the women had some connection to his studies. He had access to their files. They were oldest children and often had careers where they were in charge."

I shook my head as I tried to make sense of things. "This is what I don't understand. He snatched Clarice, who had a connection to me. He snatched Rose, who had a connection to both of us. But what about Nichole, the first woman he snatched? Why her?"

"Good question." He pulled out his laptop and began tapping at the keys. Finally, he turned the screen toward me. It was a news article on Nichole Brown. "She was 24 years old. Single. Lived with her family in Norfolk. She was the manager at a temp agency."

I looked at him. "Temp agency? Did you ever use her at the law firm?"

He shook his head. "She doesn't look familiar."

"What about while you were out of town? Could Mary Lou have called her in?"

"She wouldn't do that without my approval."

"She has a connection to you or me somehow." I stood and started pacing. "I mean, this guy's M.O. is all over the place. You said he was meticulous. Meticulous people aren't random. What about Mr. Sears? Milton Jones never killed a man. If he did, he sure didn't leave his body at home for the police to find. His method is to abduct, kill, and to leave the body somewhere to make a statement."

"You're right. Something's off."

"If we can figure out Nicole's connection, maybe we can find our killer."

"Maybe we should go talk to her family."

I nodded. "It's worth a shot."

CHAPTER
THIRTY

NICHOLE'S PARENTS lived in an upper middle class house located on the Lafayette River. In other words, it was a prime piece of real estate in a desirable area of town.

I straightened my outfit as I waited for someone to come to the door. A woman with bobbed brown hair and pink-rimmed eyes answered several minutes after we rang the bell. She didn't open the door all the way, but peered around from the other side.

"Are you reporters? Because we're not doing interviews."

Riley shook his head. "We're not with the media. My name is Riley Thomas. I prosecuted Milton Jones back in California and now I'm helping with the investigation here."

A slight smile tugged at her lips, and she opened the door wider. "Riley Thomas. Wouldn't Nichole have loved to meet you."

Riley tilted his head. "Come again?"

Mrs. Brown stepped back. "Come in and I'll explain. Get out of the blistering heat."

We stepped onto a marble entryway. Mrs. Brown motioned for us to follow her past the dining room, office, and a formal living room. Finally she stopped at a cozy-looking breakfast nook. The way the sun flooded inside through the curtains made everything seem happy and cheerful. "Would you like some tea?"

We both declined.

She sat across from us at a glass-topped table, moisture filling her eyes. "I still can't believe she's gone."

"We're so sorry about what's happened," Riley started. "All we want to do is to catch the person who did this and make sure he does his time."

Mrs. Brown sucked in a deep breath and seemed to pull her tears back for a moment. "Anything I can do to help. You have questions?"

I licked my lips. "You said your daughter would have loved to have met Riley?" That was the burning question on my mind.

"That's right. She wrote a paper on you." She let out a sad laugh. "She went to school to be a paralegal. They had to pick a prosecutor to feature for one of their assignments. This was during the Milton Jones trial. She picked you. She said you were handsome."

Nichole Brown *did* have a connection to Riley. How did Milton Jones learn of it, though?

"Nichole worked at a temp agency, correct? She didn't end up as a paralegal?" I asked.

Mrs. Brown nodded. "She wasn't a student or academically-minded, and no one could force her to be. Even going to school for a shortened degree like the one required to become a paralegal seemed to be too much for her. All she was interested in was boys and socializing. I hate to say it, but it was the truth."

"What did she do after she dropped out of school?" Riley asked.

"She started a blog and got this job with the temp agency. She was actually good at managing people. Being the oldest, being bossy came naturally to her."

Riley leaned forward. "Did you say blog?"

Mrs. Brown nodded. "That's right. She loved blogging, especially about the popular court cases of the moment. You know, Jodi Arias, Caylee Anthony, George Zimmerman. At least her time in school did her some good. She learned the ins and outs of the legal system."

"Did she ever blog about Riley?" I asked.

Mrs. Brown tilted her head. "You know, now that you mentioned it, she might have. She followed the Milton Jones case very carefully. It wouldn't surprise me."

"Could we see her blog? Do you mind?" Riley leaned forward.

"Not at all." She stood. "One moment."

As soon as she disappeared, Riley and I looked at each other. "This just keeps getting crazier and crazier all the time," I whispered.

"Tell me about it. There was a connection the whole time. I wonder if the police know."

"They very well could, and they just haven't told us. When's your next task force meeting?"

Riley shrugged. "They said they'd call me in when they needed me. Of course, I talk to them nearly every day, so anything they need to know from me, I've already told them. Offering information is really my only role on the team."

Mrs. Brown appeared with a laptop. She typed something, and then turned the screen toward us. "Here it is. She called her blog 'Brown Nosing.' Clever, I always thought."

Riley scrolled through the entries. "Is there any way we can search her posts?"

"I think there's a search box at the top right of the screen."

Riley typed in "Milton Jones" and pages of results followed.

I'd certainly say that Nichole was following the Milton Jones case and that she was following Riley's social life. There were tons of entries about Riley and all of his astute qualities.

Somehow, Milton Jones had discovered these blog posts.

That meant, this blog had ultimately led to Nichole's abduction. I bet she never foresaw herself becoming a part of the news story like this.

"I know this is going to sound like a strange question, but did Nichole ever have any contact with Milton Jones?" I asked.

"Contact with Milton Jones? No. Why would you ask such a thing?"

I kept my voice soft. "Just a familiar thread we've been following. I'm sorry. I just had to know."

Mrs. Brown shook her head. "No, she was a good girl." A sob escaped. She tried to subdue it with a hand over her mouth. It did no good. "And now that man is doing horrible things to her! If there's anything you can do to help find her, please do it. Please!"

Mrs. Brown's desperate request echoed in my head as I walked from her home to my van. Just as I pulled open the driver side door, my cell phone rang. It was Bill McCormick.

His words tumbled into each other, his normal "radio mode" voice gone. "He just called for you again."

"Milton Jones? Is he on the radio now?" I slipped inside and started to reach for the dials.

"No, he left you a message. We didn't have the chance to make Jones' call live."

My hand dropped back into my lap. "Well, what did he say?"

"He said if you want answers, he'll be at Zombie Fest tonight."

"Zombie Fest?" That was tonight, wasn't it? How could I have forgotten? It was probably a good thing his call wasn't on the air. That would have created wide spread panic. "Thanks for letting me know, Bill."

I hung up and realized that Riley was staring at me. "He left you a message?"

I nodded and filled him in.

He shook his head. "I don't like this." Riley had said that a lot lately.

"Me neither."

"It's like he's trying to lure you out."

I tried to suppress a shudder that desperately wanted to rush through my every muscle and limb. It didn't work. Why did Jones want me there tonight?

I pushed those thoughts aside and called Adams. I explained what had happened, realizing that I'd had more conversations with the detective this week than I had my best friend. A sad reality.

"You need to stay away from Zombie Fest, Gabby." Adams' voice sounded as serious as I'd ever heard it.

I nibbled on my bottom lip for a moment. "I want to be there."

"That's not a good idea, Gabby," Adams said.

"He's going to be there. He's going to be looking for me. This is our chance to get him, Detective."

"It's risky."

"You can have your men there. I can be wired. If you can grab him, maybe we'll find those women."

"Or it could go terribly wrong."

His words were a grim reminder. He spoke the truth. Things could veer off plan. In a situation like this, not going according to plan could mean life or death.

"It's worth the risk if it means catching Jones."

He didn't say anything for a minute. "Go back to your apartment. I'll meet you there and we'll talk more."

I'd go back there. But there was one place I wanted to stop first.

I thought I knew what happened to the names on our mailboxes.

Fifteen minutes later, we stood on Freddy Mansfield's doorstep and rang his bell. When he opened the door and spotted us, he tried to shut us out. Riley stuck his foot out to stop him and grabbed his shirt before he could escape.

"We need to talk," Riley muttered.

Freddy's eyes widened. "About . . . about wh—what?"

"About Thursday night," I filled him in.

"I was here. All night. No alibi, but you can check my computer logs."

"You were at our apartment building," I said.

His eyes became even wider. "Why would you think that? I don't even know where you live."

"A computer guru like you could figure it out." Riley still kept a tight fist on the man's shirt. "We can do this the easy way or we can do it the hard way. The hard way involves calling the cops and them taking you down to the station to be questioned."

Freddy raised his hands. "Okay, okay. I'll talk."

Whew. I hadn't had to pull out my gun. I was becoming

THE SCUM OF ALL FEARS 223

like *Lara Croft: Tomb Raider,* minus the tight clothes and life-less, stiff personality.

"You stole the name off of Riley's mailbox and my mail-box. Why?" I knew the answer. I wanted to hear him say it.

He stared until finally his shoulders slumped in defeat. "It could get me major money."

"You were the one who tried to get into Riley's apartment."

He shrugged. "I just wanted to take a quick look. I wasn't going to hurt anyone. Maybe I would just take one of your photos. Maybe some deodorant. Nothing that was a big deal."

"That's breaking and entering! It's stealing!" Riley's face reddened.

This whole Milton Jones case was becoming a circus.

"It's the little things that can sometimes bring the most money," Freddy insisted.

I shook my head in disgust. "You're the one who knocked that cop out."

He said nothing.

"Let me guess. You were able to trade one of the items you were auctioning for the drug. I'm sure people would jump through hoops to get some of those 'collector's' items." Everything was starting to make sense.

I could tell by the way his pupils widened and his lips parted that I'd guessed correctly.

"No one was supposed to get hurt. You wouldn't under-stand. I need more product. Milton Jones is hot right now, and people are willing to pay big time for anything related to his case."

"And you're willing to do anything to get that money," I mumbled. "It's reprehensible."

"A guy's gotta do what a guy's gotta do to make a living."

Riley let him go. "I think you're scum. A murderer? Not really. But one of the most vile people I've met, nonetheless."

As we walked back to my van—yes, I'd driven this time—I noticed the decorative plate around my license plate was missing. Sierra had given it to me, and it had said, "Keep Calm, and Investigate On."

How much did I want to bet that Freddy had taken that at some point as well?

CHAPTER
THIRTY-ONE

"I DON'T WANT you doing this." Riley stood in front of me with his hands on his hips and his eyes lined with worry. "There are so many things that could go wrong. You're going to be exactly where Jones wants you to be. You're going to be playing his game, and he's going to be controlling all of the cards. It's not going to end well."

Since a police officer was applying white makeup to my face in an effort to zombie-fy me, I couldn't escape Riley's closing argument in his case against me.

I sat in a dining room chair, which faced the window for lighting purposes, in Riley's apartment. I closed my eyes as more makeup was applied. There were so many police officers in the apartment right now, it was practically a donut shop.

I didn't say anything in response to Riley. I knew I couldn't change his mind on this, so why bother and try?

Finally, Riley stopped staring at me—I could feel his gaze leave me, even with my eyes closed—and addressed Parker. "Can't you talk her out of this? Tell her what a bad idea it is? Insist she stay far away?"

Great, he was trying to persuade the jury now.

Parker shrugged. "You don't really think she's going to listen to me, do you?"

Riley sighed. "Gabby—"

As they put the final powder puff to my cheeks, I stood. "It's going to be fine, Riley. I'm going to be careful. You're going to be with me."

I resisted the urge to bat my eyelashes and make the words drip with sugary sweetness. Because, despite how sappy my words sounded, they were true. I did feel safer with Riley nearby.

He stepped closer, probably to get my attention. It worked. Electricity crackled between us and caused me to suck in a breath.

He leaned down until we were practically nose-to-nose. "We both have targets on our backs."

I stepped back before his plan worked and I actually started listening to him. I paced instead and kept my gaze averted so I could focus. "Milton Jones doesn't use guns. He's not going to shoot us. He'll try to *abduct* us." The words really weren't that comforting.

"That's not entirely true," Parker said. He hung out against the door, twirling his toothpick. He did that when he wanted a cigarette. "We know that's what he does to women, but he's veering off of his M.O. like a meth addict in rehab. Who knows what he'll do next."

I wanted to throw a book at Parker. Maybe a tomato or a cream pie. I settled for a dirty look instead.

He shrugged and continued to twirl the toothpick in his mouth. "It's true."

I couldn't think about that right now. I had to concentrate on the things I could control, and right now that meant finding out more information.

"How many people are expected to turn out for this event tonight?" I asked.

"Hundreds," Adams said. He sprawled in Riley's leather recliner. I'd never seen him look so exhausted. Even in his tired state, I could tell he was watching everything. I'd never asked him about his personal life before, but I'd bet he was single. Divorced. Probably because his job was his life. It would make him a great detective but a lousy husband.

Apparently, down at the station, there were some under-cover cops also being zombie-fied. A police presence was already supposed to be at the event, so there would be uniformed officers on the streets. Adams and his higher ups had agreed that it would be better if I blended in. It would be harder for Jones to find me.

Of course, that also meant it would be easier for the police to lose track of me.

I guessed I couldn't have it both ways.

I was trying to appear strong, but my insides felt like gelatin. So many things could go terribly wrong in this scenario. My thoughts kept rushing toward the what ifs, but I pushed those doubts away.

Dwelling on how this could be a disaster brought me no closer to finding Clarice or Rose or Nichole. It only brought me closer to a nervous breakdown. Worry and anxiety were like that.

Time was running out. If we didn't find them by tomor-row, then Nichole would be dead.

Clarice would be next.

Rose only a day after that.

Milton Jones had created this virtual ticking time bomb, and I knew we didn't have a moment to waste.

"You're next," the officer told Riley.

Riley was stiff as he lowered himself into the dining room

chair. His jaw hardly moved as white makeup was applied to his face. Darker shades went under his eyes. His hair was teased upward.

"Your clients would love to see you now." I tried to keep my tone light. "I can see the headlines: Zombie Prosecutor Fights for the Living Dead."

Riley said nothing.

I glanced out the window. Zombies were already starting to fill the streets. There were pretty zombies and scary zombies and ninja zombies. I'm sure there were sober zombies there, but I'd betcha there were a whole lotta drunk ones, too.

I frowned. Were we putting these people in danger? No, I decided. Jones would be there, whether we were or not. Besides, the police and the FBI were on this. These streets had probably never been safer. Riley and I were the only ones Jones was after right now.

I caught a glimpse of myself in the mirror. My hair was white and bigger than a Tina Turner afro. My skin was pasty. I wore a long sleeved white button up shirt. The buttons didn't line up, and there was a rip in the sleeve. But the shirt would perfectly conceal the wire beneath it. They'd also placed a tracking device in the back pocket of my jeans.

Adams finally stood from the recliner. "We're getting out of here now. We don't want to be too obvious. But you'll have eyes on you at all times. If Milton Jones tries to get you, we'll be right there."

I nodded. My emotions weren't high. In fact, I felt rather numb and subdued. I wasn't sure the feeling could be called "peace." I just knew this was what I had to do, and I was ready to accept this challenge.

I wasn't sure if that made me wise or if it made me a fool.

I guess we'd find out in another hour.

"That's disgusting." I turned away from the food that vendors were selling along the zombie-infested street.

Sausage that looked like intestines. Cupcakes that looked like brains. Drinks that looked like blood.

Gross.

But everyone who was here *loved* it. They were eating it up. Who knew what an enterprise zombies could turn into?

I glanced around me, shielding my eyes from the setting sun. Everyone blended in with each other. If you'd seen one zombie, you'd seen them all, I supposed. But I did spot a few uniformed officers. I thought I recognized a couple of the guys from the police station dressed for the party, but I couldn't be sure.

In the background, a zombie band named "The Grateful Undead" played Michael Jackson's *Thriller*.

Riley placed his hand on my back, zapping me back to reality. "You okay?"

I nodded, not feeling all that okay.

Would I even recognize Milton Jones if he was here? I'd seen his pictures. I'd talked to him at that crime scene. I'd felt him immobilize me at my home. But if he was dressed like a zombie, I might never spot him.

This event could be a crazed killer's best-case scenario.

A ruckus down the street caught my attention. Squeals and laughs as people chased each other eased some of the tension in my chest. But it was like the calm before the storm. The quelling of my anxiety only lasted a second before coming back even stronger than before.

It looked like a game of tag had started down the street. I stayed away. The last thing I needed was for someone to grab me and for me to think it was Milton Jones.

A figure across the way caught my eye.

He was dressed like a zombie. But I'd recognize that Roman nose anywhere.

Officer Newell.

I was certain that Adams had told me the rookie was on desk duty. Was it a coincidence that he was here tonight? Had he just intended on having fun? Or was he somehow connected with Milton Jones as well?

"What is it?" Riley asked.

"It's the rookie," I nodded in the distance. "Newbie—I mean, Newell."

Just then, Newell looked up. He spotted me. His eyes widened.

He took off in the opposite direction. Running made him look guilty. He was *acting* guilty, for sure.

If he was our man, we needed to catch him. Now.

"What's going on, Gabby?" Adams said in my earpiece.

"Officer Newell is here. Is he working the event?" I pushed past two creepy lovebirds who were eating "intestines" like Lady and the Tramp ate spaghetti. As I brushed past, their food fell to the ground, and they called out an insult. I didn't have time to apologize.

"Absolutely not. He's to remain hands off in this case."

"He was taking pictures at that crime scene, Detective. Are you sure he's not in cahoots with Jones?"

I couldn't hear what he had to say over the blare of "Walk Like a Zombie," a catchy number that paid tribute to the Bangles' song, "Walk Like an Egyptian." The crowds jostled around me as Officer Newell disappeared somewhere in the direction of the Mexican restaurant Riley and I frequented.

"Can you still see him?" I yelled to Riley.

"He's still running. Come on!" He grabbed my hand and pulled me after him. I ran into someone with a "blood slushy" and red liquid covered my shirt.

We pushed farther into the crowd, closer to the game of tag. Riley stopped and surveyed everything around him. "I lost him."

I grabbed the arm of someone walking past. "Did you see this guy? This . . . this . . ." How did I describe Newell? " . . . zombie with a Roman nose?"

The girl stared at me with dull eyes. Finally, she muttered, "Brains!"

I grumbled beneath my breath. Riley and I continued to push through the crowds. Where had Newell gone?

We stopped in our tracks just in time to see a uniformed officer grab Newell and handcuff him. The officer said something quietly, and they walked away.

"We've got him in custody," Adams said in my earpiece. "We'll handle this. You just stay put. Don't call attention to yourself."

Too late for that. The game of tag pushed our way.

"Gabby . . .?" Riley pointed to my shirt, his eyes wide with surprise and concern.

I shook my head. "Blood slushy."

He pulled me toward him in a quick hug. "I can't handle this," he muttered into my ear. Just as he stepped away, a mob scene was on us.

People chanted "brains," "long live the dead," and other absurdities. I lost all sense of direction as people surrounded us. Somehow, I lost my grip on Riley.

Hands reached out. People bumped into us. Grabbed at my hair. My clothes. My sanity.

They squeezed in tighter. Their movement reminded me

of being captured in a riptide and unable to escape. Chaos. Pure chaos.

My gaze swiveled around me.

Riley? Where was Riley?

I glanced across the crowd, but each face blended into the others. Music blared. People pressed in, swallowed me.

I craned my neck to the left. To the right. Turned around.

Finally, I saw him.

The crowds had rushed between us, separating us. I tried to move but couldn't.

My heart raced. This wasn't supposed to happen. It had been one of those worst case scenarios that I'd refused to think about.

I had to get to Riley.

I had to find a police officer.

I had to do *something*.

I began to push through the squeezing, suffocating mass of people around me.

As I did so, something pricked my neck. Suddenly my body was electrified.

The air left my lungs.

My muscles cramped, became rigid, then numb.

My arms drew in toward my body. Heat filled me.

And then I lost total control and collapsed on the ground.

I'd been tasered.

As the movement of the crowd became more frantic, I realized that was the least of my problems.

I was about to be trampled.

CHAPTER
THIRTY-TWO

"GABBY!"

I heard Riley's voice rise above the crowd. I could only move my eyes to search for him. For Jones.

All I saw was an ocean of zombies.

Someone fell over me. Another person stepped onto my shoulder. Feet lingered above my face.

I was powerless to do anything about it. I could only lie there, waiting for the effects of being zapped to wear off.

"Gabby? Gabby? Where are you?" Adams said in my earpiece. "What just happened?"

I wanted to answer him, but I couldn't. Only a small gasp escaped.

Faces blurred into each other. Beer splashed on my shirt. I heard a murmured, "Sorry."

Finally, someone squatted beside me on the ground.

Riley's face came into focus. He lifted me up and carried me through the crowd to safety. As we reached the sidewalk, two uniformed officers joined us, offering crowd control. My erratic heartbeat slowed for a moment.

Finally, my jaw moved. "Jones," I whispered.

"Shh . . . the police are looking for him," Riley told me. "Worry about you right now."

Even in my electrified state, my mind was clear enough to know the police wouldn't catch Jones.

An even worse thought struck me.

Jones hadn't wanted to kill me or to snatch me. He could have easily done either.

No, he'd wanted something else.

To scare me? Maybe.

But, more than that, I thought he wanted to distract me. The question was: From what? What was I missing?

He'd taken bossy Nichole, young Clarice, always-in-charge Rose.

Who was he going to snatch next? I felt certain that it would be someone I knew.

Mrs. Mystery seemed too old. So did Mary Lou. Who else could he hurt in order to hurt Riley and me?

"Something's wrong," I whispered, resting my head on Riley's shoulder.

"Do you need to go to the hospital?"

"No, no. Not with me. With Jones."

"I know. Everyone knows that."

I tried to shake my head but couldn't. "He's going for someone else tonight. He wants me to know it. Every time he reaches out to me, that's been the reason."

"Who's he going for?"

I wish I knew. "I have no idea."

Back in Riley's apartment, I finally regained control of my muscles. Against my wishes, they'd called the paramedics to come and check me out. They'd said I was fine.

Despite that diagnosis, my limbs shook uncontrollably as I pulled myself into a sitting position on Riley's couch. The regular crew was there, Tim had returned, and I filled everyone in on exactly what had happened.

Adams had finally told me that Newell had been assigned to question all the neighbors to see if they'd seen anything after Jones broke into my place. That's why the officer had been at Mr. Sears' place. Newell also claimed that he was just at Zombie Fest for fun, not because he was trying to work the scene and especially not because he was helping Milton Jones.

I felt certain that Jones was going after someone else. We had to figure out who.

Sharon? Someone from church? The lady who cut my hair?

None of those people felt right.

A thought hit my mind with the force of a lightning bolt. I tried to stand and make my announcement, but my knees weren't ready to hold me. Riley caught me and lowered me back onto the cushions.

"What is it?" he asked.

"Teddi. Someone's got to check on Teddi. Now."

It made sense. Teddi might not be young, but Jones had apparently changed his way of doing things to better accommodate torturing Riley and me. Other than her age, Teddi fit.

Adams got Teddi's address and sent some officers over there. In the meantime, I grabbed my phone and called her cell.

She answered on the first ring, sounding sleepy and tired. I glanced at the clock. It was past midnight.

"Gabby? Is everything okay? I was just getting my beauty rest."

I gripped my phone, trying to control my emotions.

"Teddi, I know this is going to sound strange, but the police are on their way to your place. I'm afraid you could be in danger. I need you to check your locks and your windows and sit tight until they get there."

"The police? You're scaring me, Gabby. What's going on?"

Tension pulled across my chest as I prepared to drop a bombshell on her. "Teddi, I'm afraid Milton Jones might be after you."

She gasped. "The serial killer, Milton Jones?"

"It's a long story, but yes. The serial killer."

"After me?"

"I'm going to stay on the line until the police get there. You're going to be fine."

"I . . . I can't move. I can't get out of bed. I can hardly breath at the thought of that man being after me."

I knew that feeling all too well. "How about your closet? Can you stay in your closet until the police come?"

"I . . . I can do that." She rustled around. "I'm going now. I'm just going to step inside—"

She screamed.

My heart felt like it stopped beating. "Teddi? Teddi? Are you there? What's wrong?"

"Nice try, Gabby St. Claire." Someone else came on the line. "But score another point for me. You know what this means? You lose."

I'd recognize that voice anywhere.

It was Milton Jones.

I wanted to dart out of my house and over to Teddi's. Riley and Parker both pushed me back down on the couch.

"Gabby, I have to insist that you stay here. The police are all over this right now," Parker said.

"But it's Teddi! I have to call my dad."

Riley put his hand on my shoulder. "Wait until Adams calls again. Maybe the police got there in time."

But I knew in my heart that they hadn't.

I didn't say anything. In my mind, I was plotting ways to blow this joint. To slip from under everyone's grasp. To go and chase Jones myself, if I had to.

Parker glared at me. "If I can't convince you to stay here this evening, then I'm going to have to lock you up."

"You can't do that!"

"For carrying a weapon without a permit? Sure I can."

"You wouldn't."

He shrugged. "If that's what I had to do."

I threw my head back on the couch, knowing I was trapped. Now, I'd have to do the hardest thing of all. I'd have to wait.

Finally, Parker's cell phone rang. His conversation felt like it took hours as I waited to hear the update. Finally, he slid the phone back in his pocket and looked at me. I could tell it wasn't good news. "Teddi's gone."

Tears washed into my eyes. I hadn't known the woman long, but I knew she had a kind heart and that she made my dad happy. She didn't deserve this. No one did.

Riley pulled me into a hug.

"He must have gotten there right before the police. They're looking all over for him now, Gabby," Parker told me.

I shook my head. I had no hope they'd catch him. He seemed too smart for that.

Now I had to call my dad and break the news to him.

CHAPTER
THIRTY-THREE

MY DAD SOUNDED numb and in shock when I talked to him. I insisted I wanted to go to his place, despite any warnings from the police that I needed to stay put. My dad had mumbled that he wanted to be alone, so I sent Tim over to be with him.

I prayed my dad didn't turn back to alcohol. It was his go-to comfort, a personal demon that always haunted him.

By four a.m., Riley's apartment had cleared out, and I felt beside myself. Adrenaline and exhaustion mingled in my blood. I downed more than my fair share of coffee. Now I felt adrenaline, exhaustion, *and* caffeine mingling in me. I wasn't sure this combination was any better.

All I knew was that I had to find Jones. Enough was enough.

I took a shower and washed off any evidence of being zombie-fied. I didn't bother with pajamas, but pulled on a clean pair of jeans and a T-shirt instead. I wanted to be ready for action.

When I stepped out from the bathroom, I plopped on the couch beside Riley. He looked zoned out but awake. "I want to see that video again, the one that Clarice secretly took for her reality TV show."

He barely turned toward me. "Do you think there's something on the video we missed?"

I shrugged. "I have no idea. It's worth a look."

I grabbed my laptop from the dining room table and pulled up the video clips I'd saved there. I hit play.

I especially paid attention to what was going on in the background at the crime scenes. Was there something I was missing?

We got to the last part of the video. This was where we stood outside on the lawn of that first crime scene. Clarice's glasses cam had me centered on the screen. But my back was toward the street.

I carefully watched the cars that passed.

Had Milton Jones come back to survey what was going on? I mean, I had to think about it. He wasn't affiliated with those crime scenes. We'd wondered that initially. But then he'd shown up at the house and acted like the homeowner. But that was more to send a message. The actual crimes at the house had nothing to do with Jones.

"Do you see anything?" Riley asked.

I shook my head. "No, not really."

Cars drove past on the street. There were no white sedans. A few people slowed, but who wouldn't hit the brakes when there were five police cars parked outside?

I sat up straighter as I saw another car cruise by. "Go back some."

Riley hit a button and backed up the video. I pointed to the screen. "You see that car?"

"What about it?"

I didn't want to say it, but I had to. "It's your friend Dale's."

"Are you sure?" Riley asked.

"Look at it. His coat is still hanging in the backseat even."

Riley fell back so hard against the couch that I nearly yelled, "Timber!"

"Why would Dale have driven past the scene? I mean, it would have been one thing if he'd stopped to talk to the detectives. But I didn't even think he was in town then. I thought he came later." I let Riley process that in silence for a moment.

He rubbed his chin. "What should we do with this information?"

"Tell Adams and Parker. Maybe they can figure it out." I saw how pensive Riley looked and squeezed his hand. "Maybe he has a good reason for this."

"I don't know who to trust anymore. That's the truth." He shook his head. "Let me talk to Dale first."

"And if he's helping Jones? Do you really think he's going to admit it to you?"

"I just want to gauge his reaction." Riley held up his cell phone. "I'll call now."

I watched as Riley dialed his number and then put the phone to his ear. A moment later, he pulled it back down. "No answer."

"Isn't it a little suspicious for a detective not to answer? Especially a detective on a hot case like this?"

"I'll try him again in another hour. If he still doesn't answer, I'll call the police. Maybe he's just grabbing a moment of rest. You saw how tired he looked."

I leaned forward. "What do you know about Dale?"

"He seems to be a stand up guy. Everyone respected him. Been a cop forever. Joined the force out of high school."

"Personal life?"

Riley sighed. "Last I heard, he was divorced. Had a few

kids. It was a pretty ugly divorce, from what I recall. His wife accused him of some things. Being unfaithful. She was going to file charges that he'd abused her—he would have lost his job. He compromised instead and gave her full custody of the kids if she wouldn't pursue that."

I approached the next subject very carefully. "You don't think he felt some kind of kinship to Jones, do you? I mean, Jones' wife accused him of some heinous things also. She turned her back on him for all the world to see."

"Nothing would surprise me anymore, Gabby. Nothing at all."

I hated the fact that a conversation I'd initiated had caused so much strain to Riley. But the search for answers wasn't always pretty.

CHAPTER
THIRTY-FOUR

SOMEHOW, against all the odds, I must have drifted to sleep on Riley's couch. My physical exhaustion, along with the effects of the Taser, had caught up with me. When I opened my eyes, I had to blink several times.

Certainly I wasn't reading the clock right. It was 3:30 . . . in the afternoon. The paramedics had given me some Tylenol when they'd checked me out earlier. At least, that's what I'd *thought* they'd given me. I never slept that soundly though, especially not with so much going on.

I spotted Riley at his computer. He appeared to be staring at a blank screen, probably too tired to think clearly himself. Had he been able to get any shuteye? He looked clean, so apparently he'd taken a shower, at least.

"Any updates?" I muttered, running a hand through my hair.

He turned around and shook his head. "Nothing yet."

"You heard from Tim?"

"He's with your dad. They're hanging in, waiting for the police to be in touch."

"I hope Teddi is . . ." I couldn't finish. Not only did I hope she was okay, but I hoped she was *alive*. To voice the thought aloud seemed morbid.

"I know. What a night, huh? How are you feeling?"

"I really passed out, didn't I?"

"You haven't had a good night's sleep in forever. I was going to wake you, but I figured you needed your rest."

If I needed my rest, why did my head feel like it weighed a hundred pounds right now?

Someone knocked on the door. Riley crossed the room and peered out the peephole.

"It's Bill," he muttered.

He flipped the locks. A moment later, Bill plopped at Riley's dining room table, a bag of sandwiches in hand. He grabbed a ham and cheese for himself before finally shoving the bag our way.

"I figured you guys could use something to eat. Any word on Rose?"

I shook my head, grabbing a turkey and provolone and nibbling on it. My appetite wasn't great, but I knew I needed food in order to keep my energy up.

Bill frowned. I could tell he'd really liked her, and I felt bad for the big guy. Just when things had been looking up for him . . .

"I hope the police find this guy. This is crazy." He looked at me, and I thought I saw respect in his gaze. "What do you think? Are they going to catch him?"

"I hope so." I leaned against the wall and gripped my sandwich, trying to weigh my words carefully. "Time is running out."

His eyebrows scrunched together. "What do you mean?"

"Jones always kept his victims six days," Riley explained.

"Today's the sixth day for the first victim, I guess." Bill averted his gaze and stared into the distance.

I nodded. "Yeah, and we're no closer to finding this guy. We just keep getting stuck on these wild goose chases."

"What are you trying to do exactly?" he asked.

"We either need to find out who Jones is working with or where he's taking the women," Riley said. "We have no good leads at this point."

Except Dale, who still wasn't answering his phone. Riley had stuck to his end of the bargain and called Adams to tell him about the car in the video sometime before I'd drifted to sleep.

Bill shifted, finishing up his lunch. "Look, I know I was an insensitive jerk earlier, and I was thinking only about my ratings and not about your safety. I'm sorry about that. Really, I am. What can I do to help?"

"Seen anyone suspicious hanging around?" I asked.

He shrugged. "Rose's the only one I've been looking for."

"Any good guesses as to who might be working with Jones?"

He shrugged again. "Rose would probably have some pretty good guesses. She was like an armchair detective. She loved researching all of that stuff."

Is *that* what she'd told him? Not that she'd been obsessed with a killer? I kept my mouth shut. For my final absurd question, I threw out, "Know of any remote cabins in the area?"

"Rose's family has an old cabin back by the Great Dismal Swamp."

Rose, of course.

I paused and straightened. Wait. By the Great Dismal Swamp? She had mentioned that, hadn't she? Even at the cookout she'd had for us, she'd talked about going to that cabin as a child. She'd said it was by Lake Drummond, which was in the middle of what was now a protected swampland.

I glanced up at Riley. His thoughts seemed to mirror mine. "Could this actually be a lead?" I asked.

"We've got to chase down every possibility right now," said Riley. "I could totally see Milton Jones finding some twisted amusement in using the cabin of one of his victims as the place he kept his victims as well."

I turned back to Bill. "Is there anything else you can remember? The address of the cabin?"

"No, we didn't get quite that far on our first date."

"What did she tell you?"

He rubbed his chin. "She didn't really share a lot of details about her past. She asked about my radio show. My ex-wife. The apartment building."

I leaned against the wall and crossed my arms. How could we find that cabin?

I remembered being in Rose's house. I remembered seeing her mail on her kitchen counter. There'd been a middle name listed on her address. I remembered because it reminded me of Snuffleupagus.

But why?

Snuffleupagus. Snuffy. Scuffle.

Sesame Street. Big Bird.

Wooly mammoth.

Wooly.

Woolard! Except it was spelled differently.

Woollard. That was it!

An Internet search, along with calling in a favor for someone who worked for the neighboring city, brought us the results we needed. There was a "Woollard" who owned a cabin back in the area of Chesapeake near the Great Dismal Swamp. By 5:30, Riley and I had hopped in the car and taken off.

I picked up my phone. "I'm calling the police, even if it puts my reputation on the line."

Adams picked up and I told him what was going on. "I'll send some men out. You stay away."

"I can't stay away. This is my dad's girlfriend!"

"Gabby, let the authorities handle it."

I bit my lip. I'd let them handle it. But I wanted to be there when they did.

Lives were on the line. I couldn't hold back.

I stared out the car window as the landscape blurred past. There were trees, trees and more trees. The farther we got from the city, the swampier the landscape became.

I used to have nightmares about swamps when I was a kid. They just looked so spooky with all of the moss hanging from skeletal cypress trees and puddles of black water standing in every available crevice. Swamps made me think of snakes and other creepy crawlies I'd rather not encounter.

As we waited for a drawbridge, I studied the map on my phone. If I was reading it correctly, we had to turn down several desolate roads before we'd find the cabin.

That would fit Milton Jones' profile.

With the bridge back down, we continued down the road. The deeper we drove into the area around the swamp, the darker it got. The sense of dread in the pit of my stomach grew with every rotation of the tires. I felt like a soldier marching into a battle, unsure of the outcome or what he'd be getting himself into. I knew I had a choice here. I could turn around. I could go back and avoid this war if I wanted.

But then I thought of the women Jones had snatched, and I knew I couldn't sit by idly. If this were my sister, my best friend, my mom, I'd want someone to fight with everything within them to save their lives. Someone had to take up for those who were powerless to do so themselves. Teddi, Nichole, Clarice, and Rose qualified for that right now.

Though I walk through the valley of the shadow of death . . .

The verse both resonated in my mind and clutched my heart.

I will fear no evil.

Jones was about as evil as I'd ever encounter.

The Lord is with You. His rod and his staff will comfort you.

I prayed for God's wisdom and protection and comfort. Going to the cabin was risky. It was dangerous. But some things in life were worth the risk.

Riley reached over and squeezed my hand. "You okay?"

"I think God is grieving over this," I mumbled. Riley and I had talked about it to an extent already, but the thought wouldn't leave my mind. The thought of God weeping over His people. The mental picture of Him mourning.

"Grieving over death and murder? Definitely."

I shook my head. "Yes, over death and murder. But some people in society have glorified the people behind the act of death and murder. Freddy Mansfield sells serial killer mementos. Rose bought those macabre souvenirs. Someone admires Jones enough to help him with his murderous crusades. Killers have made magazine covers." I closed my eyes for a moment, grieving myself. "We've glamorized something that should be atrocious."

"I can't argue with that. And you're right. God is grieving over the states of people's hearts. Out of our hearts come our actions and words, right? Life is precious. We have to cling to whatever is good and pure. Otherwise the darkness will swallow us whole."

I lifted up another prayer. It wasn't just for Milton Jones' victims, either. It was for everyone whose heart had been blinded by false perceptions of evil. For those who called evil good. For those who didn't even realize the state of their soul.

When I opened my eyes again, a new peace washed over me. Now, I needed to focus on the task at hand—the task of saving innocent lives.

"Slow down." I stared at my phone screen, trying to decipher the markings on the map. "It says we need to turn here, but there's no road."

Riley gripped the steering wheel even tighter. "This area is so remote. Maybe the maps aren't accurate."

I scrutinized the street markings on the tiny display and then glanced back at the road. "It's weird."

"Let's try the next road."

A stretch of swampland rolled past as we drove farther into the early evening. The next road sign didn't appear for another mile.

"This can't be right. We're missing something," I insisted.

With each second we wasted, my anxiety grew. We were so close, yet so far away.

"Let's turn around." Riley maneuvered the car on the narrow road, and we headed back the way we came. We slowed at the area where the road should have been. All we saw was black water and cypress stumps and thick brush.

No road.

No sign that any road had ever been here.

We continued down the road but didn't see any other turn offs.

I pointed to a farmhouse in the distance. "Pull into the driveway. There's a man outside now."

Riley stopped by the farmer, who eyed us suspiciously. The man's dog barked at us from the edge of the driveway.

"Can I help you?" the farmer asked, wariness in his tired gaze.

I smiled brightly, trying not to seem too creepy. "Hi, there. Sorry to bother you, but I'm a little lost."

"I don't know what's happening out here tonight, but my dog won't stop barking. All I want is to go to bed." He sent his German shepherd a dirty look.

"I'm looking for 3251 Cypress Way. It says there's a turn off, but we can't find it."

He pulled up his top lip in thought, showing his stained teeth and lots of gum. "Cypress Way, you say? You're close. Hurricane Isabel sent too many trees over that street for it to be useable. Used to be an old logging road."

"There used to be a street there? Because I didn't see anything."

"The swamp's a living thing. It's always changing, Sweetheart. Mother Nature came in and filled up that road with peat moss and blueberry thickets and Devil's Walkingstick. The marsh and the swamp . . . part of its mystery is its ability to transform itself, to shift, to grow, to devour."

His words sent a chill down my spine. I pointed to the map on my phone, my throat suddenly dry. "So is there any way to get to Cypress Way now?"

He nodded. "Of course. Take the next road. Turn left. Then take the next right. You'll hit Cypress Way. It's not much of a street and there's two huge ditches running on either side of it. Hope you don't mind getting your car dirty."

We thanked him and hurried back down the road.

"That was strange," I mumbled. "Unsettling."

"He was right. The swamp is alive. The man just appreciates the land, like any good farmer would," Riley said.

That still didn't comfort me as we drove deeper into the quickly descending night. Our headlights were the only things illuminating the road. I hoped we didn't hit a dead end because the road had become even narrower.

Riley pulled to the side of the street. "We should go the rest of the way on foot. We don't want to alert anyone that we're here."

"Makes sense." What had I just said? Walk? Through the swamp? Had I lost my mind?

As soon as I stepped out, the smell of dank earth rose up to greet us. Humidity surrounded me. Bugs kissed any exposed skin.

The swamp had a welcome all its own.

In the distance, something snapped. A tree branch? An animal? A killer?

Riley reached for my hand, and we started down the dark road. Before I'd gotten out of the car, I'd shoved my cell phone in my pocket and my gun in my waistband.

Honestly, the weapon was starting to feel more like a ball and chain than a means of protection.

But a girl had to be smart. Especially a girl facing a serial killer.

The moonlight reflected on something in the distance. Something shiny. And it wasn't one of those murky puddles of water.

"What is that?" I pointed to the shimmer across the road.

We walked closer and saw a car.

A hybrid. A black hybrid.

With a suit jacket hanging in the back.

"Dale . . ." Riley muttered.

"Why's his car here?" I asked. Had the Scum River Killer grabbed him as well? Or even worse . . . was *he* the accomplice?

I stepped back and shook my head. The car had been covered up with branches, like someone was trying to hide it.

Jones or Dale?

I remembered Riley telling me at the start of this manhunt that only people who were officially connected with the case had known about the threats Jones made to Riley. Dale would have known. He was in town earlier than anyone thought. He'd wanted to use me as a decoy. He could be in on this whole nightmare.

"I don't like this," Riley mumbled.

"Me neither." From where I stood by the car, a building in the distance came into view. "Look. The cabin."

We crept closer to the structure. I ignored the sounds of nature around me, from the incessant *ribbit* of frogs, to the solemn whisper of crickets, and the shrill hum of locust.

"What's our plan?" I whispered. I grabbed his hand.

Just then, I heard a cry in the distance. Fire raced through my blood as I imagined what might be happening.

This was the right place. I was convinced of it.

We stayed low as we approached. My palms were sweaty. My heart pounded in my ears. My breathing came too quickly.

The cabin appeared to be one story, rundown with dirty white plank siding, and had window screens that were either busted or gone. I'd guess the place to be maybe 600 square feet and several decades old. It obviously hadn't been maintained throughout the years.

Just beyond the backside of the place, I spotted a car.

A white sedan.

That cry we'd heard hadn't been because of a mouse this time. That had been a scream of pure terror at the hands of a killer.

We stayed along the edges of the forest, waiting until we reached the back of the house before running toward the exterior of the building. We pressed ourselves there. My heart nearly pounded out of my chest. Slowly, I straightened, peeking carefully into the window.

Jones. Milton Jones.

I ducked back down as he turned, and I nodded at Riley. We'd found our killer. Now, we just had to figure out what to do next.

CHAPTER
THIRTY-FIVE

I PEEKED in the window again. Milton Jones was pacing the floor with something that looked like a whip in his hands. Rose sat bound in the corner. I took a good look at her. Blood trickled from her forehead, her eye was black, and her clothes torn.

I quickly noted the rickety chair where she was tied. Outdated furniture was scattered throughout the room. Fish hung like trophies on the wall.

Jones muttered something and then snapped the whip in the air.

Come on, Adams! Parker! Where are you?

Rose was gagged. So who had screamed? Where were the rest of the women? Where was Dale?

Riley moved down toward the other side of the house. As much as I didn't want to take my eyes off Rose, I followed him. We had to locate the rest of the women. Maybe while Jones was distracted by Rose, we could free everyone else.

We peered in each of the windows, but I saw no one.

Where was Jones keeping the other women? Where had that cry come from?

I turned and surveyed the area around me. Was there another cabin? A boathouse? Anywhere else these women could be?

I saw nothing.

"What now?" I whispered to Riley.

"We can't be hasty. The police should be here any minute."

"That's if they can find it. This road isn't on any map."

"Let's keep our eyes on Jones. If he starts to hurt someone, we act. Otherwise, we lay low and keep watch."

I nodded. I knew that was a better plan than mine. My plan was to burst through the front door, save Rose, and possibly get myself killed. We'd be no good to these women if we were dead.

The front door opened with a loud squeal. Shivers crept over my skin as heavy footsteps plodded across the splintered floorboards of the porch. Someone muttered. A *man* muttered.

Jones must have stepped out for a minute. Riley put a finger over his lips, motioning for me to be quiet. We remained pressed into the side of the house, daring not to move.

We listened as he stomped down the steps. Everything was silent for a moment. Was he coming our way?

My skin felt alive with tension and adrenaline and fear.

My back muscles pinched with anxiety.

Riley motioned for me to stay put, and then he slipped around the far corner, the opposite direction of the front door.

I had a bad feeling about this. About all of this.

Riley returned and leaned toward me. "He's standing near the woods smoking a cigarette."

Could we rescue the women before Jones returned? Even

if we did, we had no way to get them out of here. We'd all be sitting ducks as soon as Jones spotted us.

Psycho Scum stomped back up on the porch. The door opened and then slammed.

I remembered my gun in my waistband. I could use it, if I had to. I could take down Jones and keep him tied up until the police got here.

That sounded like a plan. A back up plan, at least.

Slowly, carefully, I peered inside again. I saw Jones walk through the living room, past Rose, and disappear somewhere.

Another scream pierced the nighttime air. Yelling followed. Something crashed.

Riley stepped closer. "We need to distract Jones."

"How?"

"We split up. Go in the woods. I'll make noises. Do something to slow him up. Make him look for me. Meanwhile, you'll be somewhere else. Somewhere safe."

"A place where I can run away and get help if you need me." I knew that's what he was thinking, but I didn't like this idea. "The plan could backfire. Jones could hear the noise and decide to accelerate the process."

Riley shook his head. "Jones takes too much joy in killing. He won't do that."

"But—"

His eyes pleaded with me. "Please. This whole thing with Jones started because of me. He wants me. Let *me* be the one to help now."

I squeezed his arm. "Don't go." Is this how Riley felt whenever I had a hare-brained scheme?

"I'll be safe. I love you, Gabby."

My chest felt like it had a boulder on it. "I love you, Riley."

With that, we split and went different directions toward the woods.

I pulled out my cell phone. It was only then I realized how badly my hands were shaking. I could barely dial Adams' number. Finally, he answered. The connection wasn't strong, though.

"This is Gabby. We found Jones. You've got to get here." I whispered. I kept my head up, on guard for any sudden sounds or movements.

"We're on our way. We're having trouble locating the street."

I gave him quick directions. So much for police equipment being more sophisticated than ours. "We should be there any time, Gabby."

Across the woods, Riley yelled. A purposeful yell. One meant to draw out Jones.

Someone moved in front of the window and peered out.

Riley had distracted Jones. But what would happen next?

Jones disappeared. A moment later, he stepped outside, dragging someone with him. Clarice? Was that Clarice? "Is someone there?"

He looked around. Walked off the porch. Pulled Clarice behind him. Walked toward Riley.

I watched as he drug Clarice across the patchy grass. She was crying. Whimpering really. She looked like she'd lost weight, and she didn't have much to lose to begin with.

I missed the Clarice who wore designer clothes, had her nails done, and her hair perfect.

This Clarice looked like a rag doll.

My heart froze. I had to stay where I was. I couldn't rush in to help. One wrong move and everything could go blow up.

Still, I looked back at the house. I remembered Rose there, tied up. I wondered if I should help her?

How much longer would the police be?

I turned back to Jones, but he was gone. Where had he gone? I'd looked away for a moment and now he'd disappeared.

I stepped back, water spreading up from the edge of my jeans. A branch snapped behind me. Before I could turn, I heard someone say, "What took you so long?"

Chills raced up my spine. That voice didn't belong to Riley.

I knew without turning around that it belonged to Jones.

Slowly, I pivoted. Sure enough, Jones stood behind me, a knife in hand and a gleam in his eyes. "I knew you'd come."

My breathing was shallow. It was hard to get air to my lungs. I turned my focus from Jones—I knew he wanted my attention, and I didn't want to give it to him—and looked at Clarice. She let out a cry. "Gabby, you're here. I just knew you'd find me."

"Clarice, where are the rest of the girls?"

"He's got them in the attic." Her voice quaked and broke as she spoke.

The attic? In this place? It must be 100 degrees up there. Something about her statement didn't hit me right. I couldn't pinpoint what.

"Where's Dale?"

"Dale?" Clarice asked.

"The cop."

"He's—" She started to answer when Jones pressed the knife into her side.

"Enough of this little reunion!" A horrid grin stretched across his face. "It's time for the real fun to begin."

"Let her go," I ordered. I'd wanted my voice to sound strong, tough. Instead, it quivered.

Clarice's eyes widened with fear, with hope, with pain.

Jones nodded toward her. "Her? Let her go? Why would I do that?"

"Because I'm going to shoot you if you don't." I raised my gun.

His grin widened. "Are you? You're a feisty little thing. A lot like my sister."

"I'm nothing like your sister. I treat people around me with love. I would never do what she did to you."

"I saw the way you were with your brother. Making him eat trash. That's not love." His voice rumbled now, any mischief gone, replaced with resentment, anger . . . vengeance.

The gun trembled as I held it in front of me. "I don't make him eat trash." Finally, it made sense. That's why Jones had turned so much rage onto me. Not only was I engaged to Riley, but he thought I was just like his sister. Explaining Tim's freegan ways would only be an exercise in futility right now.

"Do you think I'm stupid?"

"I'm telling the truth." It was even hard for me to believe that. "You need to let Clarice go. The rest of the women, too. The police are on their way."

He pressed the knife into Clarice, and she yelped. "You going to shoot me?"

"Let her go!" My voice rose in pitch as the tension stretched tight.

"You're going to have to kill me first. Which will it be? You take a life? Or I take a life?"

"I'll do it."

"Don't kill him, Gabby," Riley stepped out of the woods.

"Riley!" My heart leapt with joy.

"He wants to make sure you're just like him. He wants you to know what it's like to take someone's life."

"He deserves to die," I mumbled, staring at Jones.

"Let the justice system decide that. Keep your own hands clean."

"But . . ." In my heart, I knew Riley was right. But everything else inside me screamed to shoot. To take the life of this scum-of-the-earth killer.

For the first time ever, I wanted to shoot to kill.

I also knew that Jones was taunting me. He wanted me to take his life, to live in guilt for the rest of my days.

My finger remained poised on the trigger. I wanted to pull it. More than anything, I wanted to squeeze.

Sweat sprinkled across my forehead. Bugs swarmed around me, buzzing, biting. Swamp water continued to invade my clothes, creeping higher and higher.

I had to do something.

I had to pull the trigger.

Before I could, I saw something move at the side of my vision. Before I could turn, someone stepped out. Rose.

Rose?

That's what hadn't sat right with me about Clarice's statement. She'd said all the girls were upstairs. But Rose had been downstairs. As a decoy.

All along, she'd been the accomplice. Her abduction had just been a part of Jones' grand scheme to throw us off track.

Rose sneered before zapping Riley with a Taser. "No one talks like that to a man I'm going to marry," she muttered.

I screamed and lunged for him, praying they wouldn't harm him anymore.

CHAPTER
THIRTY-SIX

THE DISTRACTION GAVE Jones just enough time to kick my gun. The weapon flew from my hand and landed with a plop in the swamp. In one swift motion, Jones shoved Clarice to the ground, ordered Rose to take care of her, and grabbed me.

He held a knife against my neck. "Get his keys!"

"Whose?" Goosebumps raced across my skin, popping up like warning signs on a washed out road.

"Your little lover boy's!"

I carefully squatted beside Riley. Jones kept the knife at my neck, reminding me that with one wrong move, my life could be over. The blade pricked my skin as I leaned forward.

All I could think about was Riley, though. My heart squeezed with pain as I looked at him. Riley. My Riley.

I wanted to comfort him. To touch him. To tell him everything would be okay.

To tell him I'd give up everything to be with him.

Clarice's whimpers in the background only added to the strain of the moment. They reminded me that I might not have my happy ending. They reminded me that life and death were on the line.

I swallowed, my throat tight. I reached into Riley's pocket and grabbed his car keys. I mouthed, "I'm sorry," before Jones pulled me back to my feet.

"Good girl. Now move!"

I had no choice but to walk. If I didn't, I would die. Then I'd be of no use at all.

"Where's your car?" His hot breath hit my cheek. I remembered the earthy scent I'd noticed on Jones when he was in my apartment. I smelled the swamp and hadn't even realized it.

"Down the lane."

"Get going then!"

I could hardly keep up. The blade pressed into my neck. Its sharp edges cut the top layer of my skin. I could feel blood trickling down onto my shirt.

"Where are we going?"

"Away from here before the police show up," he muttered.

We reached the car, and Jones pushed me inside through the passenger door. He kept the knife at my side as he shoved me over the center console until I fell into the driver's seat. Then he slipped inside behind me and slammed the door. Something about being in the car alone with Jones increased my level of panic by about three hundred times.

"Now, drive!" He leaned beside me, one arm behind me, the other pressing the knife into the flesh at my neck.

If I hit one pothole, all of this could be over. And out on these roads, I might not even see the pothole coming.

My whole body was nearly convulsing as I stuck the keys into the ignition. I cranked the engine and then turned to him. "Which way?"

He sneered. "Just go. I'll tell you."

I put the car into drive and eased my foot off the brake. The car began rolling down the deserted lane.

"Faster!" he barked.

I pressed the accelerator, my hands shaking so badly I feared I wouldn't be able to stay on the road. But I did as he said. We traveled back down the road Riley and I had come in on.

Inky darkness surrounded us like an army of evil closing in. Only the headlights offered any glimmer of hope. Jones could kill me out here, hide my body, and I'd never be found.

I thought about Riley. Was he okay? What was Rose doing to him? How were the other women holding up?

My pulse slowed slightly when we reached the road where the farmer who'd given us directions lived. It was a little more populated, at least, and had scattered streetlights to help illuminate the way. Despite that, everything felt eerily still. At this late hour, there was no other movement out here —not even a police car.

Where were they?

Just as I turned down the road, as my hopes of heading back to civilization began to take root, the car puttered. It sputtered. It lurched.

I knew this car was just going to stop one day. Why now?

Jones showed me the knife again, as if a reminder that if I didn't choose wisely, my prize would be a stab wound in a sick version of Wheel of Misfortune. "What's wrong with this piece of rust?"

"It's old," I muttered.

"Keep going. Faster."

I pressed down on the accelerator. My heart slammed into my ribcage, each beat jarring my adrenaline into action. I had to start thinking and fast. "Why are you doing this?"

"Someone has to pay."

"Pay for the way your sister treated you?" I kept my hands on the wheel, my knuckles white, and my limbs shaking like a man on a jackhammer.

"You're all the same." His soulless eyes glared at me. I could feel them.

He wasn't even trembling, I realized as I felt the heat emanating from his arm. The realization only made the pit in my stomach grow deeper. "We're not. I love my brother. He really does eat trash. As unbelievable as it sounds, it's part of his worldview."

He snorted and his other hand squeezed the back of my neck. "All women are liars."

"What about Rose?"

"A means to an end. I needed help and she was willing. Desperate for my attention, actually." He chuckled. "Some people just have no common sense. She should know better than to trust a serial killer."

"I know you think all women are liars, but I'm telling the truth." My voice trembled, making my words lose credibility. "I haven't lied to you."

"Shut up and keep going."

I swallowed hard. The road almost seemed like a tunnel in front of me. All I could see was the illumination from my headlights. Out here was desolate. There was farmland. Glimpses of the Elizabeth River. Massive ditches on the sides of the roads. "What's going to happen to Riley?"

In the rearview mirror, I saw a smile play across his lips. "He'll get what he deserves."

Just as we turned onto another back road, I spotted the High Rise Bridge ahead. It wasn't just an every day bridge. No, it was a huge, twin-spanning structure—probably half a mile long—that carried traffic from Interstate 64 across the Elizabeth River.

The river here was wide and deep. The bridge was majestic and high. If people were allowed to bungee jump from the structure, there would probably be a waiting list every weekend.

We headed below it, toward a service road that ended with a chain link fence and a flickering light that bathed the area in a sickening shade of yellow. On the other side of the bridge was a factory of some kind and then beyond that a road that led to the Interstate.

The car sputtered again.

Then it stopped.

"Keep going!" Jones ordered. He slammed a hand on the dashboard.

I tried to start it again. The engine turned over before going dead. "I can't!"

He growled. Finally, he grabbed my arm and jerked me out of the car. He began pulling me under the bridge. His breaths came out short and quick, the sound causing nausea to roil in my stomach. His fingers dug into my arm so tightly that I almost yelped.

A sound in the distance caught my ear. Sirens. The police. They were coming. But would they find us in time?

Jones swerved his head toward the noise. For the first time this evening, I noticed that his eyes were glazed. Finally, his gaze settled on the fence in the distance. "Climb it."

I was so jittery that I could hardly hold onto the chain link. But somehow, I got over it and landed with a jarring thud on the cement slab below. Jones was right behind me, close enough that I could still hear his breathing, still smell the vapor of the swamp that had saturated his clothes and hair.

A staircase stretched in front of us. It was metal, narrow, and steep, zigzagging up—my gaze traveled to the top—probably eight stories.

Jones nudged me. "Go."

I started up the first step, my knees weaker than spaghetti noodles. Condensation had formed on the platforms and caused my feet to slip, despite the safety grooves. But with the knife at my back, I kept going.

I ignored the slits between the steps that were filled with nothing but air. I couldn't glance down. Each time I did, a wave of dizziness made my head spin. I forced one leg in front of the other and gulped in deep breaths.

I knew where this maze of stairways led.

They led to the catwalk that ran alongside the High Rise Bridge. I'd seen repair crews use it to get to the bridge tender's office located in the middle of the span. It was barely anything to walk on, only a thin piece of metal that separated you from a horrifying drop into the watery grave below.

With each step, my breathing became shallower. Jones kept a good pace behind me, that knife always close to my flesh. Finally, I reached the top.

The catwalk stretched before me, looking more like a gangplank at the moment. I made the mistake of looking down. The water was so far below that all I could see was a huge mass of black.

Falling off this bridge would be like falling into an endless abyss. Was that Jones' plan? To throw me off this bridge to my death? I'd almost rather take a bullet.

"Keep going," Jones ordered.

I took my first step onto the stretch of metal. *One foot in front of the other,* I told myself. Eyes straight ahead.

The bridge was massively high so that huge Navy vessels and barges could come and go. I didn't normally have a fear of heights, but looking down now, anxiety clutched my chest. Cars zoomed past us on the Interstate, separated only by a cement divider. Certainly the drivers were clueless.

I briefly considered hurdling the divider, but I knew I'd only end up as road kill.

I didn't know how this was going to play out, but I couldn't see it ending well. At least maybe the women would get away.

Sacrifice. Isn't that what I'd been thinking about lately? Of course, the sacrifices I'd been thinking about lately seemed petty in comparison to the sacrifice of life. I'd been thinking about giving up my dream career for my dream guy. I had to face it: Either way, I would win with those choices.

But right now, my only comfort concerning sacrificing my life was the fact Jones had me, which might mean everyone else would live.

For a moment, I remembered Jesus and His sacrifice on the cross. I wondered if He'd experienced a moment of the fear I felt now. I wondered if He had any second thoughts. I wondered if He'd wished someone could take His place.

My heart cried out for Him. It cried out with love. With understanding. With pleading that He'd intercede right now.

Against my better judgment, I looked back and saw the flashing of blue and red lights below. The police. They were here!

"Go faster!" Jones told me. The knife pressed harder.

A flash of lightheadedness hit me again when I looked at the open space beside me, a flimsy railing the only thing that separated me from falling to my death into the black water below. The wind picked up and swept over the bridge unhindered. I prayed it wasn't strong enough to push me right over the edge.

We finally reached the peak of the bridge's arch. Jones

pushed me until my head hovered over the railing. Only black air waited below. No one would survive a fall off this bridge. It was too high. The impact from the water would be too great.

"Would you like to go for a swim?" Jones' twisted humor seemed to return because he chuckled as if he enjoyed this too much.

"You're not going to get away with this," I muttered. Famous last words, right?

"No one ever thought I would get this far. Don't underestimate me. Everyone else did. My sister. My wife. My own daughter even."

I pulled back so my body weight wouldn't propel me over the edge. Jones and I faced off. He knew there was nowhere I could go without risking falling into the water below.

"I've been underestimated my entire life," I started. "I understand." Here I was, trying to find common ground with a serial killer. But still, I spoke the truth. I hoped he could see that in my gaze. It might not make any difference . . . but maybe it would.

"You don't know anything," Jones muttered.

Behind him, I saw two cops creeping down the catwalk, coming from the bridge tender's office. I kept talking, hoping to distract him. My hands gripped the railing, and I licked my lips. "Why are you treating me like your sister treated you?"

"She was a horrible person. I'm not horrible." His eyes were so wide that I could see the whites ringing his pupils. It only made him look crazier.

"Are you sure about that?"

"I'm getting rid of the people who don't deserve to be here. I'm helping to make the world a better place."

The police officers crept closer. Adams appeared on the other side of the catwalk, and I noticed that traffic had stopped flowing on the four lanes of the bridge. Cop cars blocked the road.

I had to buy time. So I kept talking. "How would the world be a better place without those women? Without Mr. Sears? Without me? What did we ever do that was so horrible?"

He pointed a finger at me and laughed. "You see? Right there. You don't even realize what a nuisance you are."

"I try to help people."

He shook his head. "You think you're superior."

"There couldn't be anything farther from the truth, Milton." I used his first name, trying to get his attention.

"Stop talking," he muttered. His words slurred into one another.

I was messing with his head, and it was working.

"Why Mr. Sears?" I asked.

He sneered. "He was a casualty. We had to get him out of the way, so we could have access to the apartment building. Rose took care of him."

"Is that what everyone is to you? A casualty?" I asked, trying to buy time.

"Let her go, Jones!" Adams shouted behind me. "We've got you surrounded. This is over."

"This will never be over," Jones muttered.

His words sent a chill down my spine. What did that mean?

Riley pushed past Adams. "Take me. I'm the one you want anyway."

Riley . . . Riley was okay. Thank God! But no way did I want to substitute myself with Riley.

Jones chuckled. "Nice try, Riley. But all along, I've had a plan."

In one swift move, Jones grabbed me and pressed the knife into my neck.

Just then, a gun fired.

The knife dropped.

The force of the bullet propelled Jones away from me. He lumbered backward a step.

His eyes widened. Blood soaked his shirt.

Then he hit the railing.

His body flipped over the catwalk. I leaned over in time to see him fall. And fall. And fall.

Finally, his body hit the water with a splash.

All the tension in my body seemed to leave it in one *goosh*. I nearly sank to the ground, but Riley rushed toward me. He pulled me into his arms and held me up. "I'm so glad you're okay."

"The women?" I whispered. "Teddi? Clarice? Nichole?"

"There's a crew there right now. They're all okay. Rose has been arrested."

My heart slowed for a moment. "What happened? What took the police so long?"

"Get this. They got caught by the draw bridge."

A soft laugh escaped. "Of course."

"It's over, Gabby. It's really over," Riley mumbled.

Then why didn't I feel so certain?

CHAPTER
THIRTY-SEVEN

RILEY and I went to church Sunday morning. We had a lot to be thankful for . . . starting with the fact we were still alive.

Nichole, Clarice, and Teddi were still alive. They might all have to have counseling, but they were still breathing. Thanks to the fact that, in his effort to torture Riley, Jones had been distracted and rushed. He hadn't had time to carry out his normal method of inflicting pain on his victims. No, they'd all gotten away with bumps and bruises, but they'd escaped the worst-case scenario that I'd feared would be perpetrated on them.

Rose was behind bars and facing so many charges I couldn't even keep them all straight.

Dale was recovering. He claimed that he came to town early, as soon as he'd heard Jones had escaped. He drove past the crime scene that first day in an effort to follow every lead, to see if Jones' calling card had been left at the crime. He'd suspected that Rose might not be as innocent as she'd claimed. He found out her family owned the cabin and had traveled out there to check it out. Jones had snuck up on him and knocked him out.

But, despite all the reasons for joy, doubt lingered in the back of my mind. Had Jones really died? Then where was his body? Washed out to sea?

My cell phone rang as Riley and I walked from the church back to our apartment. I recognized the number. Clarice.

I held up a finger to excuse myself from my conversation with Riley for a moment and answered. "Clarice. How are you?"

"I'm going to be having nightmares for a long time."

"We all are," I conceded.

"This whole thing really helped me to reevaluate my life. Life is too short for me to be someone I'm not. You really helped me to realize that. Thank you."

My heart warmed a moment. "I'm glad something good came out of all of this. And people are going to love you for who you are, Clarice. If they don't, then they're not worth your time. Don't forget that."

"I won't. And I'll see you around, Gabby. I'm always available if you need me to help you with any jobs!"

I hoped that wouldn't be the case. Chad and Sierra were coming back tonight. Thank goodness. "Got it, Clarice. Take care of yourself."

As soon as I hit END, I looked up and saw Parker waiting beside his car outside of my apartment building. Something about him being there made something shift uncomfortably in my heart.

I gripped Riley's hand as we walked up. "What's going on?"

He stuffed his hands deep into the pockets of his khakis. "Just stopped by to give you an update."

"Did you find Jones' body?"

Parker's lips pressed together in a firm line. "Not yet. There's no way he survived everything that happened,

Gabby. Our techs examined the amount of blood he lost. That, on top of trying to navigate the river in his injured state . . . there's just no way he's still alive."

"Then why haven't the cadaver dogs found his body?" Riley asked.

Parker shrugged. "For all we know, he's already been washed out to the ocean. It's going to take some time for the search to be complete." He drew in a deep breath. "You both did good work. We may not have found him without your help, so I wanted to say thank you."

"I appreciate that, Parker," I told him. Compliments weren't easy to come by with him. He'd probably rather get shot than give one out, so I knew he meant it.

"You guys should go relax, take it easy for a while. You saved the lives of four innocent people. That's nothing to scoff at."

In the midst of all the craziness last night, I'd realized that it didn't matter if I was offered that job in Kansas or not. I wasn't going to take it. It wasn't because I thought Riley's career was more important than mine. It was because I loved Riley, and I wanted to be with him. Besides, Virginia was my home, and I had unfinished business here. I hoped that more doors would open in the future so I could use my degree to its fullest. But, until then, I'd bloom where I was planted, as the saying went.

I looked up at Riley as Parker walked away. The one thing I'd realized throughout this whole Jones fiasco was that life was too short. I didn't know if I had years to live or mere hours.

"Let's get married."

He grinned softly. "I thought we *were* getting married."

"No, I mean let's ditch this whole big wedding. We don't

have the money for it anyway. Let's get married . . ." I shrugged. "I don't know. Soon."

"How soon are you talking about?"

"Well, I do have to get a dress. And I know you have a few people that you really want to be there. We should give them a little notice first, don't you think?"

He wrapped his arms around my waist. "Absolutely. How much notice is enough?"

I shrugged. "A week?"

He laughed. "You want to get married in a week?"

"Yeah. What do you think?" If we were married, we'd have no choice but to make a decision about our future *together.*

He kissed me softly. "Let's do it. One week."

"On the beach. At night. Something simple. Maybe we can have a reception later."

"I like that idea."

I grinned and squeezed his hand. "Okay, then. I'll have to remind Teddi that we're going dress shopping. I think that will be enough to lift her spirits."

That's right. Milton Jones was not going to ruin my life. That's exactly what he'd wanted to do.

Riley and I were going to say our vows. We were going to love, honor and cherish each other until we drew our last breath . . . and Milton Jones was powerless to stop us.

~~~

Thank you so much for reading *The Scum of All Fears*. If you enjoyed this book, please consider leaving a review!

Keep reading for a preview of *To Love, Honor, and Perish.*

NOW AVAILABLE

The happiest day of Gabby's life turns into her worst nightmare . . .

SQUEAKY CLEAN MYSTERIES, BOOK 6

TO LOVE, HONOR, AND PERISH

AWARD-WINNING AUTHOR
CHRISTY BARRITT

TO LOVE, HONOR, AND PERISH: CHAPTER ONE

"Gabby, you look stunning!" Teddi stepped away from the embankment of mirrors surrounding me and put her hand over her mouth.

I turned to look at my reflection and nearly gasped. "Mamma, mia . . ."

I was wearing a wedding dress. A real, certified wedding gown. It was sleeveless with a brocade around the corset and layers of white silky fabric and tulle flowing down to the floor and beyond.

"Riley's going to love it," Teddi said, circling me and taking in every angle. "Of course, I've seen the way he looks at you. He'd love it even if you were wearing a sackcloth."

"I think this is the one." I curtsied in the mirror, unable to take my eyes off the dress. I'd dreamed about this moment for so long. The day I'd find my Prince Charming, he'd realize I was his soul mate, and we lived happily ever after.

Even though Riley and I had been engaged for more than a month, my wedding planning kept getting delayed for various reasons. That's why Riley and I had decided to have a small, private ceremony in a week. Yes, one week. A little less than that now, for that matter.

Today was Monday. Our wedding was on Sunday.

We were going to have the ceremony in Virginia Beach at the oceanfront. At sunset. I didn't care about the flowers or fancy invitations. But I did want a dress that would knock Riley's socks off. What's a fairytale without a gown worthy of a princess?

Teddi tugged at the back of my gown, right at the zipper, like a seamstress might. "I don't think you're going to need to have it altered even. It's like the dress was made for you."

Teddi was my dad's new girlfriend, and she was different from any of the other women who'd been in his life since my mom passed away. What the pint-sized woman lacked in stature, she made up for in hair. The former Texas beauty queen prided herself in having earned the title of Best Gown for three years in a row. In her mind, that made her a fashion expert, and I wasn't going to argue.

Her hands rested above my hips as she peered behind me in the mirror. "Look at that tiny waist of yours. I used to have a waist like that."

I didn't mention that I'd probably dropped five to ten pounds from the stress of last week. Tracking down serial killers could do that to a girl. But that was all behind me now, and it was smooth sailing ahead.

She tugged at my red, curly hair, pulling it back away from my face. "Have you thought about your hair? How you'll wear it?"

"Probably down and curly. Riley likes it that way. No veil. Maybe a flower behind my ear."

"That sounds perfect." She grinned.

I looked in the mirror again and sighed. "I can't believe I'm getting married, Teddi."

I thought back on all the messes in my life. I remembered the moments when I thought nothing would work out. I reminisced the bad decisions, the broken paths, the train wreck that could have been. But somehow, someway, everything had worked out and had led me to this point in my life.

And now, in less than a week, I'd be marrying the man of my dreams. I knew that with Riley by my side, I could handle anything the world threw at me. Riley was my best friend, my partner in crime, the levelheaded one who balanced my brash impulsiveness.

"You are going to be one happy woman. I think marriage will really suit you. My years with Jim were some of the best of my life."

"You were married before?" As soon as I asked the question, I wanted to take it back. It was nosy, and Teddi was dating my father. I had no idea what her story was, nor should I be inquisitive about it. I'd entered the land called "Awkward," and I had no one to blame but myself.

"I was married to Jim for twenty years, Sugar. Twenty of the best years of my life."

My throat tightened. "What happened?"

"Cancer. It can get the best of us, can't it? He held on for five years, but when the disease came back the second time, he was too weak to fight." Her eyes welled with tears a moment before she smiled sadly. "I find comfort that he's in a better place now."

I squeezed her hand. I couldn't imagine what it would be like to have found the love of your life and then lost him . . . what a tragic story. "I'm so sorry, Teddi."

She shook her head and pulled herself upright. "Don't be sorry. God brought your father into my life. He's been a blessing to me."

I had trouble seeing how my dad was a blessing, but I

didn't say anything. My dad was trying to make some changes in his lifestyle. I had to give him credit for that.

Teddi motioned to the fresh-faced attendant who waited in the distance. "We'll take this dress."

"You really don't have to buy this," I started, gripping the skirt of the gown like my hands had taken on a mind of their own and might never loosen their clutch. "I'm perfectly capable of affording this myself."

She raised her hand, each finger a masterpiece from her golden, bejeweled rings to the manicured tips. "I'm not going to hear anything about it. I've decided this is how I want to help, and nothing you can say will stop me. I never had a daughter of my own, you know. And marriage is the last thing on my son's mind. He's too busy trying to make it as a country music star."

I could tell by the way she said "country music star" that Teddi didn't think too highly of his career choice. There was really so much that I didn't know about Teddi. I couldn't believe she'd stuck around for as long as she had.

"I appreciate your generosity," I finally said. If I was honest, I'd admit that money was really tight right now. I was back to crime scene cleaning, Riley was saving to buy a new car and trying to get his new law firm off the ground. Neither of us was at a place where we had a lot of disposable income.

Teddi clapped her hands together once and gave a confident nod. "Let's get this baby boxed up and paid for. Then we'll get some lunch at this little café down the street that I've been dying to try. I hear they have crepes that will blow your mind. Sound good?"

I nodded. "Sounds great."

Being with Teddi still felt a little surreal. My mom had died while I was in college, and I'd gotten used to doing things on my own. Having a mother figure to shop with and do lunch together seemed so foreign. But there was a part of me that loved it.

Maybe things were finally looking up for me. As soon as I figured out my whole career thing, I'd have absolutely nothing to complain about. You see, I'd landed my dream job with the State Medical Examiner's Office. But then budget cuts hit, so of course the new girl was the first one to go. No one else was hiring in my specialized field in the area, which brought me back to my original job as a crime scene cleaner.

I'd done an interview last week with the Medical Examiner's Office out in Kansas. I was supposed to hear any time now whether or not I got the job. It didn't really matter, though. I'd already decided that I wouldn't accept the position, mostly because I wanted to be near my family and friends here in Virginia.

The attendant knocked on the door behind us, appearing with a box in hand. Teddi nearly jumped out of her skin. She placed a hand over her heart and closed her eyes. From where I was standing, I could tell her breathing had quickened, that her muscles had tightened.

I didn't have to ask about her response. I knew exactly why she'd overreacted.

The Scum River Killer had abducted her. Thankfully, the man had been shot and fallen off the aptly-named High Rise Bridge—the structure easily stretched eight stories above the massive Elizabeth River below. Teddi and three other victims had been rescued.

I placed a hand on her arm. I'd been there in those final horrifying moments before Scum had been shot. I'd seen how terrified Teddi had been, and rightfully so. How many women had died at the hands of the man during his first terror spree out in California? I knew the answer. Thirteen.

"Are you okay?" I asked softly.

She nodded and pulled her eyes open. "Just jumpy."

"Are you sleeping any?"

The lines around her eyes tightened. "Not so much. I have too many bad memories. I keep thinking about . . ."

She didn't have to finish. I knew it would be a long time before she forgot about Milton Jones hiding in her closet and abducting her. Details of the things that had happened in that cabin in the woods were slowly coming out from the victims. I knew they'd been starved, threatened with a knife, and left in the dark. That had just been the start.

Teddi pulled me into a hug and kissed one cheek before backing up and patting the other side of my face in a way that made me feel eight. "I don't know what I would have done without you. You're one brave girl, Gabby."

I tried to smile but couldn't. "I didn't feel brave. My knees were shaking."

Flashbacks of being held by Jones at gunpoint, of being forced to drive, of being prodded out onto the catwalk of a massive bridge, flooded my own mind.

I'd encountered a lot of bad people in my life. Jones had been one of the worst, if not *the* worst. Riley had put him behind bars when he'd been a prosecutor out in California. When the man escaped custody, getting revenge on Riley had been his first priority.

As much as I hated to admit it, there was this small niggle of doubt in my mind when it came to Jones' death. I'd seen him shot. I'd watched him go over the bridge and hit the dark, black water below. If the bullet hadn't killed him, the impact of hitting the water should have. If the impact hadn't, then the river itself should have claimed him. There were a lot of layers there, which made it seem impossible that he could survive.

But I'd seen Jones do the impossible before. I knew that,

against all odds, he'd escaped from prison and made it across country in less than forty-eight hours. I knew he had a little fan club. I knew he was without a heart.

The police never found his body. They all said there was no way he could have survived the bullet wound and the fall.

Part of me wouldn't rest until his body was recovered, though. I needed that closure and resolution.

"He's gone, Gabby." Teddi put a hand on my arm, almost as if she could read my thoughts and knew I was thinking about Jones.

I forced a smile and nodded, trying to reassure her and ease some of her anxiety. "Of course he is."

But I wasn't so sure he was gone.

I'd already been told that his remains might not ever be found. From the Elizabeth River, his body could have been swept out to the James River, then the Chesapeake Bay, and finally to the ocean. Marine life could be feeding on the man now.

It wouldn't surprise me if, even in his death, the man brought destruction. All those poor sea creatures would probably turn up dead in some kind of unprecedented fish kill. After all, it just wasn't the man's flesh that could rot. His soul was already rotten.

The attendant unzipped the gown, snapping me back to the present. I stepped out of my dress—feeling reluctant to do so, for some reason—and then pulled on my jeans and Bride-To-Be T-shirt.

Just as I grabbed my purse, my cellphone rang. I hoped it wasn't someone calling me with a crime scene cleaning job that couldn't wait. Chad, my business partner, should be able to handle things for a few hours. I couldn't afford to turn down work, but I really wanted a day just to feel normal, to be a woman out planning her wedding. I still had people to call and reservations to make in order for this ceremony to happen on Sunday.

I pulled my phone out and glanced at the number. When I saw the digits there, I blinked with surprise.

Detective Adams. The Norfolk detective had worked the case against Jones.

Maybe he was calling to tell me the killer's body had been found.

Wouldn't that be a great wedding present?

I excused myself for one minute, already anticipating sharing the good news about Jones with Teddi, as I put the phone to my ear. "I hope you found him in the swamp."

"Gabby?" Detective Adams said. His deep voice rumbled across the phone.

"The beach is too peaceful and pretty," I continued. "I hope Jones got washed up somewhere dank and dirty. Somewhere fitting." I paused. "That is why you're calling, right?"

"I wish that's why I was calling, Gabby."

Something in his voice caused me to stiffen. There were undertones of tension, of sorrow. If Adams wasn't calling about Jones, then why would he be calling? "What's wrong?"

"You need to get to the hospital, Gabby."

A million scenarios raced through my mind. Time seemed to stop for a moment. I leaned against the wall, bracing myself for whatever he had to say. Had something happened to one of Jones' other victims? Nichole or Clarice maybe? Had one of them had a mental breakdown? No one would blame them after what they'd been through.

"What . . . what do you mean? What are you saying?"

"Riley was shot this morning, Gabby. He's in critical condition. Come to the hospital. There's no time to waste."

Click here to continue reading.

ALSO BY CHRISTY BARRITT:

BOOKS IN THE SQUEAKY CLEAN UNIVERSE

On her way to completing a degree in forensic science, Gabby St. Claire drops out of school and starts her own crime-scene cleaning business. When a routine cleaning job uncovers a murder weapon the police overlooked, she realizes that the wrong person is in jail. She also realizes that crime scene cleaning might be the perfect career for utilizing her investigative skills.

ABOUT THE AUTHOR

USA Today has called Christy Barritt's books "scary, funny, passionate, and quirky."

Christy writes both mystery and romantic suspense novels that are clean with underlying messages of faith. Her books have sold more than four million copies and have won the Daphne du Maurier Award for Excellence in Suspense and Mystery, have been twice nominated for the Romantic Times Reviewers' Choice Award, and have finaled for both a Carol Award and Foreword Magazine's Book of the Year.

She is married to her Prince Charming, a man who thinks she's hilarious—but only when she's not trying to be. Christy is a self-proclaimed klutz, an avid music lover who's known for spontaneously bursting into song, and a road trip aficionado.

When she's not working or spending time with her family, she enjoys singing, playing the guitar, and exploring small, unsuspecting towns where people have no idea how accident-prone she is.

Find Christy online at:
   www.christybarritt.com

www.facebook.com/christybarritt
www.twitter.com/cbarritt

Sign up for Christy's newsletter to get information on all of her latest releases here: **www.christybarritt.com/newsletter-sign-up/**

facebook.com/AuthorChristyBarritt
twitter.com/christybarritt
instagram.com/cebarritt